FORK IN THE ROAD

Book Three of The Winding Road Series

By Kerri Davidson and Mark Gelinas

A Bee and Badger Books Publication

ISBN 978-1-7779575-6-8

First Edition.

This book is dedicated to each other. The road we have traveled from online writing buddies to coauthors to true friends is stranger than fiction. Here's to us!

ACKNOWLEDGMENTS

Many thanks to:

Our beta readers, Chris, Sam, and George.

Our editor, Joanne.

Our cover artist, Jamie.

Our Bee and Badger Books logo creator, Tropi.

Chapter 1

In Which a Proposal is Discussed
Monday, August 10, 1998

"What is this?" Morgan asked, although the answer was obvious.

She took her time peeling off the rest of the wrapping paper from the box. A Club. Worst birthday present ever. She didn't even lock the doors on Zinger. She hadn't for years.

"It's for your car," Morgan's dad said with a smile.

Morgan returned the smile but could not quite manage a thank you. "Great," she said instead as the doorbell rang.

"That must be the pizza," her mom said and hurried off with her purse.

"Where's that strapping young man of yours today?" Morgan's dad asked as they waited at the kitchen table where Morgan had been unwrapping her presents.

"Strapping?" Morgan raised a brow and snickered. "He's at work and he couldn't get away for lunch. In fact, he'll be busy right up until his own birthday on the twenty-first. I won't see much of him in the meantime, but we're going to celebrate our birthdays together then."

Morgan's four-year-old brother Matthew was slowly inching the box containing the Club across the table toward him. She gave it a helpful nudge.

"No work for you today?" her dad inquired.

"Nope. First day of my holidays. Plus, I'm leaving tomorrow, remember?"

Morgan's mom returned to the kitchen with the pizza and sighed. "I just can't believe you're going all that way on your own – and to be in the hospital no less. I wish your father or I were going with you."

1

"Don't be ridiculous. I'm twenty-one years old now, and it's not a big deal. Damian's the one who's sick. Randy said he just finished his chemo, and he's in a clean room so I won't be able to see much of him, but I'm happy I'll be able to donate the marrow he needs. I'll be in and out the same day, and besides, I'm not going alone. Rab will be with me," Morgan reminded her.

"I know. I guess I'll never stop thinking of you as my baby."

"That smells great," Morgan said as the pizza was set on the table, hoping to thwart any waterworks. Her mom was awfully twitchy today. "That's one thing I'll never outgrow. Pizza lunch on my birthday."

"Go ahead and start. I've got to get Mary up from her nap."

"Such a difference from Matthew, hey?" Morgan remarked as her mom left to get her two-year old sister. No one had ever needed to wake her brother up from naps. Good luck getting him to have one at all.

"Tell me about it," her dad said, eyeing Matthew who was holding the Club in its box as if it were a baseball bat. "Matthew, put your sister's present down."

Matthew grinned and smashed it on the table, narrowly missing the pizza but making one hell of a noise as everything else jumped and clattered.

Her dad sighed and Morgan tried to hide her chuckle.

"So, Morgan, you'll call us when you get to Seattle?"

"We'll be there pretty late tomorrow, so I'll probably call the next day before my procedure."

"And after?"

"Sure, Dad." Morgan sighed. "You know it's really not a big deal, though."

"Anything involving anesthesia and my little girl is a big deal," he said.

2

She smiled, remembering a time when she'd doubted her stepfather's love for her. "And after," she promised.

Morgan's mom returned with Mary and put her in the highchair. The little girl smiled sweetly at Morgan.

"Hi, Mary," Morgan said, reaching out to smooth her rumpled hair.

"Morgan," Mary said and giggled, clutching her finger.

Morgan hadn't been kidding when she said Mary and Matthew were nothing alike. When Matthew had been Mary's age, he was an absolute terror – one of the main reasons Morgan had moved out of the house.

Mary was quiet right from the start. She rarely cried as a baby and now . . . well, she almost made Morgan rethink the whole never-having-children thing.

"Get back here right now!" her dad yelled.

Morgan looked up to find Matthew creeping away with her Club. Instead of returning with it, he let out a war cry and took off into the living room. Yeah, Mary was an anomaly. The no-kids rule was a good one.

Her dad took off to chase her brother who, by the sounds of things, had found something solid to pound on. Morgan's mom rolled her eyes as the pounding turned to yelling and screaming and crashing and . . . lord knew what they were doing in there.

Morgan grinned and took a slice of pizza before it got cold. "Boys, hey?"

Her mom laughed and got up to get Mary's lunch. "Yes. Boys." She turned back and gave Morgan a curious look. "You know . . ."

Morgan's dad returned with a screaming Matthew slung over his shoulder. However, he'd neglected to take the Club from the boy and was rewarded with a whack on the side of his head.

"That's enough!" He wrenched the box from Matthew's hand and dropped it to the ground. Then he put Matthew on his feet and pointed down the hall. "To your room, and don't come out until I tell you to!"

Matthew's face was already purple, and he continued to wail as he marched off to his room.

"Guess I'll see him another time," Morgan muttered as the door slammed hard enough to shake the house.

"That boy . . ." Her dad shook his head and sat down to grab some pizza. "I see military school in his future."

"He'll grow out of it, Gary," her mom said without conviction. "Either that or he'll follow in your political footsteps and become the prime minister of Canada. He'd certainly get things done."

Everyone, including Mary, laughed at that one.

"Morgan, do you have everything you need for your trip?" her mom asked.

"Yep. I'm mostly packed. It's not like I need much. The week is going to fly by. Tomorrow's a travel day, then I donate the marrow, then Rab and I might get to squeeze in some sightseeing before the wedding."

"Whose wedding are you going to again?" Morgan's dad asked.

"Sally Hampton's. The wedding's in Silverdale, just a short ferry ride from Seattle."

Her dad nodded and Morgan finished off her pizza, checking her watch.

"I hate to eat and run, but I have to drop off a painting at the gallery."

"Ooh, I haven't even seen your latest," her mom said. "I'll have to stop by and take a look at it. You've been doing really well selling those, haven't you?"

"Can't quit my day job." Morgan shrugged. "But yes, I can hardly keep up with the demand."

Morgan gathered up her birthday gifts and purse, gave her parents and Mary kisses, and headed for the door. "Tell

Matthew I said goodbye," she called on her way out. "And thanks for everything."

Morgan had stopped to slip on her shoes, and wasn't halfway down the driveway when her mom came bursting out of the house behind her.

"You forgot this," she said breathlessly, holding out the Club.

"Oh, um . . . thanks."

Her mom chuckled. "It was your dad's idea. I know it will end up being a doorstop."

"Hey, that's not a bad idea," Morgan agreed and turned to leave.

"Wait!"

"Mom, I told you I'll be fine. Please don't make a scene," Morgan said, facing her again.

Her mother did not look well. She pulled on strands of her blond hair that had come loose from her bun and chewed on her lip. Her eyes glimmered with . . . tears?

"What's wrong?" Morgan asked warily.

"I just . . . I can't . . . I think I need to tell you something."

"Oh, good lord. You're not having another kid are you?" Morgan blurted, remembering the last time her mom had been acting so strangely.

She surprised Morgan by laughing. "No. No, no, no. Definitely not."

"Well, what is it then?"

Her mom took a deep breath, and when she released it her words tumbled out in one long sentence. "I shouldn't say anything but I have to because I don't want you to be blindsided by it and I want to make sure you have time to think and make the right decision."

Morgan simply blinked.

Her mom looked over her shoulder at the door and then leaned close to her, lowering her voice. "He asked your father for your hand in marriage. Morgan, he's going to propose to you."

Morgan shifted the gifts in her arms and blinked some more. "Are you serious? When?"

"He asked a couple of days ago. I thought he might do it tonight, but if he's too busy with work, maybe he decided to wait."

"Wow," Morgan breathed. "I don't know what to . . . well, thanks for telling me."

Her mom pulled her in for a hug. "I know he makes you happy, and I know you're not really my baby anymore. I just don't want you making a hasty decision."

"I guess I'm not all that surprised," Morgan said. "We haven't been dating that long, but well, you know what he's like."

"Of course. He's definitely a go-getter and anyone can see how much he loves you." Her mom released her from the embrace and narrowed her eyes. "I just can't help remembering another young man who –"

Morgan held up her hand. "Don't. Don't say it. Please. Josh is gone. I love Trevor just as much as he loves me," she snapped.

Her mom nodded and bit her lip again. "Okay."

"Thanks for telling me, though," Morgan said in a softer tone. "Really. I'll talk to you soon, all right?"

Another nod and her mom waved as she walked back to the house.

Morgan waved and continued on down the driveway, her thoughts in turmoil. She actually felt bad for her mom. It was no secret how much she liked Josh. Her mom had taken his departure harder than Morgan when he left for Silverdale.

Silverdale . . . where Morgan was heading for the wedding. She hadn't given much thought to what it would be like seeing him again after so long – eight months to be exact. And that last time didn't really count. He'd basically picked up his things from the apartment that Morgan now shared with his sister Rab, and they hadn't said two words to each other.

No, she'd be fine when she saw Josh at the wedding. It wasn't like they would be spending the week together. Besides, he was the one who left, and their relationship hadn't been much of a relationship for a lot longer than eight months anyway.

But this proposal was awfully sudden. She and Trevor had only been dating for a few months. Sure, it had been an intense courtship. And as he often liked to say, he knew what he wanted and wasted no time getting it.

But marriage?

Yeesh, it was a good thing she had the next week to digest this information before having to deal with any of it. She loved Trevor, but she wasn't quite sure she would love marrying anyone.

Chapter 2

In Which Josh Takes a Moment to Brood
Monday, August 10, 1998

Josh paused outside Ezra Brock's Garage and faced east. It wasn't quite three years since he arrived in Silverdale with Morgan after their cross-continent road trip. But today was a memorable date, nonetheless.

The peak of Mount Rainier rose above the horizon in a clear sky. Contrary to popular belief, it didn't rain all the time in Washington.

He smiled to himself, remembering his relief three years ago when Morgan had turned eighteen the night before they'd entered the States. How silly he had been to worry about her being underage when they crossed the border together. He'd learned a lot since then. Regardless, they'd celebrated that evening with dinner and drinks and shared their first kiss.

His hand went up to the necklace he wore – a half-heart with her name on it. A touch of sadness washed over him when he recalled that her eighteenth birthday celebration was the best one they had shared. Even though they were a couple, the next two birthdays did not go as well as they had hoped and planned.

Between school, work, and plain tiredness, it seemed they never could enjoy each other's company. He believed he was building a future for them, but apparently it was a future she didn't want.

Yes, today was Morgan's twenty-first birthday. But more importantly, it marked eight months to the day since she broke up with him. Perhaps he shouldn't have pressed so hard, but he had needed to make a decision.

Decision made, Josh had moved to Silverdale to work as a mechanic for his uncle's friend. It was the trade he'd studied hard in order to be able to provide for a family. A family he'd believed would include Morgan. Ironically, he'd achieved this goal at the price of their relationship.

The passage of time had dulled the sharp pain to a nagging ache. Josh supposed that someday Morgan would be only a pleasant memory. But not soon. Soon, she was coming to Washington with his sister to attend their cousin Sally's wedding.

Approaching footsteps caused Josh to turn his attention away from the past. A young woman with mahogany hair smiled at him.

"Earth calling Josh," she said. "You want to help me pull this driveshaft, or do you plan to daydream for a while longer?"

"I'm right behind you, TG," Josh said and smiled as he walked toward the garage. As he followed her, he removed the chain with the half-heart and put it in his pocket. *Safety first.*

Josh and Iris had been working together at her father's garage for almost eight months, shortly after he'd driven Old Blue, his restored 1971 Dodge Fargo pickup truck, across the continent to Silverdale. It had been a memorable trip, but not as memorable as the previous two crossings.

"You seem moodier than usual today," Iris said as she engaged the lift lever. "And stop calling me TG. I am not your Tool Girl."

"I know," Josh said. "But calling you partner seems too familiar."

"Just call me Iris. The name's right on the coveralls."

"But where's the fun in that?"

She laughed and his mood lifted a bit. A rusty 1994 Ford Mustang rose off the floor, exposing its underside to them.

Iris stood a half a head shorter than Josh, even without his ever-present ball cap. Slightly shorter than Morgan, Iris was not frail. Quite the contrary, she had taken an interest in mechanics almost as early as she could pick up a wrench. Or that was how her dad told the story, anyway.

"It's her birthday," Josh said and uncoiled a drop light to examine the car. "You'd think this guy lived in Canada with all the rust under here."

"Her?" Iris said. "Morgan?"

"Yeah. There's been no one else."

Iris frowned. "You should do something about that."

Josh sighed, then handed Iris safety glasses and donned a pair. "I don't think I'm ready to move on yet."

Iris blinked amber eyes at him. "Put a chain under the shaft while I loosen the bolts."

She pulled a pair of disposable nitrile gloves from a box and slipped them on.

"I hope the Liquid Wrench has had time to work," Josh said, putting on his gloves and taking position under the car.

As Iris put a wrench to the bolt, he hooked a chain on cross members to support the drive shaft as it came free.

Josh rolled the oil collection drum under the transmission. "Did you see the Mariner game last night?"

"I was making some adjustments to my dress, so I couldn't watch the whole game."

"It was close until the sixth inning. Then A-Rod hit a three-run homer in the seventh and that sewed up the game."

"I didn't see it live, but I saw the replay," Iris said. "That was an impressive homer."

"I should go catch a game before the season is over," Josh said and glanced at the calendar featuring the Kingdome.

"Maybe you, Dad, and I could go see one on Sunday and make a day of it."

"Can't go this Sunday," Josh said as he waited for Iris to break the bolts free.

"Why not? Sally's wedding is Saturday, so we have nothing pressing," Iris said. She searched for a different socket in the rolling toolbox.

"Well, other than the fact the team will still be on the road in Chicago, Morgan doesn't leave until Monday."

"You really think she's going to want to spend time with you? Did you use my three-quarters inch socket?"

"I did, but I put it back."

"Here it is. Please put the tools back in the right spot. Looking for them wastes time."

"I'll try to remember that," Josh said and shrugged. "Anyhow, if Morgan doesn't want to spend time with me, I'll visit with Rab."

"Rab's your sister, right? I'm sure you've told me that."

"Yes, my only sibling. Her real name is Mary, but she goes by the shortened version of her middle name, Rabeau."

"I hope to get a chance to meet her. It's nice that she's coming to the wedding," Iris said and attempted to remove a bolt. "These are still pretty tight."

"Well, she's coming more to see me and travel with Morgan than attend the wedding."

"Why isn't your sister one of the bridesmaids?" Iris asked with raised eyebrows. "She's Sally's cousin, and I'm guessing about the same age."

"Sally picked only friends so there would be no family squabbles," Josh said. "Do you need a cheater bar?"

"I just need to put a little muscle into it," Iris said. Then her eyes went wide. "So that's how I became a bridesmaid. Sally surprised me when she asked. I guess Michael doesn't have the same problem."

"Michael, his best man William, and the other groomsman are all Marines. I'll be the only groomsman not in a dress uniform," Josh said.

"But you wanted to be a Marine."

"Wanted to, but close only counts in horseshoes and hand grenades."

"Still, you attempted to join," Iris said. "I respect that."

The bolt came free suddenly, and her hand struck the underside of the car and dropped the wrench. "*Baka!*"

"Are you okay?" Josh asked and took a step toward her.

"Yeah. It might leave a small bruise. You know, being asked to stand with them is an honor."

Josh picked up the wrench and handed it to her. "It is."

"You'll still be wearing a tux. You'll look nice."

"Yeah, I accepted my fate long ago. You're right, it will be an honor."

"I'm looking forward to it."

Josh laughed but tried to cover it with a cough.

"And what is so funny about that, Joshua Éveriste Caleb Hampton?" Iris asked, planting her fists on her hips.

"It's kind of hard to picture you in a frilly dress," he said, lifting his hands in defense.

"Because I wear coveralls at work you think I can't wear something nice? You should see me in a kimono."

"You have a kimono?"

"I have several, as it happens. Most are for daily wear, but I have one I wear only for the tea ceremony," Iris said.

"That sounds interesting. You'll have to tell me about that sometime."

"It is a very special ceremony. I'll be happy to perform one for you."

"I'll keep that in mind," Josh said. "Do you want me to get that other bolt?"

"I've got it. Your mind seems fixed on Morgan today. You really think you have a chance to get her back?"

"There is always a chance, however small."

"Then what?" Iris asked and positioned the wrench. "You pick up and move back to Canada? Don't you like being an American?"

"I do, but like my father, I'd give it up to be with the woman I love."

"My dad would miss you. He tells me all the time you're the best mechanic who has ever worked for him. Well, next to me, of course." She laughed.

"Of course. I appreciate the thought," Josh said, "but I'd have to do what's necessary."

"I'd miss you too. Most guys I've worked with treat me like a kid. You treat me like a person."

"I've seen your skills. You're a good mechanic. Your sex has nothing to do with your ability."

Iris paused her work and turned to face him. "Life's a journey, Josh. Sometimes the road is blocked, sometimes it is winding, but sometimes what you need is right in front of you."

"The long and winding road? I've heard that song once or twice."

A Doberman pinscher trotted into the bay and over to Iris. She reached down and ruffled his ears. The dog barked once.

"I think Toshi is saying we should get back to work," Iris said and applied herself to the wrench once again.

Toshi barked again, sniffed Josh, and went to his bed in the corner.

"I'm not going to argue with him," Josh said.

"Okay, all the bolts are out, but I'm going to have to pry this free. Hold on to the driveshaft."

Josh supported the shaft as she pried the universal. It popped free and its weight was in his hands. He lowered it until it rested on the chains he had placed.

"Go support the front end while I pull this out," Iris said.

"Right." He moved to the other end of the driveshaft and made sure the oil drain was under the rear of the transmission.

"You know, it would have been nice to be the third bridesmaid."

"Why is that?" Josh asked as she pulled.

"Then you could walk with me instead of Brook."

"Brook seems like a nice person."

"Yes, but you're my work partner. It would be a more natural pairing," Iris said.

"I'm not about to argue with my cousin on her choice. Her female cousins gave her enough of a fuss about being left out. She probably would have picked Morgan if she could be sure Morgan would be here for the wedding."

"Maybe she didn't want to risk sparks flying between you and Morgan."

"We'll find out soon enough. She'll be in Seattle tomorrow."

Iris frowned and pulled the driveshaft free.

Chapter 3

In Which Shack is Still a Dumbass
Monday, August 10, 1998

Morgan spent the entire afternoon with her thoughts jumping between the news of Trevor's pending marriage proposal and her upcoming trip to Seattle. She'd been so out of it that when she walked into the gallery to sell her painting, she'd stood there staring at the store owner for a solid minute before he asked her where the artwork was.

The painting had been in her car and if Jack – or Jacques as he used for his shop name – hadn't been so friendly and easygoing, Morgan doubted she would ever be able to show her face in there again.

Considering how distracted she was, Morgan was lucky to get to the café without crashing Zinger.

The thing that confused her the most was why Joshua Hampton kept pushing himself to the forefront of her thoughts.

When she considered what she would say when Trevor did propose marriage, why was her first thought about how Josh would feel?

When she pictured arriving in Seattle to see her biological father and half-brother, why did she wonder if Josh would be around?

Of course he wouldn't be there. She would see him at Sally's wedding, and then only briefly. She might not even speak to him.

Regardless, Josh was on her mind as she pushed her way into the café and waved at Mel, who was working behind the counter. Morgan stifled a groan when she saw Shack sitting at their usual table with his and Mel's daughter Kayla on his lap.

Yep, that had been a shocker. And no, Shack and Mel were not an item. They tolerated each other quite well, mostly in the form of bickering and fussing, but that was it. Funny, really. The way they behaved reminded Morgan of the way she and Josh used to be.

She was doing it again. What was this, National Josh Day? No, it was not. It was Morgan's birthday.

Her cell phone rang as she approached the counter and she smiled when she saw Trevor's name light up. That was more like it. If ever she needed a boyfriend pick-me-up . . .

Morgan slipped behind the counter to help herself to coffee before answering the phone. Mel slid a birthday muffin over to her and Morgan had to laugh. Kayla had definitely helped decorate.

"Happy birthday, love."

"Thanks," Morgan said to Trevor as she picked up the muffin that had been completely covered in pink icing, and quickly dropped it back onto the plate. Mel handed her a napkin for the finger-goo.

"I missed you at work today," Trevor said.

"I missed you too. How's the case going?"

"It's going. Just not fast enough. I'm so sorry I couldn't get away for lunch. I hope your parents understood."

"Of course they did. You can do no wrong in my dad's eyes," Morgan said, surprising herself at the note of bitterness in her voice.

Her dad liked her boyfriend. That was a good thing. Just because he hadn't felt the same way about Josh . . .

"Well, I'll make it up to you tenfold at our party," Trevor said. "I have a special surprise planned just for you."

Morgan's blood pressure shot through the roof. Maybe her mom shouldn't have told her what this surprise might be. She'd be a ball of nerves for the next few weeks now.

"I'm looking forward to it," she said quickly. And it wasn't a lie. She loved that he was throwing a party at his

16

parents' house, casual style, instead of renting a stuffy hall or something like someone else she knew probably would have done . . . *Stop thinking about him.* "No chance you can get away for a bit tonight?" she asked Trevor.

"Not likely. This is my first big case and I'm guaranteed junior partner if I don't screw it up. Everyone thinks I'm a shoo-in because my dad owns the law firm, but I still need to prove myself. I'm sure I could grab a quick break later if you wanted to stop by . . ."

"No. I'll be turning in super early. I just stopped by the café to see Rab and Mel . . . and Robert, apparently. Then I'll be heading home. Besides, I'm making the most out of my week away from the office. We'll have a lot of catching up to do when I return from my trip . . ." Morgan trailed off suggestively.

"You can count on that," Trevor replied. "Absence makes the heart grow fonder, right?"

"Not always." *Dammit, think before you speak. This is not about Josh!* "But I'm sure it will for us," she added.

"I'm not sure my heart could grow much fonder of you. You're certain you're going to be okay all alone in Seattle?"

"Not going to be all alone," Morgan reminded him. "Rab will be there. And Randy, Damian, Sally . . . lots of people to see."

"Right. Well, just remember I love you and I'll be thinking of you the whole time."

"I love you too," she said.

"Oh, since my brother's there, do you think I could talk to him for a sec?"

"Sure," Morgan said and headed over to the table. "I'll call you when I get to Seattle tomorrow."

They exchanged phone-kisses and Morgan handed the phone to Shack. "It's your brother."

Morgan walked back to the counter to get her coffee and muffin. Knowing she wouldn't be allowed to pay for anything as usual, she shoved a twenty into the tip jar while Mel's back was turned.

"Stop that," Mel said.

"Holy hell, woman! It's true; mothers do grow eyes in the back of their heads!"

Mel pointed up to the security mirror.

"Right," Morgan said. "But I'm not taking it back."

Mel returned to the counter with a toasted sandwich and put it on a tray. "I'm assistant manager now. I'm not a charity case."

"Tipping is not a charity case," Morgan said. Since she'd already been caught, she stuffed another five into the jar and stuck her tongue out at her friend as she turned to leave.

Shack had finished with her phone by the time she got to the table. But Kayla had not.

"Gross! There's slobber all over my phone!"

Shack grinned up at her. "Hey, Morg." He took the phone from Kayla – not without a struggle, that kid was a devil – and set it on the table.

Morgan put down her coffee and muffin and leaned back in her chair, crossing her arms. "Want to try that again, Robert?"

Shack cringed. "Relax, Morg-aaaaan. It's just a nickname."

"We've been through this a dozen times. I don't like it. Call me Morgan or don't call me anything at all."

"I just did," he pointed out happily and stuck his finger into his coffee cup, swirling it around.

"Rab hasn't been by yet, has she?" Morgan asked. She was late and that was not like her. "Hold it!"

Shack froze with his finger in the air. "What now?"

"Tell me that coffee-coated finger is not on its way to your kid's mouth."

Shack kept his finger where it was, his face screwed up in concentration. Morgan couldn't tell if he was trying to

18

figure out the naughtiness level of giving coffee to a two-year-old, or if he was thinking of a way to deny what he'd intended to do.

As it turned out, it was the former.

"It's like a few drops," he said, looking genuinely confused.

"Mel!" Morgan called as she passed by with her tray. "Are you cool with Kayla drinking coffee?"

Mel didn't even slow down. She just rolled her eyes and shook her head.

"Snitch," Shack muttered. "Sorry, kid. She's no fun at all, is she?"

Kayla squealed her agreement and whacked her father on the side of the head.

Morgan watched until Shack had wiped off his hand – he was more work than an actual kid – and wondered yet again how Shack and Trevor could possibly be brothers. Morgan doubted Shack had ever stepped foot into their father's law office. She'd certainly never seen him there. His life goals consisted of studying hockey or some crap in Toronto and acting like the two-year-old who sat on his lap.

The front door opened and Morgan turned to see Rab entering.

"Sorry I'm late," Rab said. "David just left for school, and he and I were saying our farewells. I see the gang's all here." She handed Morgan an envelope. "Happy birthday."

"Thanks."

"You look good today," Shack said to Rab in his typical way – with a full body eyeballing.

Rab raised a brow and sat down, pulling her light sweater closer around her.

"Man, you two are a pair," Shack grumbled. "What was wrong with that?"

"Why can't you say anything nice without it being creepy?" Morgan asked rhetorically. He made her so tired.

"Fine. I like the way you let your hair grow out," he said to Morgan.

"Really? Thanks." She'd been on the fence about letting her curly blond hair reach halfway down her back. Josh had always liked it short – *Woah, not about Josh* . . .

"If only you'd do the same with your chest," Shack added with a huge grin.

Morgan smacked him on the back of the head.

Two groups of patrons left at the same time and Mel came over to their table with Rab's coffee. "Just the usual?" she asked.

"Yes, thank you," Rab said and took the coffee.

The only customers left in the café were an elderly couple sitting a few tables away, so Mel sat down. Kayla reached out for her but she shook her head.

"Mom's got to work for a few more hours. You stay with Dad."

Kayla squirmed and tried harder to wiggle free of her father's grip.

"Burn." Morgan chuckled as she scraped some of the pink frosting off her muffin.

"It is not a burn," Shack said. "She . . . gets some stuff confused."

Mel nodded. "She thinks I'm both M-O-M and D-A-D."

"Well, I'm going to teach her that before I leave for school. Dad." He set Kayla in the booster seat beside him. "Can you say Dad?"

"Dad!" Kayla exclaimed proudly, pointing at Mel.

Shack threw his hands up in defeat. "We've still got a few weeks to work on it. Hey, are you coming to the bash of the year?" he asked Mel. "Friday, August twenty-first. My place. Trev's pulling out all the stops for his birthday. Everyone who is anyone is going to be there." He turned to Morgan. "You up for babysitting?"

"You really are a dumbass," she said.

Again, Shack sat and looked confused.

"I will be at the party. Trevor is my boyfriend. It's a birthday party for both of us," she told him, choosing to keep her sentences short and ridiculously simple.

"Oh, right." He laughed. "Forgot for a sec. But you have the same birthday as him? That's weird."

This time Mel smacked him on the back of the head. "Her birthday is today. She's holding a birthday card. She's eating Kayla's birthday muffin."

Shack frowned and studied his coffee cup, processing everything he'd just been told.

"So, you two are off to Seattle in the morning. I am so jealous," Mel said.

"Well, the first bit's not going to be exciting," Morgan said, "but I can't wait to actually have some fun in Seattle. Last time I was there . . . well, anyway, I'm twenty-one now."

"I'm not," Rab pointed out.

"Close enough. We can drink in the hotel room," Morgan said, even though she knew Rab wasn't a big drinker.

"Sally called earlier," Rab said. "They're having a shower for her Wednesday night."

"Really? Do we have to go?"

Rab shrugged. "It would be nice. If you feel up to it after your procedure, that is. It's kind of a last minute thing. They already had the big shower weeks ago, but Michael is having a bachelor party that night, so they decided to do something for Sally too."

"It's more like a stagette party then?" Morgan asked hopefully.

"That's not really Sally's style, but there'll probably be liquor," Rab said.

"Then I'll probably think about it," Morgan agreed.

Shack perked up at the mention of liquor. "Where's this party?"

All three women sighed.

21

"Nowhere near here," Mel answered. She turned to Kayla. "Okay, my girl, Mom's got to get back to work." She pointed to herself. "Now who's that over there?" She pointed to Shack, who grinned.

Kayla smiled and yelled, "Dumbass!"

Even the elderly couple at the next table broke out laughing and no one, least of all Shack whose grin had only grown larger, could bring themselves to correct her.

Chapter 4

In Which Josh Faces a Force of Nature
Monday, August 10, 1998

Josh guided Old Blue onto the highway and turned north. He usually arrived home about the same time as his Uncle Bill, who worked at the shipyard. Home. It seemed strange, yet natural to think of his uncle's place as home.

He had lived there almost a year now, and perhaps the best part was that they were letting him stay for free. His uncle made the provision that Josh put half of his check into a savings account for future schooling.

Josh wasn't sure he would take any more schooling, but didn't rule out the possibility. If he didn't, the money would be there for a life expense, perhaps a down payment on a home of his own one day.

As things stood, Josh didn't anticipate needing more than the room his cousin William had left behind when he went to join the Marines. He'd been transferred back to the area, but with a wife and daughter, they had their own home in town.

He turned off Silverdale Way onto the street where his aunt and uncle lived. His uncle's truck was already in the driveway when he pulled in.

"I'm home," Josh announced as he entered the house and kicked off his shoes.

"Go ahead and wash up. I'm putting supper on the table now," Aunt Peggy called from the dining room.

Josh did as he was told, his mouth watering at the delicious smells coming from the kitchen. His aunt was an excellent cook.

Dinner conversation centered primarily on the upcoming wedding. Sally oozed excitement while her mother masterfully kept the conversation where it needed to be.

Until Sally turned to Josh. "Did you call and wish Morgan a happy birthday? She turned twenty-one today, you know."

"Trust me, Sal, I of all people am aware of that," Josh said and inwardly cringed, knowing his cousin wouldn't let him off that easy.

"You didn't answer my question," she said.

"I tried this morning, but there was no answer at the house and her cell phone is no longer in service. That girl changes phone numbers as often as some people change their oil."

Sally jumped up from the table to grab her purse. "I have her most recent number."

"It's too late there to call now; she's probably already in bed," *with him*. A pang of jealousy stabbed Josh's heart.

"Yeah, right. If I know her, she's still out partying," Sally said.

"Maybe not this year. She does have to be in Moncton pretty early to catch a flight."

"That's right! That's right. They're coming tomorrow. They'll be here for the shower. How could I forget?"

"Maybe because you are going to be the guest of honor at a wedding in a few days?" Josh said.

Sally laughed. "That's one way of putting it. But seriously, you should call her. It would set things up for her arrival."

"But she'll need her sleep," Josh said, hoping Sally would accept that.

"Oh, come on, cuz, she can sleep on the plane. She told me it's going to take like eleven hours to get to SeaTac. Are you going to meet her at the airport?"

"No. She and Rab have their own arrangements to get to

Seattle. She has to be at the hospital early Wednesday. I don't expect to see her until the wedding."

"Better put on your best appearance. You can start by scraping the fuzz off your face."

"You don't like my beard?" Josh rubbed his hand over his chin. He hadn't shaved since last December.

"You'll look like a barbarian next to the other groomsmen," Uncle Bill said.

"I don't want you looking like a caveman at my wedding. Shave," Sally said.

"Really, do I have to?"

"My wedding, my rules. The fuzz goes."

"I'll shave before your wedding," Josh promised.

"Start early so the inevitable nicks will be gone by Saturday."

"I'll consider it."

Sally handed him a sticky note with a number on it. "Here you go. Give her a call."

"Not while we're eating," Aunt Peggy said.

Josh sent out a silent thank you to his aunt.

***

After supper, Josh retreated upstairs. He took a shower and put on a pair of sweats. The TV was on downstairs and he heard a game playing, but was not in the mood to go down and watch it tonight.

He looked at the sticky note Sally had given him and set it on the nightstand next to the phone. Resting on the nightstand was the scrapbook of pictures Morgan had given him. Josh sat on the bed and pulled it onto his lap. Flipping through the pages took him back to that magical trip in 1995. A touch of sadness washed over him. It was the best time they'd had during their entire relationship.

Living together was good, but even before he went to

college in Moncton, he was barely home and then he was always tired. Morgan worked full-time at the law office and part-time at the café, but had far more free time than he did. Or perhaps just more energy.

A knock sounded at the door and Sally called, "Are you decent?"

Josh closed the book and set it next to him on the bed. "Yes. You can come in."

She opened the door and entered the room.

"You okay, Josh? Mom is a bit worried about you."

"I'll be okay. Some days are harder than others." *Like today.* He rested a hand on the scrapbook. "Was there something you wanted?"

"No. William stopped by with this for you." She held an envelope in her hand.

Josh took the envelope and opened it. Inside was a homemade invitation to a bachelor party for Michael that was being held at William's place. The letter included directions to his house.

"You going to go?" Sally asked.

"I don't know. It doesn't sound like my type of party."

"Well, Heather is throwing a bridal shower for me here, so we're chasing the men out. You'll have to find something to do."

"What's your dad doing?"

"I think he's going to a movie," Sally said. "Maybe you could go with him."

"*Saving Private Ryan* is playing, isn't it? I wouldn't mind seeing that."

Sally shook her head. "Dad doesn't watch war movies. He says being in the real thing was enough. He'll probably go see *Mask of Zorro*."

"I can understand that, but I think I'll pass anyway. I want to keep my options open."

"In case Morgan has a complete change of heart and decides to have a one-night stand with you?"

"Sally!" Josh gawked at his cousin.

"Hey, now that you aren't working your ass off, maybe you could show her you can stay awake during a date."

"I appreciate the thought, but she may not even look at me. She has some party boy on her hook now."

"In any case, I made sure to invite Morgan and Rab to the bridal shower. So she'll probably be here," Sally said, tilting her head slightly.

"Rab's looking forward to meeting you," Josh said, changing the subject.

Sally didn't bite. "What really happened between you and Morgan?"

"I'm sure she's told you all about it," Josh said, lowering his head.

"Not so much, other than to say you weren't together. And here I was sure you two would be married by now."

"Me too. At least engaged, but it didn't happen."

"So tell me about it," Sally said and plopped into a chair.

"After we got back to Bathurst I started working, but to pay the rent my parents were charging me I had to work more than one job. Naturally, working all those hours and the midnight shift left me very tired. I wasn't able to give Morgan the attention she needed," Josh said. He lifted his hands, hoping she would understand.

"She should have understood you were doing it for her future."

"I told her several times, but Morgan was into the now and preferred to let the future take care of itself."

"She may have changed," Sally said.

"Maybe. We'll see."

"You went off to college not long after that, didn't you?"

"Yes. Mechanic training in Moncton," Josh said. "It's not far from Bathurst, but far enough that a daily commute wasn't practical."

"So you ended up seeing her even less," Sally said.

"Yes, and when I was back at the apartment, I spent much of my time studying and sleeping. That didn't help the relationship at all."

"Is that when she broke up with you?"

"No. Your dad called me with the job offer last December, just after I graduated. I had to make a decision, so I called Morgan and asked her if she wanted me to return to Bathurst. She told me no," Josh said and covered his face with his hands.

"So neither one of you officially said the relationship was over."

"Not in so many words, but I took that as her ending it."

"What did you do after that? Did you try talking with her again?" Sally asked.

"I packed up Old Blue and went to Bathurst to get a few things from the apartment. I didn't speak to Morgan at all. I just said goodbye to Rab and gave her my apartment key."

"Did you go see your parents?"

"Mom pretty much disowned me after I refused to dump Morgan in exchange for a college loan. So I just left Bathurst and drove west. With all the snow, I almost didn't make it here before Christmas."

"Wow, that's pretty harsh. I'm still rooting for you two, cuz. She's coming here. Make an effort or you'll regret it later."

"And if she doesn't want me?" The words tore at his heart.

"Then you'll have to learn to live without her," Sally said matter-of-factly.

28

As Josh climbed into bed later, he remembered he hadn't tried to call Morgan again. He looked at the alarm clock, shrugged, and decided it really was too late now. It may have been too late for a long time.

Chapter 5

In Which Things Don't Seem to Fit
Tuesday, August 11, 1998

"Good lord, what was I thinking?" Morgan muttered to herself.

She was knee-deep in the contents of her keepsake chest – aka her regifting trunk – and had come across some of her early sketches. They needed to be burned. Quickly.

"What are you doing?" Rab's voice came from the open door.

Morgan tossed the sketches in the direction of her bed and smiled sweetly, knowing she was about to get a lecture regarding either neatness or promptness.

"I'm all packed. Promise," she said, pointing to her suitcase by the door. "I was just looking for a gift for that shower if we end up going. You think Sally would like a Club?"

"I think we could find time to stop and buy something. Let me guess; you'll clean this up when we get home?"

"There's nothing to clean," Morgan said as she began gathering armloads of things to shove back into the trunk, proving her point.

Rab sighed, picked up some of the items by her feet, and handed them to Morgan. An envelope slipped from the pile, spilling photographs onto the floor. Morgan bent down to retrieve them.

"You okay?" Rab asked when Morgan sat on the floor and began flipping through the photos.

"Sure," Morgan said, barely aware of Rab's presence.

They were the pictures from her and Josh's trip to Seattle three years ago. She was completely lost in the photo of her

and Josh on the ferry. They looked so happy. Morgan felt happy just looking at it. She felt safe. She felt . . .

"Morgan?"

Morgan saw her teardrop fall onto the picture and flipped it over to dab it on the carpet.

Rab sat beside her and put a hand on her shoulder.

"I'm okay," Morgan sob-laughed. "I just don't understand why everything I touch lately reminds me of him. Well, the picture makes sense, I guess. But why do these things keep popping up?"

"Maybe you're just anxious about seeing him again," Rab offered.

"Probably." Morgan picked up all the photos and placed them in the trunk behind her. "I honestly didn't expect to be affected at all. I mean, we had some good times together, but they ended long ago. I have a life of my own now. I have Trevor."

"Trevor's a great guy," Rab agreed. "So is Josh," she added quietly.

Morgan chuckled. "It's been a while since you snuck in one of those."

"Can't help it. Maybe I'm biased because he's my brother but you two . . . well, I just thought you two would stick."

Morgan shrugged. "You know what happened."

"Actually, I don't. All I know is the long-distance thing wasn't working and you broke up with him over the phone."

"There was a bit more to it," Morgan said. "But what it really boils down to is I think we just had some good times on a road trip three years ago and that was that."

"I beg to differ. You were living together."

"Well, lucky you because now you get to live with me."

Rab only frowned at Morgan's light-hearted comment. She wasn't going to let her get away with it today.

"All right," Morgan said. "The truth of the matter is that we had nothing in common. Not our pasts, not our presents, and not our futures. Sure, the biggest point of contention between us was that he was always busy or tired, but you know your brother. Even if he wasn't exhausted, he would pick staying in over going out any day."

Rab opened her mouth to say something, but Morgan decided it was time to get it all out – put the subject to rest. "The long-distance relationship definitely didn't help, but it certainly couldn't have been a good sign that I dreaded the weekends when he did come home."

"Well, no . . ."

"And that break up over the phone, as you like to call it? We hadn't spoken for days, then out of the blue he picks up the phone and demands I tell him whether or not I want him to come home ever again. He sounded absolutely miserable and in that moment I knew I didn't want him to. Not even for a visit. I'd had enough of the negativity and the . . . the boringness. I envisioned our future together and it was bleak. No, more of a nightmare. Housewife drudgery and babies on each hip." Morgan shivered.

"He said that's what he wanted?"

"Not specifically, but it had been implied. Truly, the most spontaneous thing I ever so much as heard of him doing was taking off on that trip to Seattle with me. Even then, for him, it was planned. Not for me. I was on an adventure – it was scary, exciting, thrilling. He was on a mission to restore honor to the family." Morgan rolled her eyes. "Then when that delusion was cleared up, plan B was to secure a career in order to provide for a family."

Rab chewed on her lip. "You know how important family is to him."

"Not really. What was the deal with him and your parents anyhow? All he told me was he'd had enough and didn't want anything to do with them anymore."

32

"It wasn't just one thing. No one has been getting along with each other in that house for years. I mean, I still love them and I believe he does too, but Dad's . . . Dad, and Mom likes to get her way. Do you know why they wouldn't help pay for his schooling?"

Morgan shook her head.

"Because our mom refused to give him so much as one cent for school unless he broke up with you."

Morgan's mouth fell open. "I knew she didn't like me but . . . really? She hated me that much?"

"She never got to know you. She wanted her son to end up with someone of her choosing. That's her fault. But I don't like to speak badly of my parents. I just thought you should know that he did sacrifice a lot for you."

"Ouch. But that really doesn't change the big picture. We didn't work out and . . . I didn't get a chance to tell you or Mel yesterday, but I think Trevor is going to propose to me."

"Seriously? What are you going to say?"

"I don't know. Yes, probably?"

Rab's brows shot up.

"I only found out yesterday. My mom told me that he'd asked my dad for permission, and I'm glad she did. I'll have plenty of time to think about it. I more than suspect he might ask me at our birthday party. Just don't tell anyone yet."

"Of course not," Rab said. "But I thought you didn't want to get married."

"I'm not sure I do. But I love Trevor. And we both want the same things in life. No kids, at least not anytime soon. We want to travel and leave Bathurst one day. I'm still thinking about going to school for journalism and he fully supports that. With Trevor, it feels like it would be more of a beginning than what I'd envisioned with your brother – an end."

"Right, all the drudgery."

"Rab, I'm serious. I did have feelings for your brother – I thought I was in love with him, but it wasn't enough. Trevor is who I'm meant to be with. In fact, I already miss him and we haven't even gone anywhere yet."

"He's been working a lot."

"Sure, but I get it. It's only temporary – an important case. And even when he is tired, he doesn't let that stop him. We still go out and do things – fun things – and what's more important is he has fun too. With Josh it always felt like he was doing me a favor."

Morgan got to her feet and pulled Rab along with her. "Enough about him, okay? Help me toss the rest of this crap back into the trunk before we really do end up being late."

"Sure," Rab said. "But I just want to make sure you'll be okay when you see him again."

"Of course I will. It's just been a crazy couple of days. Hey, what do you think about this for a shower gift?"

Morgan held up a still-in-the-package set of . . . something kitcheny.

"I think you might want to consider brushing up on your Home Ec skills."

"Aren't these rolling pins?"

"They're dog toys," Rab said, turning the package over.

"Why in the hell did someone give me dog toys? I haven't had a dog since I was ten."

Morgan's cell phone rang from somewhere underneath the pile of things.

"Just give me those," Rab said. "I'll put this stuff away and you get that."

Morgan grinned gratefully at her friend and followed the ringing sound to find her phone. Trevor.

She answered just before the call was sent to voicemail. "Hi!"

"Woah, sounds like you had a lot of coffee this morning."

"Nope. Just about forgot my phone. I'm glad you called. And not just for that reason. I'm really going to miss you."

"Me too. At least you're going at a good time. I'm missing you enough already and I can't wait until this case prep is over."

"Ditto."

"Are you two on the road yet?"

"Nope. We're leaving right away."

"Well, I won't keep you. I just wanted to tell you that I love you and I wish I was going with you."

"I love you too. And you have no idea how much I wish you were coming with me."

"I'd drop everything for you in a heartbeat if you really wanted me to, you know," he said, suddenly very serious.

Morgan smiled because she did know. She never felt like she needed to compete for Trevor's attention. "Not this time, but thanks for saying it."

"Always."

"I'll call you tonight." She blew a kiss into the phone, heard him do the same, and hung up.

Rab had finished putting everything into the trunk from the floor and stood staring at it, puzzled. There was no way it would close.

"Um, Rab?"

"Yeah?"

"The stuff on the floor wasn't all keepsake stuff."

"I figured. It's a wonder we don't have mice in this place."

Morgan grabbed Rab's arm and began dragging her to the door. "It's not like it's going anywhere, but we need to. I promise I'll let you disinfect your heart out in here when we get back."

"You're too good to me," Rab muttered.

Chapter 6

In Which Josh Gets a Makeover
Tuesday, August 11, 1998

Josh sat in Old Blue in the employee parking at Brock's Garage. He had been there since first light, which during August in Washington comes quite early. He had a set of keys to the shop but wasn't ready to start work.

He wasn't sure why he had left the house so early. Maybe to avoid telling Sally he hadn't called Morgan the night before. More likely it was because he couldn't sleep. Their talk last night weighed on his mind.

He'd spent the better part of two hours lying awake and thinking about things said and done with Morgan. The words Rab had written last February tore at his heart. "I hate to be the one to tell you this, but Morgan is seeing someone else."

Was he that easy to forget? Did their time together mean nothing? Had he just been a placeholder until someone better came along?

How long would he wait for her to say, "I don't love you anymore," when her actions were saying as much? But she hadn't yet, so he held on to that tiny spark, that minuscule glimmer of hope.

And sometime today she would be back in Washington.

A pink Volkswagen pulled into the lot, signaling Karla's arrival at work.

Ezra's counter attendant and secretary was a middle-aged woman with mousy brown hair. As she unlocked the door, Josh climbed out of his truck.

"You're early this morning," Karla said as he followed her into the lobby.

"Couldn't sleep much. Morgan's arriving at SeaTac today."

"Do you mean 'the' Morgan?"

"Yeah, she's coming to visit family in Seattle. She plans to attend Sally's wedding while she's here," Josh said as he filled the coffee pot with water.

"But not to see you?" Karla sat and checked the answering machine for messages. There were none.

"Not specifically, but I'm sure I'll see her at the wedding." Josh poured water into the coffee maker.

"Then you need to speak with her. Will you ever get an opportunity like this again?"

"Probably not," Josh replied and frowned. It was an accurate assessment. Morgan had little to do with her biological father and his new family. If it weren't for Damian's illness, she wouldn't be coming today. That Sally was getting married at the same time was serendipitous.

"If you want her back, Josh, make the effort," Karla said.

"Everyone keeps telling me that." He dumped the filter with the old grounds into the trash and put in a new filter and fresh grounds.

"Then you should listen," Karla said. "What time is their flight?"

Josh looked at his watch and mentally adjusted for time zones. "They should be in the air soon."

The door opened with a chime and Iris walked in. She shrugged off her jacket and hung it on the coat stand. "Good morning. You're in early this morning, Josh."

"He was sitting in his truck brooding over that woman," Karla said.

Iris rolled her eyes. "What did I tell you about that?"

"You told me a lot of things," Josh said with a shrug and a lopsided smile.

"Step over there and let me look at you," Iris said.

Josh punched the start button on the coffee maker and complied with Iris's directions.

Iris studied him with a critical eye. "You're going to need to do better if you want to impress *her*."

"I'm dressed for work," Josh said, "What do you expect?"

"Parts of you are the same whether you're at work or not."

"Such as?" He wasn't sure what she was driving at but had a notion.

"I know you're not that dense, Josh," Iris said with a scowl.

He rubbed his face. "Well, Sally says the beard has to go."

"Yes, and the hair needs to be cut. You'll need to clean up your hands and trim your nails too," Iris said.

"When am I going to have time to do all that?"

"Look, at lunchtime I'll run over to the house and get a few items and we'll take care of it this afternoon. Do you have pants that aren't made of denim?" Iris asked.

"Other than the tux, which is rented, I have a few pairs of dress pants. Can I get off the pedestal now?"

"Yes, you can," Iris said with a laugh.

"You're a handsome young man, Josh. With a little effort, you could seriously impress Morgan," Karla said.

"Or any other woman looking at you," Iris added with a soft smile.

Josh smiled back. It was nice to be complimented.

"Iris is right, that woman better think twice about what she's doing."

"Go home at lunch and get your dress shoes and I'll shine them for you," Iris said.

"You shine shoes, too? Is there no limit to your abilities?" Josh asked.

"My dad's a Marine. I learned from him. When I'm done, you'll be able to see your reflection in them."

"You don't have to go to all this fuss. I have a thing at home that can shine them."

"Pfft. One of those sponge things? About all that does is knock off the dirt."

"Okay, so why're you doing all this?" Josh asked.

"Because you're my partner; I want you to be happy. I'm doing it so you'll either get back together or get over her."

"Okay, I'll get my shoes at lunch. Now let's get some coffee and get to work."

***

Josh sat on a mechanic stool in the shop with a plastic apron draped around him. Piles of hair already littered the floor.

"I didn't know you could cut hair, too," Josh said. The presence of Iris's body near his was causing mixed feelings. He missed the closeness of Morgan and was slightly uncomfortable as Iris worked on his hair.

"I used to watch when my mom cut my dad's hair. When I was old enough, she allowed me to try, patiently pointing out my mistakes and helping me improve."

"Hey, I don't want a high and tight."

Iris laughed. "Are you sure? It's my best cut."

"I used to wear my hair super short. I need it long enough to show Morgan I've changed."

The clippers paused for a second.

"Is everything okay?" Josh asked. He wanted to run his hand through his hair to feel for mistakes, but didn't.

"Yeah. Just thinking about my approach here. You'll want to leave your hat at home so she can see your hair."

Josh wanted to nod but feared losing more hair than he cared.

Her touch was gentle as she turned his head to the left and right.

"Okay, now let's get that beard. I'll knock it down, but you'll have to finish it with a razor. You do have a razor?" Iris asked.

"I do, but I haven't used it since I've lived here."

His mind flashed to the morning on the road home when Morgan had sat on the tub and watched him shave before they visited his *grand-mère*.

When most of his beard had fallen to the floor, Iris ran her hand across the scruff. "You shouldn't have any problem getting your face smooth."

"Are we done?" Josh asked.

"Not quite yet." Iris rolled another seat to a position in front of him. "Let me see that right hand."

Josh held his hand out to her and she clipped the nails close. Then she used a nail file to get any remaining dirt from under the nail. "You will wear gloves today."

"Shouldn't we be working now?" Josh asked.

"I told Dad we were taking a couple hours off. We can make it up next week."

"What if I'm gone by then?"

Iris focused intently on his hand. "Then I'll make up your time as well. Now give me your other hand."

Josh complied and wondered if he might really be on his way back to Bathurst. He would drive Old Blue rather than fly. At least it would be warmer than his drive here.

While Iris worked on his other hand, she asked, "Do you have a nice sports coat – something made from a natural fiber and not polyester?"

"What's wrong with polyester?" That ruled out at least one of his jackets.

"Nothing, if you want to look like Leisure Suit Larry."

"Never heard of him," Josh said.

"He was a character in a game in the late '80s. Trust me, you don't want to look like a lounge lizard."

"I think I have one or two jackets that could work."

"If not, buy yourself one. A nice one. It would be a good investment and you'll look good," Iris said.

"For Morgan?"

"Yes, for *her* and any other time you need to look sharp."

"Maybe what happened was all a big misunderstanding, and we can sort it out," Josh said, although he wasn't sure he believed it.

"Or *maybe* she dumped you and *is* with someone else."

"No need to be negative." He didn't want to admit that she might be right.

"I don't want you to crash hard if things go south," Iris said. "I'm trying to help you here, aren't I?"

"Yes, you are, and I'm not sure I can adequately thank you."

"You can thank me by scrubbing those hands with a brush until they're pink and clean. You're a mechanic, but you don't have to look like one after work."

"Could it all be a misunderstanding, though?" Josh asked.

"I honestly don't know. I'm not Morgan and I only know what you've told me. But if it is, then wouldn't it have been better to fix it months ago?"

Josh lowered his head. "Yeah, that would have been ideal. If things don't work out, I have only myself to blame."

"That's not true. It takes two to tango, remember. Did Morgan make any effort to fix things?"

"No. There were no calls, no letters, nothing. I wouldn't even have known she was seeing someone else if my sister hadn't told me."

"Did you write your sister back and tell her you weren't seeing anyone?" Iris asked, holding onto his left hand even though she had finished working on it.

"Yes, but I don't know if she told Morgan."

"Didn't you say they were best friends?"

"Yes. Rab moved into the apartment sometime after she turned eighteen. It's one more thing my mom blames me for," Josh said.

"Then Morgan knows, especially if your sister's on your side."

"I believe she is. She practically knocked our heads together when we had an earlier misunderstanding."

Iris stood and touched his shoulder. "Well, maybe lightning will strike twice."

Chapter 7

In Which Times are Turbulent
Tuesday, August 11, 1998

Morgan clamped her eyes shut tightly and leaned her head against the window. "Changed my mind again," she groaned.

Rab sighed. "Just pull the shade down so you can't see out."

Morgan kept her eyes closed and shook her head, fighting a wave of nausea. "Won't help. I still know it's out there."

"Morgan, switching seats will not make the ground go away, nor will it change its location. We're in an airplane."

Morgan turned to Rab and squinted at her. "You think I don't know we're in an airplane? I am well aware that we are thousands and thousands of feet in the air, mowing through clouds. It's just not right! Something this big should not be able to fly. It doesn't make any sense!"

"You need to settle down. Why don't you take those motion sickness pills the flight attendant offered us? They'll relax you."

"Oh, no." Morgan shuddered. "I need to be alert. I'm not sick, I'm vigilant. If this thing starts veering toward the – ugh."

She'd made the mistake of looking out the window again. Rab grabbed the barf bag from the seat pocket in front of them.

"I don't need that," Morgan insisted, though she had broken out in a cold sweat. "I need to switch seats with you."

To give Rab credit, she didn't even sigh. She simply stood and waited for Morgan to crawl out into the aisle.

"Better?" Rab asked once they were settled again.

"Minimally. Can you close that thing?"

Rab pulled the window shade down.

"Any chance you can get everyone else in here to do the same?" Morgan chuckled wearily.

"Just don't look. Here." She handed her a brochure from the seat pocket by the barf bags. "Read this."

"It's flight safety instructions. Believe me, I committed the lecture to heart. And you can also believe me when I say there's no way in hell I'm tucking my head into my crotch and kissing my ass goodbye. I'll be screaming my head off and hoarding all the floatation devices."

Rab put a hand to her mouth to try cover her laugh. Morgan glared at her.

"I'm sorry," Rab said. "I just can't believe how weird you're being. I've never flown before either, you know."

"Well, good for you. You win. You're the bravest. I wonder how much they'd charge to take a rental car all the way back to Bathurst?"

"I don't think they do that."

"Whatever. Maybe I'll just buy a new car now that Zinger's gone."

"Zinger is not gone," Rab said as she pulled a package of gum from her purse. "He said your car will be fixed by the time we get back. It's just the radiator."

Morgan shook her head at the gum Rab offered and closed her eyes again.

That had been a real treat. They hadn't gotten five minutes out of town that morning when Zinger's engine had overheated.

At the time, Morgan had no clue what was happening except that smoke was pouring out of the hood of her car. However, it was clear Zinger would not be taking them to the airport. After calling the useless roadside assistance number her dad insisted she carry, they discovered the wait time for a tow was more than an hour.

After a quick debate of who they should call instead, Morgan discovered she still had the number for Cal's garage in her phone. She didn't remember carrying it over to her list of contacts when she got her newest phone. Why would she? Josh didn't work there anymore.

Nevertheless, Cal's number was there and she ended up calling him. He'd made it out in record time, towed Zinger to the garage, and even dropped them off at home to pick up Rab's car – Josh's old one. Bob.

So it had been another Josh-filled morning. And they were left with more hellos to pass along to Josh when they saw him.

Luckily, they'd made their flight just in time. If one could call *this* lucky.

The plane lurched and began plummeting toward the earth. Morgan's eyes flew open and she was halfway out of her seat heading . . . she had no idea where.

Rab placed a hand on her arm. "It's just turbulence."

Morgan laughed. "Just turbulence?"

She continued to laugh hysterically until Rab gave her a gentle shake. She snapped her fingers in front of Morgan's face and then made her take deep breaths until she'd calmed down enough to sit back in her seat.

Morgan felt oddly detached from herself as she softly muttered a string of curse words, expressed a desire to be with her mother, and asked Rab to change the subject to anything that was not airborne.

"It's too bad David couldn't come with us," Rab said.

"Yeah. Why did he have to go back to school so early?" Morgan asked, though she was pretty sure she should know the answer to this.

"He didn't have to. He chose to take a summer class before the fall semester starts."

"Right. I knew that. Sorry."

Silence reigned for a moment and Morgan picked nervously at the armrest, sweating again.

"I got a letter from Trixie the other day," Rab said.

"No kidding. How's she making out?" Morgan asked with genuine interest.

"Not bad, for her. She's got her own place now, which is good, and she's working."

The past Christmas, right after Josh had left, Trixie had had a terrible falling out with her mother. Morgan had not been keen on taking her in for a few days. Needless to say she was not a fan of Josh's ex-girlfriend, who had gone into full stalker mode and tried to break them up shortly after they'd gotten together.

However, Morgan learned a lot about Trixie during her short stay. She had not had an easy life by any means. Her mother's problems with drug and alcohol abuse, as well as her choice in men that she brought home, were at the top of Trixie's list of woes.

"I still worry," Rab continued. "It sounds like she's barely getting by with two waitress jobs, but she's not qualified for anything else. I guess my biggest concern is that she has no interest in . . . well, anything. She seems resigned to a life much like the one she grew up in."

"I do feel sorry for her. She's still in Halifax then?"

"Yeah. Her mother took off but she decided to stay. I wish she would have returned to Bathurst. At least she has friends there, not that she listens to them much. I really think she needs to be treated for depression."

Morgan chuckled. "I never thought I'd be considered one of her friends, but I guess it's true. I saw a whole other side of her when she stayed with us and I have to admit I like her, underneath it all. Goes to show you just never know. I mean after what she tried to do to Josh and me . . ." Morgan trailed off. Yep. Another Josh-fest was right around the corner if they continued on this path.

Rab caught her discomfort quickly. "Did you decide about Sally's shower tomorrow?"

"Sure did. I've decided we're not getting her a Club or dog toys."

Rab laughed. "That's a good start. How about deciding if we should go?"

Morgan shrugged. "I guess we have to let her know soon, hey?"

"Yeah. I think we should go. It'll just be a bunch of girls and I'd like to spend as much time as I can with Sally. I've never even met her in person."

"I only met her the one time," Morgan said, "but we clicked right away. She's incredible, and I'm so happy we stayed in touch over the years."

"I'm just happy I *got* in touch with her, thanks to you. It kind of feels like I'll be meeting a pen pal."

"She's definitely fun from what I remember . . ."

Yes, fun. Sally had enjoyed tormenting Josh and his "girlfriend Morgan," who wasn't quite yet his girlfriend at the time but had wanted to be.

Josh. Josh. Josh.

Morgan gave her head a hard shake. "Anyway, you're right. We should go to her shower. No boys allowed. Wait. Do you think they'll have balloons?"

"Uh, chances are good. I forgot you're afraid of them. Surely you'll be all right around just a few?" Rab narrowed her eyes in the direction of Morgan's wide ones. "You really are a handful, you know."

The two girls broke out laughing.

"I'm a mess!" Morgan declared. "But I have an idea."

She pressed the service button to call the attendant.

"Change your mind about the motion sickness pills?" Rab asked hopefully.

"Nope." Morgan grinned. "But I'm willing to sacrifice a bit of my alertness in the name of alcohol."

Rab sighed and reclined her seat as the flight attendant appeared to take Morgan's order of as many travel-sized liquor bottles as possible.

It was a male flight attendant. He didn't appear to be much older than a teenager. He had bright blue eyes and sandy brown hair that rebelled with a cowlick in front.

But the cowlick wasn't what had Morgan laughing so damned hard that Rab shot up in her seat, probably thinking Morgan had reverted to hysterics again.

The guy's nametag read "Josh."

Chapter 8

In Which Family Matters
Tuesday, August 11, 1998

When Josh arrived home that evening, two extra vehicles were parked on the street. One was a green Toyota Rav4 and the other a red Corvette, but a newer model than the Shackmobile. Both sported a sticker with the Eagle, Globe, and Anchor on the rear window. Right, William and Michael were over for supper. William's wife, Molly, and daughter, Ashley, would be with him.

Josh had forgotten there was a family dinner at the Hampton home tonight. Being a Hampton and living there, he was naturally invited. He had thought of begging out of it, feeling like an outsider, but he knew his Aunt Peggy wouldn't hear of it.

After turning off Old Blue, Josh took a deep breath. He exhaled slowly before getting out of the truck and walking into the organized chaos inside.

Sally was busy setting the table. She had convinced Molly to help her while Aunt Peggy carried her blond-haired granddaughter on her hip and supervised.

Josh took the hallway to the living room to avoid getting in the way. He found Uncle Bill, William, and Michael there, who were also staying out of the way.

Uncle Bill sat in his recliner while the two young men stood. William resembled his father, but Josh could easily have passed as his brother. All the Hampton men, Josh's father included, were cast from the same mold.

"Hey Josh," his cousin said, "did you get into a fight with a lawnmower? Your hair is almost as short as ours." He ran his hand across his forehead to emphasize his point.

"Iris cut my hair. She said I needed to look good for . . . the wedding."

"She wasn't wrong, but I suspect Morgan's arrival may have had something to do with it, too."

"Now where did you hear that?" Josh asked.

"You know, telephone, telegraph, tell a Sally."

"I heard that, Billy," Sally yelled from the dining room.

"I'm in for it now," William said and laughed. "Maybe I can talk my wife into placating her."

"It'll cost ya, honey," Molly replied. "Now how about y'all come on into the dining room and get yourself set down."

"You boys go ahead. I'll be right behind you," Uncle Bill said and started to get out of his chair, favoring his good leg.

The three young men went into the dining room and sat waiting for the head of the family to arrive. Ashley had been placed in a highchair between her mother and Aunt Peggy.

As soon as Uncle Bill had eased himself into his chair, Aunt Peggy, sitting at the opposite end of the dinner table, began to pass the food around. Everyone at the table was related by blood or marriage, except Michael. That would change on Saturday.

Yet Josh still felt like an outsider. Uncle Bill's family was together, happy, and growing. Josh's family was fragmented and unhappy. Sure, Rab and David were dating, but the prospect of them getting married was years away.

And Josh didn't seem to have any prospects.

Josh would have expected Sally to ask the question, but her attention was fully focused on her fiancé. Instead, it was Aunt Peggy who asked, "Do you think the girls have arrived yet?"

"Their flight is scheduled to arrive at eight, and it'll take them a bit to deplane and get their luggage," Josh said. *If Morgan packed anything more than her duffel.* "Rab is supposed to call me, but I'm not sure if she plans to do that from the airport or when they get settled at the hotel."

"Now, Rab's your sister, right?" Michael asked. "Is the other woman your sister, too?"

"Rab is my sister," Josh said. "Morgan is a friend who is traveling to Seattle to see her family, but she'll be at the wedding."

"Don't listen to him," Sally said. "Morgan is more than a friend. She was his girlfriend until she dumped him last year just before Christmas."

"Thanks for the update, Sally," Josh said. "Your future husband didn't really need to know that."

"You know, Josh, several eligible young women will be at the wedding," William said. "You've been carrying that torch for far too long."

"Are you crazy?" Sally said. "This weekend could be the last chance he has to win Morgan back. He can't be out there playing the field."

William nudged his future brother-in-law. "See, I was right. Morgan. If she wasn't coming, he'd probably show up looking like some hippy."

"My hair would have had to be a lot longer than it was for me to look like a hippy," Josh grumbled.

"It was long enough," Sally said. "If I had to wrestle him to the ground and attack him with my sewing scissors, he would have looked decent for my wedding."

Josh gave his cousin a wide-eyed look. He wasn't sure she was kidding.

"Oh, my word," Molly said. "Your sewing scissors? Now that's some serious stuff there."

"I'm glad I had it cut then," Josh said, regaining his composure. "I wouldn't want to dull your scissors."

"Speaking of sewing," Aunt Peggy said, "have you had your uniform adjusted, Bill?"

"Yes, dear. Sally is going to pick it up from the cleaners tomorrow," Uncle Bill said. "It really didn't need much adjusting."

"It needed more than you think it did," Aunt Peggy replied. "Sally doesn't want to walk down the aisle with her dad in an ill-fitting uniform."

"He's my dad and I'm thankful he's here to walk me down the aisle."

"She's right," Molly said. "I'm so happy my daddy was able to walk me down the aisle when I married William."

Everyone remained silent for a moment, remembering Molly's father had died shortly after her wedding. Josh had never met the man, but respectfully shared the silence.

***

When dinner was done, Aunt Peggy took Ashley to the living room. The young men cleaned up, supervised by Uncle Bill. Molly and Sally withdrew to her room for a private discussion.

While Josh was loading the dishwasher, he checked the clock. It was already eight-thirty and he hadn't heard from Rab yet. He wasn't too concerned because it was still within the time window he estimated they would arrive.

Nevertheless, he jumped when the phone rang.

"It's probably for you, Josh," Uncle Bill said. "We don't usually get calls this late."

Josh quickly wiped his hands dry and picked up the phone. The caller ID read "Morgan Parker."

"Morgan?"

"Wrong answer, bro," Rab replied.

"Rab? Why are you calling from Morgan's number?"

"Because the payphones are tied up and it had Sally's number in it."

"Is Morgan with you?" Josh asked.

"No, Josh. Morgan handed me her phone and let me fly all the way to Seattle by myself – of course she's with me."

"I mean right next to you."

"She's feeling a little ill so she's in the bathroom," Rab said and sighed.

"Is she okay?"

"She's going to be okay, and she'll be fine for the procedure tomorrow. Flying just didn't agree with her. But I didn't call to talk about Morgan."

"Right. Do you want me to take the ferry to Seattle and meet you at the terminal after you drop her off in the morning?" Josh asked.

"There's no sense in paying for a round trip. I'll park and walk onto the ferry. You can meet me at the Bremerton terminal."

"About what time?" Josh asked.

"Morgan has to be up early to get to the hospital. I could catch the seven-thirty ferry and be there at eight-thirty. Would that be too early?" Rab asked.

"No, I can be there by then. I usually get to work by eight, but I have tomorrow off. Are you sure you don't want me to come to Seattle? There's more to see over there than here."

"I'm sure. I'd like a chance to visit Sally before the wedding. I imagine she'll be a bit busy that day."

"It's already getting a little crazy over here," Josh said.

"Exactly my point. People over places. Are there any decent stores over there? I need to get a wedding gift and something for the bridal shower."

"You haven't picked that out already?"

"Didn't want to drag it across the continent and I figured I had time. It won't be like shopping on Christmas Eve," Rab said.

"The Kitsap Mall has a Sears and a JCPenny. I think Sally and Michael are registered at Sears." Across the kitchen Michael nodded an affirmative.

"That should work. Hold on a minute." Rab's voice became faint as she asked, "Are you okay?"

The phone picked up Morgan's voice. "Yeah. I just needed some private time with the commode and to wash my face. Do me a favor and don't ever let me do that again."

"You're a grown woman, and older than me. I can't stop you from doing anything," Rab said.

"Is that Morgan? Can I speak with her?"

"Are you still talking to Josh?" Morgan asked in the background.

"Yes. He wants to speak with you."

"Oh, no, not now. I'm in no shape for that. I'll be at the wedding."

Rab's voice became clearer. "Morgan isn't up to it right now. She says she'll be at the wedding."

"I heard," Josh said with a sigh. "I better let you go. Love you and see you tomorrow."

"Love you too, bro."

The connection ended and Josh hung the phone back on the wall.

Strike one.

Chapter 9

In Which Good Deeds are Their Own Reward
Wednesday, August 12, 1998

"Too early," Morgan grumbled as she pulled the blanket over her head.

Rab quickly snatched the blanket off and Morgan burrowed her head under the pillow. Her pounding, throbbing head.

"Morgan, it's already after ten back home," Rab said and yanked the pillow off as well.

"I hate planes, I hate hospitals, and I think I might hate drinking."

"No one likes hospitals, but I'll give you the drinking one."

Morgan sat up slowly and rubbed her eyes. "Can you at least close the curtains?"

Rab walked over and pulled the curtains shut. Morgan sighed with relief.

"I don't care what time it is back home. It feels like the clock says – six. And lies! You like hospitals. You're planning on being a nurse."

"I meant most patients. Are you going to be like this all day?"

"I don't know," Morgan said. "But at least you won't have to put up with me. Actually, no one will. I'll be out cold, right?"

"Yes. But you shouldn't have had any alcohol yesterday. I told you that."

Morgan waved a hand dismissively. "It was the only way to get through that plane trip and I'll be doing the same on the way back unless I actually do buy a car. It's not going to affect the bone marrow."

Rab only shook her head. "The bathroom's all yours, but you really need to get moving if you want to see your brother before you're admitted."

Morgan lowered her feet over the edge of the bed and watched as Rab, fully dressed and looking fresh as a daisy, settled into a chair and flipped through the newspaper.

Morgan felt a pang of envy. She loved her friend, but often wished she could be more like her. Rab was always so confident and composed. Most days Morgan felt like a basket-case on the verge of hysterics.

But today was not the day for a mental makeover, even if it were possible. Morgan got out of bed and rooted through her suitcase. It didn't really matter what she wore since she'd be in a hospital gown for most of the day, but she did want to look good for when she saw her father and half-brother.

She settled on a pair of non-ripped jeans and a pink T-shirt with a light-weight cream-colored sweater. Despite having let her hair grow out, it still needed nothing more than a quick combing for it to settle in neat waves around her face.

"All ready," Morgan announced. "I just want to call Trevor really quick and then we can go."

Rab nodded and continued to peruse the newspaper. Morgan grabbed a cup of coffee that Rab had brewed.

"Drop it," Rab said.

Morgan set down the phone and went to sip the coffee, wondering what was going on.

"Not the phone, the coffee. You can't eat or drink anything this morning," Rab said with the patience of a saint.

"Right." Morgan gave the coffee one last longing look and dialed Trevor's number.

It went straight to voicemail and Morgan couldn't help but sigh. He'd told her he would likely be tied up with work, but she really would have liked to hear his voice before leaving for the hospital. She was a lot more nervous about the procedure than she'd admitted to anyone, including herself until right now.

Morgan settled for listening to the recording of Trevor's voice, closed her eyes and pictured him all tall dark and handsome, and left a message saying she loved him and would call him when she was done at the hospital.

***

"You're certain you don't want me to come in with you?" Rab asked yet again as she pulled up to the Children's Hospital.

"Nope. I'll be fine. I'm going straight to see Randy and Damian anyhow. I'll call Sally's place as soon as it's over."

"Okay. You'll probably be done and awake by noon, but your throat might be a little sore."

"My throat? Why would my throat be sore?"

"You're having general anesthesia. They need to . . . didn't you read any of the pamphlets?"

"I skimmed them. They need to what?" Morgan's voice rose along with her anxiety.

"Intubate you."

"The tube down the throat?" Yep, hysterics. The hysterics had arrived. "I thought they just gassed me out and I woke up after it was all done!"

"Relax. They do sedate you. In fact, you likely won't know it happened at all except for a bit of a sore throat. They'll tell you more inside."

"Okay. Thanks. Have a good visit." Morgan hopped out of the car, shut the door, and walked quickly toward the building before Rab could see the tears in her eyes.

She was at the doors before she heard the car pull away.

After several deep breaths in the lobby, Morgan had composed herself enough to approach the reception desk. It really was a nice building. Not scary at all. Not out here, anyway.

Damian's room wasn't hard to find, but Morgan wasn't allowed to just barge on in. He was in a clean room, having received his chemo, awaiting the precious marrow Morgan was to provide. That much Morgan knew. Everything else was a surprise.

There was a huge window that covered most of the wall to the hall, with a phone hanging next to it, through which Morgan could see her twelve-year-old half-brother sitting up in his bed. He was smiling, but that was the only good thing about his appearance. He looked like he'd barely grown at all since Morgan had last seen him three years ago. His skin was yellowish, there were dark hollows under his eyes, and his head was completely bald.

Randy and his wife Lisa were sitting on either side of the bed dressed in scrubs and masks. It was Damian who noticed Morgan first and pointed at the window, his smile widening. Randy jumped up and approached the window as all three waved at her.

She waved back and did her best to smile. Randy picked up a phone and pointed for her to do the same.

"Morgan! It's so good to see you." He turned to Damian before she could say anything in reply. "Look, Munchkin, it's your sister."

Morgan's heart plunged and then began to pound furiously as she felt her face redden. She knew Damian and Lisa had called out greetings to her, but she hadn't heard them. She continued to hold her smile in place and wave like an idiot.

"Hang on, I'll be right out to talk to you," Randy said and hung up his phone.

Morgan hung up as well.

All her life, for as long as she could remember, that had been her biological father's special nickname for her. Munchkin. He wrote it in every letter or card he'd sent. He even called her that when she finally showed up on his doorstep uninvited three years ago.

Apparently, it wasn't so special after all. As she waited for Randy to emerge from the room, she idly wondered what the requirements were to have that name bestowed upon a person. Would anyone under a certain age qualify, or did they need to be his offspring?

"Hey, you're here! How was your trip?"

Morgan looked into Randy's dark green eyes that mirrored her own and didn't know quite what to say. She settled for a lie.

"It was fine."

"I – we – can't thank you enough for coming and doing this. Where's your friend?"

"Oh, she went to visit her brother today."

"Good, good. Did you get checked in yet?"

"No," Morgan said, leaning to peer around him into the room. "I thought I'd come see Damian first."

"Oh. Well, it's best you don't go in. He's very susceptible to, well, everything right now. Why don't we go chat in the waiting area down the hall? There are some people there you might like to meet." He chuckled. Nervously, Morgan thought.

She didn't say anything else as he led her down the hall, but she couldn't help the bitterness that flooded her. Sure, her bone marrow was good and healthy for them, but heaven forbid they allow her germy presence in her half-brother's room.

"Morgan?"

"What?" Lost in her thoughts, Morgan hadn't heard what Randy had said. Or maybe she had, but just dismissed it as something that made no sense at all.

"These are your grandparents," he repeated.

Morgan's mouth fell open ever so slightly as she gazed at the elderly couple standing awkwardly in front of her. They looked like they were dressed for church. They both had short gray hair. The green-eyed man was tall and thin, the brown-eyed woman short and plump.

No one moved or spoke for a solid minute as eyes darted uncertainly back and forth.

So, these were the mysterious parents of Morgan's biological father. Her grandparents who lived about a half-hour out of Bathurst, New Brunswick. The mythical relatives who had never once even bothered to contact her despite the close proximity.

Her grandfather was the first to extend his hand and offer a smile. "Pleased to meet you."

Morgan returned the greeting, which was followed by a similar one from her grandmother, and before she knew it Randy was whisking her off to Admitting.

"We should have plenty of time to catch up later," he said. "But we want to get you checked in and ready, right?"

Morgan, in a slight stupor, followed where he led.

She snapped out of her daze when she saw he was about to leave her at the Admitting desk.

"Where are you going?"

"Back to sit with Damian," he replied. "You'll be in good hands here."

"But . . . right. Can you do me a favor?"

"Of course."

Morgan dug her cell phone out of her purse and handed it to him. "For emergencies. Can you hang onto it for me?"

Randy appeared relieved she hadn't asked for anything else and took the phone. "Sure. I'll check in on you soon, okay?"

He was gone before Morgan could answer. As she turned back to the desk, she realized that she hadn't even learned her grandparents' names.

Chapter 10

In Which Josh Hangs With the Girls
Wednesday, August 12, 1998

After a joyous reunion at the ferry terminal in Bremerton, Josh drove Rab out to Ezra's garage since not much else was open that early. While they traveled, his sister caught him up on things back home – how her first year of college went, how her boyfriend was doing, the letter she'd received from Trixie, and how she rarely visited the Hampton home. Some things she had covered in her letters, but the latter was news.

"It seems like every time I go over there, Mom and Dad are fighting about something," Rab explained.

"Not physical violence, I hope?"

"No, not like that, and not even screaming. But there are a lot of tense, harsh words and accusations."

"Accusations? Like what?"

"I really don't want to get into it, Josh. Mostly stuff about money, but a little about how we were raised and all that."

"I wonder what set that off after all the years they've been together," Josh said.

Rab shrugged. "It's almost like our leaving the house removed whatever restraints they had in place."

"I can't feel sorry about that. We're adults now and have to forge our own lives."

"I love them both, even if Mom makes me nuts, and I hope they don't try to make me take sides."

"I know what you mean. Although, I'm afraid Mom would have ruled me out as an ally anyway," Josh said.

"You said Mom and not *Maman,*" Rab said.

"You noticed that. America is not a bilingual country, so I'm cutting down on my French, but learning a bit of Spanish and Japanese. I don't even remember the last time I said *merde*."

"Japanese? Now, there's a switch. Say something in Japanese."

"*Hai*!" Josh said.

"Hi? Does it mean the same thing it does in English?"

"It sounds the same but is spelled h-a-i. It means yes."

Rab laughed. "So, why do you have this urge to learn Japanese?"

"Because Iris, my co-worker, is of Japanese descent and will slip into her mother's language sometimes. Her dad's an American, though. He served in the Marines with Uncle Bill."

"Sort of like our dad, except the serving part."

"How so?" Josh asked.

"Well, Dad is an American and married a woman from another country. When we were growing up, we learned to speak French and you, at least, slipped into French from time to time."

"Has Father gotten your American citizenship papers yet?"

Rab sighed. "He's asked, and I don't want you to take this the wrong way, but I'm not sure I want them. I'm Canadian by birth and don't see myself ever living in the States."

"You know you don't lose your Canadian citizenship if you accept them."

"I know. I remember you telling me that when you got yours. It just seems like a lot of hassle for something I'll never use."

"It won't bother me if you choose not to get the papers. I'll support you no matter what you decide."

"I know, Josh, just as I have respected your decisions. Well, most of them."

"But not all?" He believed he knew which one.

"Maybe you should have come back to Bathurst to live after school, regardless of what Morgan told you," Rab said. "Your chances of getting back together would have been better."

There it was, the elephant in the truck, but he didn't have time to address it because they had arrived at the garage.

After introducing Rab to Karla, he led her into the repair bay. Iris was bent over the front end of a green Jeep.

"Iris, this is my sister, Rab," Josh said. "Rab, this is my co-worker, Iris."

Iris extracted herself from the engine compartment of the Jeep and pulled off her nitrile gloves. She approached the siblings and offered Rab a hand. "It's a pleasure to meet you, Rab."

Rab accepted the hand. "It's a pleasure to meet you too, Iris."

Iris looked down and spread her arms. "I wasn't expecting to have a guest. I mean look at me in greasy coveralls, no makeup, and my hair all tied back."

"You look fine. I don't know why that dumbass brother of mine never mentioned how beautiful you are."

"Because your brother is *baka,*" Iris said turning toward Josh.

"*Baka*? I'm guessing that's Japanese. What does it mean?" Rab asked.

"It's hard to translate, but it sort of means fool. It's a very strong insult in our language," Iris said.

"That's my brother, all right."

"You do realize I'm standing right here?" Josh said.

"And probably thinking of Morgan," Rab replied.

"Well . . ."

"*Baka*!" both girls exclaimed and then laughed so hard they clung to each other to keep from doubling over.

Josh blushed furiously.

The two young women chatted for a few more minutes before Iris had to excuse herself and get back to work. Josh marveled at how they talked to each other as if they'd been friends all their lives.

"Bye now, I hope we can talk some more before you go back home," Iris said.

"Me, too. I'm sure we'll have a chance at the wedding," Rab said.

"Will you be at the bridal shower tonight?" Iris asked.

"Yes. I still need to pick up a present, but I plan to attend – Morgan, too."

Josh's ears perked up. Maybe he could get home early and catch her before she left.

"I was going to ask," Iris said.

"I know. Saved you the effort."

"Don't party too hard tonight, partner, we need to be ready to work first thing in the morning," Iris said, patting Josh on the shoulder.

"Right, the bachelor party," Josh said.

"I doubt my brother will even finish the first beer, not that I blame him."

"I'll be here, don't worry about it," Josh said.

When they got back in the truck and began the drive north toward the mall, Rab was silent for a moment.

"Something wrong, sis?" Josh asked.

"Iris is a lovely person and I feel sorry for her."

"What do you mean?"

"If you get Morgan back, you're going to break her heart," Rab said.

"You're not talking sense. Iris isn't my girlfriend."

"Maybe not, but she's got it bad for you."

"No way. We're just co-workers and we get along well," Josh said.

"Think what you like, but while we were talking, she kept looking at you. She likes you – a lot. I could see it in her face."

"Well, when Morgan and I make up, I'll be driving back to Bathurst. Iris will be fine."

"You mean if you make up," Rab said.

"Hey, I've got to think positively."

"I'm still rooting for you and Morgan, but if that doesn't happen, don't rule out Iris."

"But not Trixie?" Josh asked.

"She's my friend and she needs help, but she's not good for you. For once your instinct was right."

They arrived at the mall, but it wasn't open yet. They took the opportunity to get some coffee at Starbucks and sat in the truck talking about Josh's new life in the States.

Rab seemed surprised at how Americanized her brother had become.

Whenever he tried to talk about Morgan, Rab steered him away from the subject.

After a couple of hours of shopping, they crossed Silverdale Way to Osaka Restaurant where they had arranged to meet Sally.

They had hardly been seated and were looking at the menus when Sally came bustling in. It didn't take long for her to spot Josh and Rab in the small restaurant.

"Rab!" she exclaimed as she rushed toward the table.

"Sally," Rab said as she jumped up from the table and they hugged.

"You're wearing your hair longer than you did in the last picture your mom sent us," Sally said.

"Mom never sent any," Josh said. "After Grandpa's funeral, I kept in touch with your folks and sent our school pictures."

"You must have seen some from my Goth phase," Rab said, cringing slightly. "Let's sit."

"How was the flight?" Sally asked as they took their seats.

"My God, it was so long, but it seemed like we spent as much time waiting on flights as we did in the air. We were up early yesterday and didn't get to the hotel until after midnight our time," Rab said.

Josh followed the conversation intently, hoping to catch something more about Morgan.

The waitress arrived and brought Sally a menu.

"And you had to be up early this morning, too?" Sally asked.

"Yes, Morgan had to be at the hospital early to get prepped. Speaking of which, has she called yet?"

Josh checked his watch. She should have called by now.

"No," Sally said, setting her cell phone on the table, "but Mom is at home watching Ashley, so I asked her to call me as soon as she does."

"Okay, good. Her part shouldn't take too long, so she'll be out of recovery soon, I expect. So how are you? You must really be excited."

"Oh, I am," Sally said. "I'm sorry, Josh, we're not letting you say a word."

"It's okay, I talked with Rab this morning and I see you every day," Josh said. "You two get acquainted."

"Thanks, you're a dear," Sally said and turned back to Rab. "It's hard to believe that in three days I'll be a married woman."

"Where are you going on your honeymoon?"

Josh allowed his mind to drift, wondering where he and Morgan might go on a honeymoon. She may want a small wedding, but she deserved a grand honeymoon.

"We're going to spend the first night in Seattle; I'm not saying where. Then we'll board the Bering Princess and take a cruise up the coast to Alaska."

"Will you be moving after you're married?" Rab asked.

"We've rented a small apartment in Poulsbo. That's about all we'll really need for a few years, at least until

Michael gets his next assignment. So tell me about Morgan and this Trevor guy."

"Sally! Not while Josh is here," Rab said.

"No, it's okay, Rab. I need to know what I'm up against," Josh said.

Sally placed a hand on his shoulder. "I'm still rooting for you, Josh, but you're right, you need to know."

The waitress came back and took their orders. As they waited and while they ate, Sally and Rab chatted away like two old friends.

Josh listened for more hints about Morgan but was disappointed when Rab refused to discuss her or Trevor any further.

After the dishes were cleared away, Rab looked at her watch and frowned. "Morgan should have called by now. I'm hoping she just got so busy visiting she forgot."

"Let me call Mom," Sally said, picking up her phone. "She may have been preoccupied with my niece."

Josh and Rab waited while Sally dialed.

"Mom, has Morgan called yet? She hasn't? Okay, thanks. I'll be home soon. Love you."

Rab reached across the table. "May I borrow your phone?"

"Sure."

Rab dialed a number and waited until it rang. "Morgan?"

A muffled voice spoke at the other end.

"Randy? Where's Morgan? Still unconscious? Let me speak to a nurse."

There was a pause.

Josh was already standing and removing his wallet.

"If there is no nurse, tell me exactly what they told you."

As Randy spoke, Rab's frown grew deeper.

Josh passed several twenty-dollar bills to Sally. "Pay our bill for us, please, we need to leave."

"Have you called her parents?" Rab asked. "No? Look for Parker, their number should be right on Morgan's phone."

More muffled words.

Rab stood and nodded to Josh, who was already at the door. "Look, we're on our way. We'll be there as soon as possible."

She hung up the phone and handed it to Sally. "Thanks, Sally. You probably heard, but Morgan hasn't come out of the anesthesia yet. Sorry we have run like this."

"Go, be with your friend. I'll see you soon."

Rab gave Sally a kiss on the cheek and joined Josh at the door. "When's the next ferry?"

"We're not waiting for a ferry. We're going to drive around," Josh said.

"Won't that mean driving over that bridge you told me about?"

"Morgan's in trouble. I'll focus on that."

Chapter 11

In Which Everything is Fuzzy
Wednesday, August 12, 1998

The light was blinding, even through Morgan's closed eyelids. Where was she?

More importantly, what was on her face? Panicked thought after panicked thought swirled through her brain as she tried to lift her arms that refused to comply. They were so heavy. She was so weak. She needed to get that thing off her face.

She heard more than felt herself whimper. She could breathe, but for how long? Another mighty effort to reach her face and remove the blockage resulted in another pathetic sob.

She needed to open her eyes, but the lids wouldn't budge. The only sound was her own blood rushing through her head, hard and fast.

Someone had drugged her. That was the only explanation. Good lord, she must have been abducted!

Morgan struggled futilely to move something, anything. She tried so hard she broke into a sweat and was left even more weak than before.

And she hadn't even managed to open her eyes. But through her still-closed lids, she could see the light was dimming and she thought she heard something beeping.

***

Voices coming from down a tunnel. No, make that one voice. It was a nice voice. An elderly woman?

"Morgan, sweetie, can you open your eyes?"

Sure she could. But she didn't want to. They needed to take that spotlight away first.

Someone groaned. Maybe it was her. There was something on her face, over her nose and mouth. Oh, maybe

69

this woman would save her. Could she not see what was on Morgan's face? Why wasn't she helping her?

"Honey, the doctor's on his way to see you."

Doctor? She couldn't wait for a doctor. She was going to suffocate! Since her hands were limp and useless, she tried rolling her head from side to side, hoping to dislodge the object.

Hands came up to restrain the minimal progress she was making. Oh, no. The woman wasn't helping her at all. She was trying to kill her!

"Morgan. You need to relax. Can you take a deep breath for me?"

Was this woman serious? Of course she couldn't. But then, reflexively, she did. Weird. There was still plenty of air to breathe. Might as well get as much as she could while she had the chance.

Morgan gulped air repeatedly until that beeping sound increased in intensity, the old lady started yelling at her, and the light began to fade. Too bad. She'd been planning to give opening her eyes a try next.

***

Morgan's eyes fluttered open and she shut them immediately. Too bright.

A wave of nausea washed over her and her eyes flew open. She squinted against the harsh lighting and turned her head to the side. The nausea passed. Good thing, too, because there was a plastic mask strapped to her face.

A hospital?

Yes, she could make out enough of the room to tell it was a hospital.

But why was she in one? What happened to her? Had she been in an accident?

Slowly and carefully – she didn't have much of a choice because she was so damned weak – Morgan stretched out her arms and legs. They seemed fine. The only thing amiss was a dull ache in her pelvic region. And her throat. Water. She needed water.

A plump woman with gray hair wearing scrubs poked her head through the doorway. She was kind of pretty. Maybe she'd come to give Morgan water.

"Morgan, you're awake." She smiled and hurried over to the bed. "Can you stay with me this time?"

This time? How long had she been in here? Morgan tried to answer that she'd do her best, but all that came out was a muffled croak. That stupid mask. She rolled her head back and forth again and frowned at the woman.

"Here. Take it easy. That's just oxygen."

Finally, she reached over and took the thing off. Much better.

"How are you feeling?" the nurse asked.

Morgan didn't waste her breath trying to answer that one. She wasn't even sure of the answer. There were too many questions she needed to ask.

"Why . . . who . . . water?"

Yes. The rest could wait. She needed water.

"Okay, dear. We'll need to sit you up a bit first."

The head of the bed began to rise ever so slowly and the room spun. Morgan cried out and started choking. She felt tears leaking out of her eyes as she shut them.

"Easy, easy. When you're ready."

Ready for what? Morgan didn't care about why she was in the hospital anymore. She didn't care about her aches and pains and vertigo. She just didn't understand why she was here alone. Did anyone even know she was here?

Morgan didn't know how long she'd been sobbing before it turned into full out choking and the nurse had to intervene. She kept her eyes closed as she was held up and a cup was brought to her lips. So good.

It was quickly taken away.

"Sweetheart, you need to calm down. You're still groggy from the anesthesia, but I need you to try stay awake until the doctor gets here."

Morgan peered through slitted eyes at the nurse, afraid to try speaking again.

She smiled brightly. "Your friends are here in the waiting room. They're very eager to see you."

Well, who was out there? Why didn't she just send them in then? What was she waiting for?

Morgan watched as the nurse bustled about checking machines and . . .

***

Damn that light was bright. Someone was shaking her.

Morgan squinted up into the face of a . . . doctor? He didn't look friendly at all. His eyes and skin were dark and he looked like he'd just rolled out of bed, his black hair sticking out in all directions. She was about to yell at him and tell him to take his damned hands off her, but he backed away just in time.

That was good, actually, because Morgan wasn't sure she could speak.

"Do you know where you are, Miss Parker?"

Was he for real?

He folded his arms and stared at her. Yep, he was serious.

"Hospital," Morgan choked out. "Water?"

He motioned to an elderly smiling nurse, who held a cup of water up to her lips. Morgan sucked as much as she could before it was taken away.

"You had some troubles with your anesthesia, Miss Parker. Delayed emergence is what we call it. We'll need to keep you overnight." The doctor spoke with his eyes trained on a clipboard. "Your emergency contact has been notified."

Who was her emergency contact? Where were they? She squeezed her eyes shut. "Light . . . off?"

"Sorry, you're in the post-anesthesia care unit. The lights have to stay on. Just try to get some rest."

How in the world did they expect her to sleep when her room was lit up like a stadium?

***

Morgan awoke irritated. What was with the blinding light?

She groaned and tried to roll over. The first thing she saw when she cracked her eyes open was Josh. He looked strange. Like a deer caught in headlights. She frowned and reached her arm out to him. It didn't get very far. It was so heavy. Why was he sitting so far away and looking at her like he'd never seen her before?

She was in a hospital?

"What happened?" Morgan hardly recognized her own voice. It was as weak as the rest of her and scratchy as hell.

Josh jumped to his feet but didn't approach the bed. His eyes remained wide and . . . freaked out? He looked from her to the door, then back to her and back to the door.

"Josh?"

She started coughing and closed her eyes. When she opened them, Josh was beside her with the cup of water.

"Just a little bit," he said. "Don't try drinking too much."

She did as he said then smiled up at him. "What's wrong?"

"You . . . I can get the doctor."

"No. What's wrong with *you*?" She reached out again and waited until he took her hand and held it. "You look scared."

"Just worried about you," he said.

Finally, he smiled and so did Morgan. She closed her eyes and decided she could wait until later to find out what had happened to her. Obviously some sort of accident. Oh, well. At least Josh was here with her and he appeared to be uninjured.

She was almost asleep when she felt his hand slipping away. She opened her eyes and tried to sit up in a panic. She didn't get far. "Where are you going?"

"I was going to let you rest."

"Don't go," Morgan said, frustrated. "You can't leave me."

"Of course. But they won't allow me to stay in here for more than ten minutes at a time."

Morgan frowned and her eyelids began to droop. "Don't go far then. Promise me."

"I promise."

"Okay." She allowed her eyes to close. "I love you."

"I love you too, Angel."

Chapter 12

In Which There Is a Reunion
Wednesday, August 12, 1998

Josh sat in Morgan's room, watching the heart and respiration traces across the monitor next to the bed. The gentle rise and fall of the hospital gown told him she was breathing, but he wanted reassurance.

Thoughts crowded his mind while he watched her sleep again, grateful she had been awake for even a few minutes.

How many times had her heartbeat filled his ears as he rested his head on her chest? How many times had he lain awake next to her as she slept softly beside him?

"Don't go," Morgan had said.

But he had left her months ago. He had crossed the continent. He had gone three thousand miles away from home, from her. How he wished she would have said this eight months ago. He would have still been in Bathurst, but happy because they would have been together.

Was she finally giving him the answer he'd sought last December? He had been ready to live with Morgan in Bathurst then, and he was ready still.

She'd said, "You can't leave me."

Did she mean right now or never again? Oh, how his heart hoped she meant the latter. He had left her, but only because she didn't want him to return home. Had those long, lonely months softened her heart? Had she changed her mind? Was this Trevor fellow only there to ease the ache she felt without him?

Or was he deluding himself?

No, Josh, you can't think that. You can't let the negative thoughts drive out the last shreds of hope you have.

He had promised her he would not go far. Did he mean from this room or her life? He wasn't sure he could keep the former promise; the hospital staff was strict about visiting hours. He had been asked to leave the room several times and was surprised they didn't make him leave the hospital.

And she had said, "I love you."

He had almost forgotten how those words from her lips thrilled him. His heart had almost burst with joy the first time she had spoken them outside his parents' house at the end of the trip home. He had told her time and again that she would have to tell him she didn't love him before he would ever stop loving her, and even then he might not.

Rab entered the room with two cups of coffee.

"Morgan woke up a few minutes ago," Josh said. He saw no reason to tell his sister about their conversation.

"That's a good sign," Rab replied. "She probably just needs to rest now."

Josh took a sip of his coffee while Rab examined the various displays that Josh had been watching. She would comprehend better than he what each one was telling them about Morgan.

"Morgan's vitals look normal," Rab said. "I see no reason why she can't leave in the morning. Then again, I'm not a doctor."

"I certainly hope she can."

A knock sounded at the door and a middle-aged man stepped into the room. His eyes were the same color of green as Morgan's, so it could only be Randy Pearson.

"Mr. Pearson?" Josh asked, just to be sure, standing as he did.

Randy smiled at him. "Yes, and you must be Trevor. You know, this will be the first time I've ever met one of Morgan's boyfriends."

"Mr. Pearson, this is my brother, Josh, and I'm Rab. Morgan and I came together. Trevor couldn't make it."

"That's right, Trevor couldn't be bothered to travel with her," Josh said.

"Ah, a simple mistake. I should have known. She said Trevor was taller than her, and I can see that you aren't."

"What do you want, Randy?" Josh snapped. The dig on his height tugged at his temper.

"I just wanted to pop in and see how our girl was doing," Randy said.

"Why should you care? You abandoned Morgan's mother when she was just a newborn."

"I did what I did and can't say I'm proud of it," Randy said and shrugged. "But it was where my head was at the time. Besides, she turned out all right."

"Only because her mother met a man who loved her and accepted Morgan as his own daughter. But you couldn't know she would turn out okay."

"Look, you little shit, I told Ingrid I would pay for her to take care of the problem."

"Problem? How can you look at this beautiful, intelligent young woman – your biological daughter – and call her a problem?" Josh's voice rose with his temper.

Rab glanced toward the nurse's station, not far from Morgan's room.

"She was then," Randy said with a dismissive wave of his hand.

"And how many other 'problems' did you leave scattered across the country?"

"Josh, I think that's quite enough," Rab said, placing a hand on his shoulder.

Randy shrugged again. "Love 'em and leave 'em was the way then."

"Tell, me Randy, was Lisa pregnant before or after you married her?" Josh persisted.

"Joshua Éveriste Hampton, you will apologize to Mr. Pearson right now or I will walk out that door and it will be a long time before you ever see me again," Rab said. To emphasize her point, she stepped to the couch and picked up her purse.

Josh looked between the two. The air was filled with tension as he took a deep breath and said, "I apologize, Mr. Pearson. I let my frustration boil over and said things I shouldn't have."

"Think nothing of it, kid," Randy said. "Take care of my girl for me."

"Mr. Pearson," Rab said, and held out her hand. "I will take Morgan's cell phone."

"Why should I give it to you? You're no kin of hers."

"We may not be related by blood," Rab said, "but Morgan and I have lived together, laughed together, and cried together. We've hugged more in a week than you have in a lifetime. Now please give me the phone, or I'll let my brother loose again."

Josh snapped his head toward his sister, half hoping she would.

"He doesn't frighten me," Randy said, but he stepped back and pulled the cell phone out of his pocket.

"Thank you," Rab said when he handed it to her. "We will make sure Morgan is well taken care of. Now, did you call her parents like I asked you to?"

"Good question," Josh muttered.

"Sure, but I didn't know what to say. Ingrid was plenty upset, so I told her to call the hospital number and ask the doctor." At the look on Rab's face, he quickly added, "I was busy with my son."

"Perhaps you should go see how your – son – is doing now that you know Ms. Parker is okay," Rab said.

Josh bit his tongue to prevent himself from telling the man to just leave like he always did.

Randy left the room without saying another word.

Josh lowered his head and closed his eyes. He took several slow, deep breaths.

"I'm sorry, Rab," he said, "the man just pushed all the wrong buttons."

"You didn't scream at him, you didn't swear at him, and, most importantly, you didn't punch him, although God knows I wanted to myself."

"I might have if you weren't here," Josh said.

"I believe you're past doing things like that now," Rab said and rubbed his shoulder. "I'm going to step into the hall and make a phone call."

"I hope Morgan didn't hear any of that."

"I think she's pretty well out."

"I may need to borrow the phone and make a call later," Josh said.

"We'll need to call Sally too and let her know we're okay."

Josh nodded and sat next to Morgan again, taking her hand in his. He hoped she would wake up again; he wanted to hear those words once more.

Outside the door, Rab had the cell phone to her ear. He couldn't really hear what she was saying, but the name "Trev" reached him several times before Rab said goodbye and started another call.

Josh rested his head on the edge of the bed. "Morgan, I don't know if you can hear me, but maybe these words will reach you somewhere deep inside there.

"I know we had a rough time when we were together. I was always working, studying, or sleeping. Always tired. But that's changed. I'm not the 'scrub boy' anymore. I have my certificate; I can be paid a trained mechanic's salary and I have a year's work experience."

Morgan shifted some and squeezed his hand but didn't open her eyes.

"If you want me back, I'll be happy to drive you home in Old Blue so you don't have to fly again. I'll work one job and only one job. We wouldn't have to get married if you didn't want to. I'd be happy just to have you in my life again."

Josh hoped he would be able to say all that when she was awake and that she would say yes.

Rab returned to the room. "I called the Parkers and let them know Morgan's okay, and I called Aunt Peggy's and apologized that Morgan and I missed the shower, but they understood and hoped she would be better soon."

"And you called Trevor too?" Josh asked.

"Yes, I called Trevor too. I'm your sister, but I'm also her friend. He would have been expecting to hear from her."

"I suppose that's fair. Still, I'm here and he's there. I have a chance."

"Trust me, you have this weekend. That's it, Josh. The clock's ticking."

"Let me borrow the phone, please, I need to make a call."

"Better use the payphone," Rab said. "I'm sure those calls cost her a bunch."

"Where are the payphones?"

"There's one in the lobby. I'll sit with Morgan, but visiting hours are almost over."

"Just give me the cell phone then. I'll make it quick and I'll pay for the call."

Rab handed over the phone and Josh stepped into the hall before he dialed the number to Brock's Garage. No one would answer at the garage, but someone would have the cell phone.

After two rings, Iris answered. "*Mushi, mushi*. Brock's Garage."

"Hi, Iris," Josh said. "Are you at the shower?"

A peal of feminine laughter answered his question before she said, "Yes. We heard about Morgan. Is she going to be okay?"

"I think so. The nurse says she'll probably be released sometime in the morning."

"So you won't be at work in the morning?" Iris asked, but it was more a statement.

"Might not be there all day."

"I'll let Dad know. I'll miss you, but it sounds like Morgan needs Rab's support."

"Maybe mine too. Enjoy the party," Josh said.

"Take care of yourself, okay, partner?"

"I will. See you later." He disconnected and headed back to the room.

"You just missed it, Josh. Morgan woke up and was a bit agitated wondering where you were. She calmed down when I told her you just stepped out to make a call."

The nurse came in and said, "Visiting hours are over. I have to ask you to leave."

"Do you have some paper and a pen? I'd like to leave her a note," Josh said.

"Sure," the nurse said and dug a pen and paper out of her pockets. "Please be quick."

"I will." He accepted the paper and wrote, "Angel, I wanted to stay with you all night, but the nurse is making us leave. I'll be just down the road with Rab. We'll return first thing in the morning to be here when they release you. Love, your Sunshine."

He put the note on her tray and walked away feeling a mixture of elation and anxiety.

Chapter 13

In Which Morgan's Eyes are Opened
Thursday, August 13, 1998

"Good morning, sunshine."

Morgan's eyes popped open. *Josh?*

No, of course not. Why on earth would it be Josh? It was a woman – the nurse. Morgan gave her head a shake and tried to sit up.

"Easy now, you're bound to be a bit sore."

"And dizzy," Morgan admitted.

The nurse set a breakfast tray on the nightstand and hurried to raise the bed for her.

"Wait a minute," Morgan said. "Breakfast? It's still morning?"

The nurse finished adjusting the bed and pulled a swiveling table over. "Still morning? Do you mean you don't remember any of last night?"

Morgan frowned as she tried to figure out what the woman was talking about. Last night she and Rab had been at the hotel, hadn't they? She'd called her parents and Trevor and then . . .

No!

Sketchy bits of what Morgan could only hope were dreams skittered through her mind.

The breakfast tray was placed in front of her on the table, but the smell made her nauseous. She pushed it away before asking the question she wasn't sure she wanted an answer to.

"How long have I been in here?"

"Almost twenty-four hours. You had some trouble with the anesthesia. Everything looks good now, but you experienced a delayed emergence after your surgery. It's something you'll need to keep in mind for the future in case you need anesthesia again, but you're out of the woods now."

Morgan swallowed hard. "Did I have any visitors last night?"

"Oh, yes. A handsome young man and his sister were here right until visiting hours were over. Had to practically crowbar the gentleman out. He left you a note."

The nurse retrieved a piece of paper from the nightstand and held it out to her, smiling.

Morgan set the note by her breakfast tray. "Did . . . my father come by?"

"Um, yes. He did. Anyhow, I'll leave you to your breakfast. Just ring if you need anything. The doctor should be by for morning rounds shortly and then I'm certain you'll be cleared to leave."

"Okay. Good. Thanks."

The nurse left and Morgan stared at her rubbery scrambled eggs and toast. Not happening. She needed coffee before anything else.

Okay, so she'd dreamt about Josh. Probably because he'd come to see her with Rab. No big deal, right?

Morgan plucked the note off the tray and unfolded it. She read it three times.

Well, shit. It couldn't be true. He must have known that whatever she'd said last night was because she was drugged.

Or maybe she didn't say what she thought she might have and it really was a dream after all. Maybe Josh was just . . . not over her?

Regardless, this was not a pen pal letter. It was a love letter. There was no ignoring that.

There was a light rapping on the open door and Morgan stuffed the note underneath her breakfast tray.

"Visitors," Nurse Smiley announced and disappeared.

Morgan's heart stopped beating. There he was. Josh. Her Josh. No, not her Josh. Not anymore.

But how in the world had she thought she'd be okay seeing him again like it was nothing? It was definitely something. She vaguely registered the fact he'd stepped into the room and that Rab was with him as memories assaulted her, one after the other.

The first time she met him at Cal's garage to get her oil checked and she realized he wasn't bad looking at all. Their first day on the road together heading to Seattle – him napping in the car looking all cute and peaceful. Their first kiss. Their first . . .

Rab had said something she hadn't heard. She was standing right in front of Morgan, who couldn't tear her eyes from Josh's ice blue ones. He was smiling and looking . . . hopeful?

"Morgan? Can you hear me?"

Morgan forced herself to look at Rab and blinked hard. She was pretty sure she looked terrified. And she hadn't remembered to breathe in a while. She drew in a deep lungful of air and exhaled.

"Sorry. What did you say?"

"I asked how you were feeling this morning." Rab frowned. "The drugs should be long gone from your system by now."

"No – yes – I mean I feel fine. Just a bit sore and confused. I had no idea I'd been in here overnight until the nurse told me. I don't remember anything at all. Nothing," she stressed, being careful not to look at Josh again.

"Well, you gave us a scare, that's for sure," Rab said and pulled Morgan's cell phone out of her pocket. "Here. You'll need to make some calls home."

"Oh God, no! They called my parents?"

"Uh, sort of. I told Randy to. I also called Trevor."

"Did you at least call them back when you found out I was okay?"

"Morgan, relax," Rab said, glancing at the heartrate monitor that was beeping like mad. "I did call them back. Everyone knows you're okay now."

"Ugh. I wish no one had called them in the first place. I guess we missed Sally's wedding shower then?" Morgan chuckled nervously.

"This is not a laughing matter. You weren't waking up, Morgan. It was a very serious thing."

"Okay, okay. I don't need a lecture today." Morgan took her phone and scanned through her recent calls. "Holy hell. Did you call everyone? My phone bill is going to be through the roof."

"Sorry. I didn't think about the cost. We were worried," Rab said.

"It's not a big deal. Thanks for caring," Morgan said, realizing she was being incredibly rude. She forced herself to turn to Josh.

Dammit. Those eyes. She couldn't remember the last time she'd seen them, at least not filled with love like they were now. But he'd lost his smile. Her heart threatened to break in two as she tried to come up with something to say. She was drawing a blank. For the life of her, she couldn't remember why they'd broken up. Seriously, had they even technically broken up?

Morgan swallowed her panic and decided to pretend she hadn't received Josh's letter. There was no other way.

"Thank you for coming along to keep Rab company. You didn't have to," she managed to say in a voice she didn't recognize as her own. It was so flat. Time to pep it up a bit. At least be friendly. "How have you been?"

Josh's eyes darkened. "I've been getting by."

Morgan had no more words. Thankfully, another rap on the door saved her from having to come up with any. It was Randy.

"Hey, there," he said with a nervous glance at Josh. "Feeling better this morning?"

"I think so," Morgan answered. "Have you met my friends?"

"Uh, yes. We met last night."

"Oh. Right. Well, how's Damian doing?"

"Fantastic." Randy beamed. "He'll be in the hospital for quite a while yet, but the doctors are optimistic for a full recovery. I can never thank you enough for coming out here to do this."

"I'm happy I could help. The doctor should be by to see me soon, and then I'll stop and see him before I leave."

"Oh, that's not necessary," Randy said, shifting uncomfortably. "He's not going to be up for visitors anytime soon. But I should really get back. Those nurses weren't happy I'm violating the two at a time rule here . . ."

So that was it. He was done with her again.

"Sure," Morgan said. "I guess I'll see you later then."

Randy's smile returned. "For sure. We'll keep in touch."

He waved and disappeared as quickly as he'd come.

"So, breakfast?" Rab peered at the disgusting mess of eggs and wrinkled her nose slightly.

"Not a chance. I would love some coffee, though. Would you mind? There's change in my purse."

"I'll get it," Josh said and stood to leave.

"Thanks," Morgan said.

Rab gave Morgan a strange look that probably wasn't all that strange, considering what Morgan was pretending not to know. "I'll go with him," she said.

"Just a sec. Can you help me with this rail and the IV? I need to use the washroom," Morgan said.

"Sure. Go ahead, Josh. I'll stay and help her."

"No, no. I'll be fine. I just need out," Morgan said.

Josh waited in the doorway while Rab lowered the bedrail, removed Morgan's finger monitor, pressed something to shut the machines up, then got her IV rolling.

"You sure you don't want me to stay?" Rab asked as Morgan shuffled to the bathroom.

"I'm fine. Seriously. I'm not even dizzy anymore, just a bit weak. Go on." She smiled at Rab and held the smile in place until they left.

Morgan released the breath she'd been holding and entered the bathroom. Okay, maybe she could have used a bit of help. It was plenty awkward with the IV in such a small bathroom. But she needed a minute alone. God, she needed a few weeks alone.

By the time she emerged from the bathroom, Rab and Josh had returned. Her eyes went to where the note had been sticking out from beneath the breakfast tray, and then to Josh who was stuffing something into his pocket. She just wanted to cry.

***

The doctor had shown up surprisingly early and cleared Morgan to leave within minutes. Rab had driven the three of them back to the hotel in the rental car with Josh sitting in the back seat. That three-block trip felt longer than her entire morning in the hospital. No one seemed to know what to say.

When Morgan found out Josh had brought Old Blue the night before, she expected he'd take his leave as soon as they were back at the hotel.

This was not the case. He and Rab sat speaking quietly by the window while Morgan returned her Bathurst calls at the table by the door, using the hotel phone.

She couldn't take her eyes off the two of them and wondered how she'd come to deserve such great friends – one of whom had once been something so much more.

From what she'd seen of their parents, she couldn't understand how they'd turned out so well. Their mother was

– well, Morgan had no word to describe her other than a bitch. She hadn't spent much time around their father at all, but from what she'd seen he was a grumpy, miserly old man.

But look what those two had created. Two polite, mature, hard-working, self-sufficient people with hearts of gold.

No, Morgan wasn't sure she deserved the friendship of either one at all. She certainly didn't deserve any form of goodwill from Josh. Yet there they sat, waiting to make sure she was okay.

She doubted she would ever be okay again. How could she do this to Josh? How could she deceive him about what she – kind of – remembered from the previous night? How could she not tell him that she'd read his note? Why in the world did he still care?

Geez. She was an absolute mess. Her mom had been talking the entire time she'd been contemplating Josh and Rab and she hadn't heard a thing. She was brought back to the conversation when she heard her mom talking about flights.

"Mom, it's over. I'm completely fine. There is absolutely no need to come here."

"I've already arranged for Mel to look after the kids. Your dad would be there too, but he just can't get away from work."

"You're not listening. Even if you did come out there would be nothing for you to do. You're not invited to the wedding, remember?" Morgan half-joked.

Her mom sighed. "You're right. I know. I just had a bad feeling about this whole thing before you even left. I knew as soon as Randy called that I never should have let you go."

"Don't be ridiculous. Besides, Damian is doing well. I helped him, Mom. He's a great kid." No way was she telling her about the way Randy had behaved.

"You're right, of course. Would you please call back later when your dad gets home? I can't tell you how worried he's been."

"I'll try. No promises. Just tell him I'm one hundred percent fine now. I've got to call Trevor, okay?"

"Okay. I love you."

"Love you too."

One down. One to go. Morgan crossed her fingers, hoping to get Trevor's voicemail.

"Morgan?"

No such luck.

"Hi, Trevor. You were expecting me?"

"Of course I was! There's no one else from this area code I've been wanting to hear from. You're really okay?"

"I'm great. It was nothing," Morgan said.

"Oh, it was something. Do you have any idea how terrified I was when Rab called? I was on my way to the airport before she convinced me you were going to be all right."

"Yeah, a lot of people were. I'm really sorry, Trev." And she really was. Oh, how she wished he'd been able to come with her. Oh, what a mess she'd made of things so quickly without him.

"There's nothing to be sorry about," he said. "Just don't ever do that to me again. How's your brother?"

"He's doing great, apparently. I wasn't able to see much of him, but my work here is done. I really miss you."

"Me too. I've been missing you for way too long, what with work and all. I can't wait until you get home."

"I'll be home before you know it. You're still expecting to be done prepping that case by your birthday?"

"Hell, I'm ambitious to get that promotion, but not that ambitious. The case will be done or I'll damn well quit." He chuckled. "I really can't wait for *our* day. I love you so much, Morgan," he said, deadly serious now.

The sentiment hit Morgan hard.

"I love you too," she said and meant it with her entire being.

But as she hung up the phone, her eyes went straight to Josh's that were trained on her. How was she going to get through these next few days without screwing everything up even more?

Well, to start with, she needed to keep her distance from Joshua Hampton. No matter what.

Chapter 14

In Which Aunt Peggy Insists
Thursday, August 13, 1998

Josh sat at the desk and gazed at Morgan seated on the bed nearby. This felt very familiar to Josh, even though they hadn't spent a night in a hotel room together in almost three years. And she hadn't been here with him last night.

Morgan had been sleeping in the hospital while Josh had slept in her bed at the hotel, alone. When they had left the hospital the night before, Rab had talked him into staying in the room she and Morgan were sharing instead of getting his own room.

Morgan's scent had lingered on the pillowcase. More than once he had reached for her in the night only to touch cold, empty sheets.

Now she looked at him with eyes devoid of emotion. He wanted to tell himself that it was an after-effect of the medications. But the doctor had assured them the anesthesia was out of her system and she was good to go home.

So, what was he supposed to make of last night? She had said she loved him. But he was sure she had just said the same to Trevor, even though she was talking softly. He wasn't trying to eavesdrop, but it was hard not to hear when she was in the same room.

What had Rab said to him earlier? "The clock is ticking."

He suspected that his sister knew something she couldn't tell him because of her friendship with Morgan.

But why did life have to be so damned complicated? He had loved her, and she had loved him. Wasn't love supposed to be eternal? Josh stuck his hand into his pocket. The note he'd snagged from Morgan's table in the hospital seared his flesh.

Josh meant every word of what he had written. He had meant every word he'd said to Morgan in that room. He had told his co-worker he'd go back to New Brunswick for her, and he'd meant those words too. Every one of them.

It was already Thursday. With work and the rehearsal tomorrow, and the wedding on Saturday, time wasn't just running out; it was practically nonexistent.

"Josh? Are you okay?" Rab asked. Her face was right in front of his.

How long had she been there? "Yeah, yeah. I guess I didn't sleep well last night." It wasn't exactly a lie.

"I was saying you should call Aunt Peggy and let her know Morgan is out of the hospital."

"Yeah. That's a good idea," Josh said, blinking a few times to get his mind back to the present.

"Use the hotel phone. We ran up quite a bill on Morgan's cell phone."

"Number one reason I don't have one." Josh picked up the phone and dialed a number from memory.

"*Mushi, mushi,* Brock's Garage. How may I help you?" Iris asked.

"Iris? I dialed my aunt's house."

"You might think you did, but you dialed the shop. Maybe you were thinking of me," Iris said.

Josh could hear her smiling.

"I guess I must have misdialed. I was trying to reach my aunt," Josh said, a bit confused.

"Well, I'm in the shop, *quite alone*. Karla called in sick this morning and Dad's out on a call. Can I do something for you, Josh? Did Old Blue break down?"

"No, no. I need to reach my aunt."

"Well, since I have you, how is – she – doing?" Iris asked.

"Morgan was released this morning. Rab and I got her back to the hotel and we're playing catch-up. I expect to be coming back to . . . Silverdale soon." *Why didn't I say home?*

"Do you intend to work tomorrow?"

"Yes, I should be there at the regular time," Josh said.

"See you then, partner," Iris said and hung up.

"Wrong number?" Rab asked.

"Yeah, I dialed the shop." Josh disconnected, then focused intently on punching in the correct numbers for his aunt and uncle's house.

"Hello?" Aunt Peggy, thankfully, answered.

"Hey, Aunty, it's Josh."

"How is Morgan doing?"

"She's been released from the hospital, but she may be a bit groggy and sore," Josh said.

"I am *not* groggy," Morgan said. "I'm only trying to process what happened yesterday."

"She doesn't need to be staying in a hotel," Aunt Peggy said. "You bring her over here. She and your sister can sleep in your room. You can sleep on the couch."

"Let me ask them." Josh put the phone on his shoulder and turned to the girls. "Aunt Peggy says you should come and stay there. She says you two can sleep in my room and I'll get the couch."

Morgan began to shake her head vigorously and waved her hands back and forth.

Rab looked at Morgan. "You told me you stayed there before and they accepted you more warmly than the Pearsons," she said.

"I really don't want to intrude. Besides, with the wedding, it must be a madhouse," Morgan said.

"Nonsense," Josh said. "Aunt Peggy has everything under control. Besides, it'll make up for that phone bill we ran up and save you a few trips across the water."

"Come on, pack up and let's check out," Rab said. "If we get there and it doesn't work out, we can find a hotel in Silverdale. Since you're no longer needed at the hospital, we don't need to be as close."

"Yeah, not needed there," Morgan said. Disappointment clouded her face. "You're right. Let's go."

Josh put the phone back to his ear. "Sounds like the girls are coming, Aunty."

"Good. I'll be sure to make extra for supper," Aunt Peggy said.

Josh exchanged farewells with his aunt, then hung up the phone.

Morgan was already standing by the door. "Let's get going then."

"It won't take me long to pack," Rab said. "Do you want to ride over with Josh?"

"In Old Blue? I'll pass," Morgan said. "The rental is much more comfortable and has better AC."

Josh grimaced at the slight to his truck. "Do you girls need any help?"

"You go on ahead so you can help Aunt Peggy set up for us," Rab said.

"I'll be taking the ferry across. Maybe you can catch the same one?"

"We'll be sure to look for Old Blue when we board," Rab said.

"Later then," Josh said. He stole a glance at Morgan, but she had moved from the door and wasn't facing his way. *With them staying at Aunty's, I'll have that much more time.*

He closed the door behind him and headed to his truck with a spring in his step.

***

They didn't make the ferry with Josh. Disappointment threatened to crush his heart. He had hoped he and Morgan could go out on the deck and watch Seattle recede as they sailed toward Bremerton, like they had done three years ago. He would leave his hat in Old Blue this time.

Instead, Josh sat alone in his truck while the ferry crossed the Puget Sound.

***

When Josh walked into the house and announced his arrival, Aunt Peggy called him into the kitchen. Out in the living room, Sally sat on the floor with her cell phone and an address book in front of her. Her hair was in disarray and her expression was not a happy one.

"What's going on with Sally?" Josh asked when he arrived in the kitchen.

"You missed all the excitement last night," Aunt Peggy said. "But you would have anyway since you wouldn't have been at the bridal shower."

"What happened? Is everyone okay?"

"Yes, everyone's okay. I'll tell you more in a minute. Rab called and said they'd be arriving on a later ferry."

"Did they have a car problem?" Josh asked. "I should have waited for them."

"They're fine, but Rab said Morgan wouldn't let her leave Seattle until they stopped at Pike's Place Market. I guess she wanted to get some sightseeing in."

"Makes sense. I'm sure they'll avoid the balloon man. So, what happened?"

"Right in the middle of the bridal shower, Brook went into labor. Sally contacted Brook's husband while I got her to the hospital," Aunt Peggy said.

"Is she okay?"

"Oh, yes. She gave birth to a baby boy at about five this morning. They were flown to the NICU in Seattle."

"I can see how that could upset a party, but it doesn't explain why Sally looks so upset," Josh said.

"Brook was one of the bridesmaids. Now she won't be able to attend the wedding."

"Oh, I see. Sally's looking for a last-minute replacement."

"Yes. If she can't find one, we may have to cut you from the wedding party," Aunt Peggy said. "Brook was supposed to walk with you."

"I seem to remember that. I can accept being cut, if necessary. I was kind of the odd man out, anyway. But why did Sally choose a bridesmaid that was due on her wedding day?"

"That's the problem; she wasn't due for another two months. The baby came prematurely."

"I hope the baby will be okay," Josh said.

"Brook told us the baby is doing well and should be able to go home in a couple of weeks."

"Well, that's good."

"Now, let's get your bedroom set up for the girls," Aunt Peggy said, going to the stairs.

As Josh wrestled the cot and foam mattress down from the attic, Aunt Peggy stripped his bed. There was no way she was going to let a guest sleep on dirty sheets – even though he had changed them yesterday. After they'd made up the cot, Aunt Peggy left him to finish tidying up.

Josh dusted, then took his laundry down to the utility room and started a load of wash. Back in his room, he decided to rearrange his pictures. He swapped out the newer photographs and replaced them with older ones that prominently showed Morgan and him when they were happy.

Josh had framed the picture Morgan had drawn of him to replace the one that was stolen during their trip home from Seattle. No need to rearrange that – it hung on his wall as it always had.

Sitting at his desk – he dared not sit on that freshly made bed – he took the note out of his pocket and read the words he'd written to Morgan at the hospital and started considering his chances. He debated placing the note on the pillow where she couldn't fail to see it. But then she'd know he had taken it from the hospital, and who knew what kind of fuss that would start.

He almost tossed it into the trash can, but slipped it inside his copy of *Robert Frost's Poems* instead.

Josh was still brooding when the doorbell sounded. Believing it was Morgan and Rab, he left his room to go downstairs. As he was descending, he heard the patter of bare feet and Sally exclaiming, "I've got it!"

She pulled the door open. "Morgan!"

The two girls embraced and squealed with delight.

Rab stepped past them and leveled her eyes at Josh. "You didn't warn me about the flying fish."

"I didn't know you were going to that market. Come on, let's go meet Aunt Peggy."

In the kitchen, Aunt Peggy wiped her hands on a towel. "Mary, dear, it's so good to finally meet you."

"I go by Rab, please, Aunty. It's good to finally meet you, too."

Sally dragged Morgan into the kitchen. "Look who's here, Mom."

"We weren't expecting to see you until the wedding," Aunt Peggy said. "How are you, dear? You had quite a day yesterday."

Before Morgan could reply, Sally said, "Oh my God. That's it! Morgan, oh Morgan, you've got to be one of my bridesmaids."

Josh held back a laugh at his cousin's enthusiasm.

"What? No! Your wedding is in two days. I'm honored, but there's no way I could be fitted and have a dress made in time," Morgan said.

"We have a dress. You're about the same size as Brook. A few adjustments and it should fit perfectly."

"Except Morgan's not seven months pregnant," Josh said.

"Shush, cuz, you don't know anything. The dresses for the bridesmaids all have an Empire waist, so we could allow for Brook's tummy."

"What's an empire waist?" Josh asked.

"It means the waist is tucked right up under the boobs," Sally said.

"Sally, we have guests."

"Yes, Mom, both of whom have boobs," Sally said. "Come on, Morgan, you have to try it on so we can see what adjustments we need to make."

"Give the girl a chance to relax. She had a rough day yesterday," Aunt Peggy said.

"I haven't even said I'd do it," Morgan protested.

Josh debated adding his encouragement, but decided to see how things played out on their own.

"Wearing a maternity dress won't get you pregnant, Morgan," Rab said with a smirk.

"Are you sure? Because it seems to keep happening to my mom. I made her get rid of them after my sister was born."

Everyone laughed.

"I'm studying to be a nurse, trust me on this."

"Well, okay," Morgan said.

Sally threw her arms around Morgan again. "Yes! You've saved my wedding! Oh, thank you, Morgan, you're my hero."

This time, Josh couldn't help chuckling.

"Wait . . ." Morgan said and tossed a look at Josh.

"Come on. Let's sit down and have some tea and you can tell us all about what happened to you at the hospital," Sally said and led Morgan away.

"I'll help you get the bags to your room, Rab," Josh said.

As they went out to the rental, Josh was smiling inwardly. Not only was Morgan there, but she'd be in the wedding party. And walking down the aisle next to him.

There was no way he was going to tell her that before she was too committed to back out.

Chapter 15

In Which Morgan Wakes Up in Josh's Bed
Friday, August 14, 1998

Morgan lay staring at the portrait she'd drawn of Josh. It was framed – displayed prominently in his room. She was still convinced it was nothing like the first one she'd drawn. It wasn't as good. This one didn't capture his eyes properly. Or his smile.

But every other goddamned picture of the two of them in his room did. Had he done that on purpose, or had this stuff been here all along? Whatever the reason for the pictures and his behavior in general, why in the hell had he left Bathurst in the first place if he was so hung up on her?

Morgan rolled over despite her soreness to bury her face in the pillow and block out the sight of all the happy-couple pictures. But the images remained seared into her brain. Even worse, she caught a whiff of that scent again – the one she'd been smelling all night. What *was* that underneath the laundry detergent smell?

Well, it was Josh. Not cologne, not shampoo or soap, just Josh. Even though she was irritated beyond belief, Morgan couldn't help inhaling deeply and remembering. Everything.

She never should have come here. She should have simply checked off the "no" box on the RSVP. She could have hung out in Seattle while Rab attended the wedding and sampled the city's nightlife all on her own.

But Seattle hadn't proven to be any safer than Silverdale when it came to Josh-drama. The day before, in a desperate attempt to avoid riding the ferry with Josh, Morgan had talked Rab into going to Pike's Place to find a unique belated shower gift for Sally. She hadn't even liked that place when she and

Josh had gone there years ago, but it was the only market she knew of that the Silverdale stores couldn't compete with.

From the second they'd entered the parking lot, all Morgan could think about was Josh. She'd wandered around in a daze and she couldn't even remember what Rab ended up picking out for Sally's gift.

Doomed. She was just doomed.

Rab had risen long ago and slipped out quietly. Morgan had been awake but not in any hurry to get up and greet the day. The sounds and smells of breakfast being made reminded her she couldn't very well hide up here for the duration of their stay.

And getting the hell out of this room was probably a fantastic idea.

Morgan started to get out of bed as she normally would and cried out as her lower back throbbed. Damn. They said she'd be a little bit sore for a week or two, but this was more than a little bit. Maybe she could use it as an excuse to get out of bridesmaid duty . . . perhaps the whole wedding.

Morgan sighed and finished hoisting herself out of bed. No, she couldn't do that to Sally. Surely she'd be able to pull herself together, get through the next couple of days, and get back on that plane.

Yes, air travel had suddenly become the lesser of all evils.

Morgan enviously eyed the cot beside the bed as she gathered her things to take to the bathroom. Of course, Rab had insisted on taking the cot because the bed would be much more comfortable for post-surgery Morgan.

She'd been wrong. Morgan was taking that cot tonight if she had to flip Rab right off it.

After a quick shower, Morgan descended the stairs into utter madness. Breakfast was already over, but Aunt Peggy insisted on fixing her a plate. Morgan told her she only wanted coffee, but her protests fell on deaf ears. At least she got coffee, though.

Morgan sat sipping it, refusing to feel any sense of disappointment that Josh had already gone to work, and tried to nod and smile at all the people around her while she picked at some toast. Of course Josh was at work. It was good news. She certainly didn't want to see him. He probably should have been at work yesterday, too.

Morgan was introduced to Sally's sister-in-law and immediately forgot her name. There was a little girl about the same age as Morgan's sister who was constantly being passed from woman to woman. Another name forgotten. Two other women in addition to Rab were in the living room, working on what looked like blueprints with Sally.

Morgan shuddered. She needed to get out of here. Too much estrogen.

But it was not to be. The second she was finished with breakfast and started planning an escape, Sally and Aunt Peggy herded her up the stairs to work on the bridesmaid dress.

Once they'd stuffed her into it, Morgan thought that would be it. It was peach-colored, so there was no helping that, but otherwise it seemed to fit decently.

Apparently, she was wrong. The two women fluttered around her with measuring tapes and pins. Morgan tolerated it as long as she could before begging to be released. The biggest problem was, of course, the top of the dress. Simple solution: she promised to stuff her bra.

Surprisingly, that appeased them. But then they sat her at a vanity table and started fussing with her hair and suggesting makeup options.

After half an hour of that nonsense, Morgan promised to take their suggestions into consideration, then resorted to claiming her fatigue and soreness was just too much and she needed to rest. It wasn't a complete lie. And it did get her out of Sally's room.

Right back into Josh's.

Morgan flopped onto the bed, smelled Josh, and leapt back up. Yes, those were a couple of painful maneuvers, but she barely felt them. The hard wooden chair by the desk where Morgan had her cell phone charging was the best seat in the room. She turned it so it faced away from the portrait of Josh, placed the photos of the two of them that were on the desk facedown, and picked up her phone. No calls.

Morgan was tired but definitely not sleepy. It was – *holy crap* – only one o'clock. What was she going to do all day until the rehearsal and dinner tonight? She hadn't brought anything to entertain herself with. She'd been expecting . . . not this. She and Rab were supposed to be sightseeing and partying in Seattle. She thought she'd be visiting with her little half-brother . . .

Morgan picked up her phone, dialed the number for the hospital, and asked to be put through to Damian's room.

Randy answered and they exchanged greetings. Awkwardly. How silly Morgan felt thinking he would recognize her voice. She had to identify herself by name before he caught on.

"Oh, Morgan. Good to hear from you. How was your trip?"

"My trip? Short. I'm in Silverdale," she said.

"Oh. I thought you'd already gone back to Bathurst."

"Um, no. I'm here until Sunday. My friend's getting married tomorrow, remember?"

"Oh, of course. Well, I hope you have a good time. You can tell me all about it in your next letter, okay?"

It sounded like he was about to hang up. "How's Damian doing?" Morgan asked quickly.

"Same as yesterday; everything looks promising. We'll get him to write you a thank you letter once he's up to it."

"That's . . . great. I guess I'll see you another time, then."

"Yeah, for sure. When things settle down, we'll work something out."

Morgan held in her sigh and shook her head. "Goodbye."

She didn't wait for him to respond before disconnecting.

Morgan's finger hovered over Trevor's number, but that's where it stayed. She had no idea what to say to him. Tell him how her trip was going? Uh, no. Not right now. Why did she feel guilty? She had no reason to feel this way. Yet she did.

Morgan tossed the phone aside and picked up a book Josh had left on his desk. Robert Frost. Nice. She hadn't read any of his stuff since high school.

She took the book over to the cot and made herself comfortable then opened the cover.

She slammed the book shut. Nope. Nope, nope, nope. She had not just seen that. Not the letter Josh had left for her at the hospital and then taken back. Not the one he'd stuffed into his pocket that should have ended up in a trash can. Not the paper that had been painstakingly smoothed out with only a few wrinkles and preserved in this book.

This couldn't be happening. Why did it bother her so much?

The answer was simple. Because she couldn't pretend not to care anymore.

Morgan shoved the book away and lay staring at the ceiling.

She loved Trevor. She loved his arms, his hands, his eyes. She still shivered every time he kissed her. She was never bored around him. Even at work they managed to have fun. He loved her. He wanted to marry her, for Chrissake.

But when did she stop loving Josh? The simple yet terrifying answer was that she hadn't. She never had the chance. She still loved him. How could she not? They'd been through so much together. No one had ever made her feel safer and more adored. There was nothing he wouldn't do for her, even now.

But how could she be in love with two people at the same time? It just wasn't possible. Yet here she was. And there was no more denying it.

There was only one question she needed to ask herself. What would she do if there was no Trevor – if she'd just shown up single after all this time and Josh had been waiting for her?

Morgan got up off the cot, returned the book to the desk, and grabbed her cell phone and purse. Maybe she was being a complete idiot, maybe not. Regardless, the one thing she did know was that she couldn't leave without talking to him.

Maybe there was still something there. Maybe there was nothing. But goddammit, their time together hadn't been nothing. All she knew was that she had to find out what was left between them, and the clock was ticking. Rehearsal dinner tonight, wedding tomorrow, and then she'd be on her way home. It was now or never.

Morgan marched down the stairs, found Rab, and pulled her aside.

"I need to know where Josh works."

Rab gave her a funny look. "I told you; he's a mechanic at a garage owned by one of Uncle Bill's friends."

"No, I need the address."

"Now?" Rab's eyes widened.

"Yes, now. Please don't make a big deal of this and don't tell anyone else, okay? I just need to talk to him."

Rab chewed on her lip. "Morgan, you should –"

"Rab, please!"

"Okay, okay. Just hang on."

Rab disappeared and Morgan stood by the door to the living room watching the happy wedding planners. She wanted to be happy. She deserved to be happy. She just wasn't sure with whom.

And that made her feel terrible.

Rab returned with a slip of paper. "Are you sure –"

"I just need to talk to him," Morgan said and kissed her friend on the cheek before dashing out of the house.

Her heart pounded as she got in the rental car and headed out. There was still time to turn back. The sane thing to do would be to turn back.

But as she drove, Bathurst receded further and further away in her mind. Fate had brought her here. All she had to do now was figure out why.

Along the way, she passed the junkyard that she and Josh had gone to three years earlier. It was where he'd found the piece he needed to fix Zinger. Morgan pulled over and spent some time picking a bunch of wildflowers. The resultant bouquet was cheesy, but pretty. She couldn't show up empty-handed after the way she'd treated him yesterday.

As she got back into the car, she could clearly picture Josh's face when he saw the flowers. She laughed aloud as she imagined his astounded look that would only last a minute or so. Then slowly but surely it would transform into the smile that started at his eyes and worked its way down to his mouth.

Morgan stepped on the gas.

Chapter 16

In Which the Wrong Lips Lock
Friday, August 14, 1998

Josh's day started off uneventfully. Morgan had still been asleep while Rab and Sally sat in the living room talking about wedding stuff. He'd had his usual bowl of Fruity Rings – a food he'd introduced to the pantry – and departed for work.

He'd arrived at the garage at the usual time. Iris was already there, setting up to remove the hood of the Mustang they'd been working on. The owner of the vehicle wanted the engine rebuilt, so Josh and Iris were pulling the engine out today and stripping it down to the block.

As the day went on, it seemed almost foreign to Josh to be back in the shop. He'd only been off for two days, but it might as well have been two months. Today could be his last day of working here if Morgan wanted him to drive her back to Bathurst, back home.

He'd prefer to give two weeks' notice because Mr. Brock had been so good to him. He was a wonderful mentor, a good friend, and much like he'd wished his father to have been. Of course, he was willing to admit that part of that strained relationship had been his fault.

Regardless, Josh would forgo his last check if he had to leave abruptly.

Maybe he could talk Morgan into visiting for two weeks, but she probably had to be back at work. He wasn't even sure she'd have time to drive with him across the continent. He might have to fly back instead.

Flying would mean leaving Old Blue behind, but he could come back once things were settled and drive the truck home . . . maybe even bring Morgan with him for another wild road trip. He'd love for them to stop at some of the places they'd talked about but never got the chance to visit.

Okay, Josh, let's dial it back some. Before he could have a wild, cross-country honeymoon with Morgan, Old Blue, and his trusty blanket, she'd have to accept him back.

"You didn't get a chance to listen to the game last night, did you?" Iris asked.

"Huh? No."

"Just as well. The White Sox creamed the Mariners fourteen to two."

"Uh-huh," Josh said.

"Okay, Josh, back out of the engine. We need to talk."

Josh stood and turned to her, setting the socket wrench down. "We do?"

"Yes, dammit, we do. You've hardly said two words at a time all day, and even then I had to pry them out of you," Iris said.

"I'm concerned about Morgan."

"She's going to be okay. Otherwise she'd still be in the hospital and not staying with you."

"How'd you know where she's staying?" Josh asked.

"Sally and I talked last night when she called about some small wedding detail." Iris crossed her arms. "She said Morgan's staying at your aunt's place and you're sleeping on the couch."

"Well, yeah. Couldn't let Morgan stay alone after what happened."

"I thought you might be tired from sleeping on the couch, but you're working like normal," Iris said.

"I had a lot of experience working while tired when I was in college."

"So it can't be that. What is it?"

"If you must know, Morgan said she loved me," Josh said, keeping his face neutral.

"When? A year ago? Three years ago?"

108

"No, no. The other night, when she was in the hospital."

"Was she wide awake?" Iris asked.

Josh scrunched his face together. "No, she kept drifting in and out of sleep."

"So you're brooding over her because she said something while still working the drugs out of her system."

"She seemed awake enough. Morgan asked me not to leave, but the nurse wouldn't let me stay," Josh said.

"Stop right there, Josh, and look at me."

Josh looked at Iris, puzzled. "Okay, I'm looking at you. What am I looking for?"

"What do you see?" Iris asked.

"I see my co-worker and a damned fine mechanic at that."

"But you don't see the woman beneath these coveralls."

"I see you in your jeans and T-shirt when you take the coveralls off for the day," Josh said.

She let loose an exasperated sigh. "You see a person, but do you see the woman?"

"I don't understand what you're getting at. I know you're a woman."

"Yes, exactly. You have that tiny bit of knowledge locked somewhere up there in your brain," Iris said and pulled his hat off. "Let's see if taking this off lets that notion free."

Josh realized she was standing quite close to him now. Sure, they worked side by side, often in contact, but this was different. He didn't know what to think.

"I don't feel any different," he said, even though he kind of did.

"You're looking for a future but don't realize it could be right in front of you."

"I'm not sure what you mean," he said, but remembered what Rab had told him. A notion was forming.

Without warning, Iris grabbed the front of his coveralls, stood on her tiptoes, and pressed her lips to his.

Josh stared wide-eyed for a second. Then he closed his eyes and kissed back, his arms wrapping around her.

His mind was screaming this was wrong, wrong, wrong, but he felt the passion in those lips. This was the closest any woman had been to him in almost a year, and he wanted to – needed to – respond in kind. He'd allow this and sort out what it meant later.

He didn't know or care how long they'd been locked together when the sound of the door closing caused them to separate. Josh turned to the door but didn't see anyone standing there watching them fraternize. The shop's fan ruffled his hair and he searched for his hat. It was still in Iris's hand.

"What just happened?" Josh asked.

"Well, I don't know about Canada, but down here in the States, we call that a kiss," Iris said with a wry smile. "It is often performed by two people who like each other."

Josh shook his head. "No, I mean I heard the door close."

"I don't see anyone, and no one threw cold water on us, so I wouldn't worry about it."

"We shouldn't be kissing in the shop," Josh said. "We're being paid to work."

"But you haven't kissed me any other place."

"We shouldn't be kissing at all."

"Why not? I like you a lot and I suspect you like me more than you're letting on," Iris said. "Your kiss was certainly affectionate."

"But this isn't the time or the place for that."

"Listen, I had to go for it now. There may never be another time or another place."

"What are you talking about?" Josh asked.

"We have worked together, eaten together, laughed together, and even cried together when Kobi was killed by that *baka* driver. I may be falling in love with you, and I want the chance to explore that."

110

"But . . . Morgan."

"Yes, *but Morgan*. Even when she was three thousand miles away, her presence was in this shop every damned day. Not physically, but here nonetheless. And I'm damned well tired of it."

"I never . . ." Josh began.

"Yes, you did talk about her all the time, but you didn't think anything of it because I'm just one of the guys. I don't mind being treated like one of the guys in the shop, but I want to be treated as a woman, too."

"But . . ."

"Every day, while we worked, it was Morgan this and Morgan that and Morgan something else. At first, I was interested. But then I dreamed it was me having those adventures and good times with you. Now, I don't want to hear about her anymore," Iris said and popped him in the chest with his hat.

"I have to take a chance . . ."

"I know, I know, and the next two days are going to be a torment for me. I won't know whether we'll get a chance to learn if we belong together or whether you'll ride off into the rising sun with her." Tears started to form.

"I never knew you felt this way," Josh said, placing the hat back on his head.

"Because your mind was three thousand miles away and you couldn't see what was right in front of you. I should have said something before, but I thought it was obvious enough. Your sister knew how I felt the moment we met."

"She did say something like that."

"I'm glad she did. Maybe it'll get your heart working again," Iris said. "Look, I don't want to be your plan B. If Morgan says no, make a clean break and start again with me as your new plan A."

"And if Morgan chooses to take me back, what'll happen to you?"

"Not your concern. Don't base your decision on my feelings. You have to take care of your own heart." She shrugged. "Life will go on. It always does. Maybe your departure would be what life has in store for me."

"I wouldn't forget you," Josh said.

"You damned well better not, but don't send me any cards or letters unless Morgan also signs them."

The door opened and Karla stuck her head in. "Iris, I need you to watch the desk for a few minutes. I have to run to the bank."

"Sure," Iris said and peeled off her nitrile gloves. "Be right there."

"Where is your guest?" Karla asked.

"Guest? We've had no guest back here," Iris said.

"I thought I heard the door close, but didn't see anyone," Josh said.

"A young woman came in and wanted to speak with Josh for a minute," Karla said.

"Young woman?" Josh said turning toward the door. "Did she give a name?"

"No. Since she asked for you by name and had a bunch of flowers, I figured you knew her."

"What did she look like?" Josh asked.

"She had long, blond hair, but I mostly noticed her eyes. They were the most amazing shade of green I've ever seen."

"Morgan." Josh's heart plunged. "She's not in the lobby?"

"No. She must've left when I stepped into Mr. Brock's office."

"Well, shit. I've got to go catch her and explain," Josh said and dashed out the door into the lobby, passing Iris on the way. Her crestfallen face caused him to pause. A second ticked by and his eyes went to a bouquet of wildflowers on the floor.

But Morgan.

"I'll be back," he shouted as he ran from the building and climbed into the cab of Old Blue.

He left the parking lot and took a chance that Morgan had headed back to Silverdale.

There was also a chance that she'd head south and drive back to Seattle. But he believed Morgan would at least talk to Rab before leaving.

He drove all the way to Aunt Peggy's. When he didn't see the rental there, he turned around and headed back toward work, driving more carefully while he searched for Morgan. He didn't see her or the rental.

He would have to try explaining things to Morgan later, but was sure he'd just swung and missed for strike two. Or worse – he may have hit into a double play.

Game over?

Chapter 17

In Which Morgan is in the Dumps
Friday, August 14, 1998

Morgan had just over a thousand dollars saved up for a down payment on a new car. She loved Zinger, her '86 Pontiac 6000, but it was time for a change. The attempted trip to the airport on Monday had proven that.

She'd done her research and had her eye on a brand-new Toyota Celica – blue in color.

Now, as she wandered through the junkyard examining all the vehicles abandoned to rust and rot and molder, she was having second thoughts.

Buying a new car was a ridiculous idea. Save up for a down payment, get a loan, then make payments for nearly a decade and what do you get?

A piece of junk that ended up here. They all ended up here, eventually.

Morgan kicked at a tire blocking her path. It didn't move. She didn't care. It felt good to kick. She kicked it again. And again.

By the time she finished beating on the tire, she'd worked up quite a sweat. She wasn't sure when it had started raining but it was pouring now. Strands of hair had come loose from her ponytail and were plastered all over her face.

Now that the tire was good and dead, she let out a cry of primal rage and flopped down on the ground beside it. Still, she didn't shed tears. Or think.

When she'd left the garage, she'd been numb – in total flight mode. She'd driven in the direction of Sally's house until she came across the junkyard again. When she'd stopped earlier, she hadn't noticed the two signs on the small building.

CLOSED and FOR SALE.

They might as well have said WELCOME and VACANCY because she immediately steered her car in that direction.

Morgan had parked right up close to the aisles of abandoned vehicles and gotten out, walking aimlessly for . . . she didn't have a clue how long, but her mind was blessedly empty.

However, just like anesthesia, this numbness was bound to wear off too.

Morgan sat cross-legged on the ground, which was beginning to turn from dirt to mud, and looked up to the sky. Rain drops splattered on her face causing her to squint. It felt good.

Okay, bright side. There had to be a bright side. Finding it would be a good way to start this whole thinking process.

Voila! She hadn't screwed up her life back home with Trevor on a whim of idiocy.

But that didn't make her feel any less guilty. Or angry.

Really, angry wasn't the right word.

She'd walked into that garage with a handful of flowers, a bright smile, and hope in her heart. When she'd first peered into the shop she couldn't find Josh. But she had been surprised to find two people making out back there. It was hard to tell who was the boy and who was the girl, and Morgan thought for a second it was two guys entwined in that heated embrace.

That was until something in the closer guy's stance – the set of his shoulders – reminded Morgan of someone. As things got steamier, the couple shifted around some and Morgan went straight from happy and hopeful to absolute devastation.

It was Josh. Her Josh. The Josh who used to hold her and kiss her and – Morgan gave her head a shake. If she had to think – fine. But she did not have to think about that.

Devastation had turned to rage as she stood there staring at that never-ending kiss. She'd crumpled the flowers and let them fall to the floor before getting the hell out of there.

And now the thing that was enraging her the most was the fact that Josh had never kissed her with such ardor.

Who was that tramp, anyway? And what the hell had Josh done to his hair? It was likely the slut's doing. There was nothing left of it.

Okay, so her feelings had been acknowledged. Morgan gave herself a mental pat on the back for her hard work. But there were still some questions that needed to be answered.

Morgan got up and automatically brushed the dirt off her jeans.

No, she didn't. She just smeared the mud around. Whatever. She continued to wander through the junkyard searching for answers.

It was no secret that Josh had always been a bit slow when it came to all things romantic. But even he couldn't be this clueless.

He had told her he loved her. Twice since she'd been here. Once out loud – she was pretty sure – and once in writing. That note was concrete evidence, not that she'd have any need for such evidence since she wasn't planning on speaking to him ever again.

It just didn't make sense, though. When she'd set out to find him that morning, Morgan had had doubts about her true feelings for him. But she hadn't had any doubts about finding acceptance were she to extend that olive branch or perhaps admit they had some unfinished business.

She had been wrong. And there was only one explanation for Josh's behavior. He was a two-timing creep who had only been looking to get some action while she was in town.

Morgan walked on, and the more she thought about it, the more she convinced herself he'd probably always been this way. He'd likely been cheating on her the whole time they'd been dating – except for when they were on the road. She wondered how many floozies he'd had on the side out in Moncton while she waited for him at home in Bathurst.

Sadly, things were starting to make sense now. No wonder the spark between them had fizzled out. Morgan had to admit that spark was probably just raging teenage hormones. And no wonder he was always tired and broody when they were together, never wanting to do anything remotely exciting or fun.

And that blasted phone call he'd made to her last year – the one that had ended up placing all the blame on her for their breakup. He knew damn well she wouldn't have asked him to return to Bathurst only for her. He just didn't have the balls to break up with her himself.

So there it was. Not that hard to figure out after all. Once she had loved Josh. Now she hated him.

No need to seethe any longer about the other girl. It wasn't her fault she hooked up with an unfaithful jerk like him. Still, Morgan couldn't scrub the image of their kiss from her mind. She certainly wouldn't turn down an opportunity to throttle the bitch should one ever arise. Not a likely scenario, but it sure would feel good to throttle something.

A crazy giggle escaped as Morgan turned down another row of crap and ran right into a truck. Not just any truck. An old blue truck. Not an exact replica of Old Blue, but close enough.

Without a thought, Morgan balled her fist, pulled back her arm, and shattered the driver's side mirror. Delightfully therapeutic. She smiled and went to work on the body of the truck, punching and kicking until she was satisfied.

Okay, she had to admit she'd probably gone a bit overboard. Her head was still far from clear, but she was starting to feel the effects of the damage she'd inflicted upon herself. Junkyard time was over.

Morgan pulled a few shards of glass from her hand as she headed in the direction of her rental car. What to do now?

The only person in the entire world she wanted to see at that moment was Trevor. He was her future. He was also thousands of miles away. But that could be corrected. She could head straight for the airport, get the next ticket home, and by tomorrow she'd be back in Bathurst.

No. She couldn't completely ditch Rab here on the other side of the continent.

But she could easily head back to Seattle without her. She had plenty of excuses. There wasn't enough room in the house. She wasn't up for the wedding because she was in pain from her surgery. She could even lie and say she wanted to spend time with her father and half-brother. Honestly, it wasn't like she even needed an excuse. She was a grown woman and didn't have to answer to anyone.

Except herself.

Morgan arrived at the car and sighed. Who was she kidding? She wasn't going to turn tail and run. She would return to the house and suck it up. It wouldn't be that bad. There were so many people around it wouldn't be hard to avoid Josh.

She'd tough it out for Sally's sake. Tonight's rehearsal dinner and the wedding tomorrow would be even easier. Big old public places – no need to see him at all.

Morgan opened the car door and glanced down at her jeans. Yeesh. She'd either need to clean the car before returning it or pay a hefty fee. Well, there was nothing she could do about it now. She got in and grimaced at the squishing sounds her mud-covered clothes made against the fabric of the seat.

Morgan found a box of tissue on the floor and yanked a bunch out to cover her blood-stained and – looking closer – still bleeding hands. She started the car, flicked on the windshield wipers, and drove back to the Hamptons' house.

By the time she reached it, the driveway was full and cars were parked on the road. Excellent. She hadn't realized she'd spent so much time in the junkyard, but this was great news. Now if only she could slip in unnoticed.

Morgan parked the car and tried using the falling rain to wash up a bit. Terrible idea. It only made her muddier and the blood from her hands – yes, her dad had trained her to punch with both – mixed with the mud so it looked as if she'd been in a terrible car wreck.

Which was not that far from the truth.

Although she normally knocked, Morgan slipped in the front door and took off her shoes as quickly as she could. When she straightened up, Rab was standing there, mouth agape.

"What happened to you?" Rab asked.

"Got caught in the rain," Morgan replied cheerfully.

Rab narrowed her eyes and said nothing.

"Look, I don't want to talk about it. Please, please, please, just let it go."

"Let it go? Have you . . . seen yourself? You can't walk through the house like that. You'll get the carpet filthy."

Morgan followed Rab's eyes down to her feet and knew she was right.

"What am I supposed to do? Strip naked right here?"

Rab sighed. "Don't move."

She hurried away and Morgan stood impatiently, hoping no one would round the corner and see her. The house was filled with chatter and laughter.

Rab returned with two shopping bags and knelt down. "Give me your foot."

Morgan did as she was told and was soon outfitted with plastic booties held up by elastic bands. Rab reached into the closet and pulled out some cleaning rags to give her a quick mopping.

"Let's go."

Morgan followed as Rab led her past the living room and kitchen, where she had no choice but to smile and wave at the curious people there, to the stairs. At least she hadn't recognized any of the houseguests.

Morgan headed straight for the bathroom, which was thankfully unoccupied, and tried to close the door behind her. Rab held it open. Morgan raised a brow.

"I'll get you a change of clothes and the first aid kit. Any preference?"

"No stitches, please," Morgan said.

"This isn't funny."

Morgan nodded. Rab was right. She began to shiver and said, "I have another pair of jeans, and a sweater will be fine."

Rab left again and Morgan sat on the edge of the tub to wait. She scraped mud off her watch and saw it was already after four. *Ugh.* By the time she cleaned up, she'd have to change into her fancy clothes and try to fix her – *woah.*

Morgan had stood to look in the mirror and realized she hadn't actually seen herself, just as Rab had implied at the door. She picked up a gnarled strand of her sopping, muddy, bloody hair and cursed her temper. Her face wasn't much better off, and she was surprised to see she'd managed to get a decent number of scrapes and cuts on it too.

Rab knocked on the door before opening it. "Here." She deposited the clothing along with Morgan's toiletry kit and a garbage bag on the counter. "Hurry up and shower so I can tend to your cuts. People are going to need the bathroom."

Morgan only nodded before shutting and locking the door. She started the water in the shower and stripped off her makeshift shoes and clothes, placing them in the garbage bag.

The hot shower was heaven. It eased her shivering and soothed her muscles. For a minute. Scrubbing the mud off around her wounds was not easy to do without screaming, but she managed.

Morgan dressed quickly and opened the door to let in Rab, who had remained just outside the door.

"Ready to talk about it yet?" Rab asked as she took one of Morgan's hands and got to work.

Morgan didn't say a word.

"Josh called the house looking for you earlier. He seemed upset."

"Rab, if I talk about it I will yell about it, and I just can't do that right now."

Rab shrugged and finished bandaging one of her hands, then started on the other. Morgan held up the finished one and groaned.

"I'm going to look like a mummy."

"Yeah, well, right now you look like Frankenstein's monster."

To give Rab credit, she didn't ask a single question throughout the lengthy process of fixing Morgan's cuts and scrapes. She only called out, "Just a minute" every time someone knocked on the door.

By the time they were finished, the aches and pains had really set in. Morgan thanked her friend, who took the dirty clothes with her, and retreated to their room for a bit of solitude before she would need to get ready for the evening.

The first thing she did was gather all the photos of her and Josh and shove them into a drawer. She took down the portrait she'd drawn of him and turned it so it was facing the wall. She then took her duffel bag and plopped it onto the cot, staking it as her own.

Satisfied, Morgan decided to brave the kitchen and snag a cup of coffee to warm her bones. If she were to lie down now she doubted her aching muscles would allow her to get back up. Maybe they'd have some liqueur kicking around down there to add to the coffee.

She left the room, walked down the stairs, and put on a cheery face for the kitchen folks. Aunt Peggy came in from the living room and noticed Morgan's bandages immediately. To be fair, they would be hard to miss.

"Morgan, dear, what happened?"

That was a good question. Now, how to answer . . .

"Car trouble," Morgan said with a smile. "Nothing to worry about. Rab fixed me up good."

The explanation seemed to suffice, but Aunt Peggy continued to fuss about her as Morgan turned to hunt down that coffee.

Instead of coffee, she found Josh, who had just entered the kitchen. He was wearing his "I'm so innocent and confused" expression.

Morgan shot him the coldest look she could muster and marched right out of the kitchen and back up the stairs.

Chapter 18

In Which Chaos Ensues
Friday, August 14, 1998

The rain had stopped by the time Josh left work, but low dark clouds still scudded across the sky like the thoughts swirling through his mind.

Iris had left shortly after he'd returned to the garage. She claimed that she needed to get ready for the rehearsal and dinner. But between the kiss and her departure, she'd hardly spoken except when necessary for the work they were doing. She'd also seemed to be avoiding any physical contact.

Josh hadn't been sure what to think, so he'd allowed his mind to drift to thoughts of Morgan. He wasn't eighteen anymore, so he damned sure wasn't going to let this misunderstanding fester.

When he'd arrived back at Aunt Peggy's, he had to park Old Blue on the street, not coincidently right behind Morgan's rental.

As he'd walked past the car, the heavy mud on its sides puzzled him. Even with the heavy rains this afternoon, there was no way the car should have gotten that muddy on the streets.

Inside, he was met by the chaos that had been promised by the collection of vehicles outside. When he entered the kitchen, he practically ran into Morgan, who had multiple bandages on her hands and arms. He had opened his mouth to ask what happened, but she'd given him a look that would have made a polar bear shiver.

He turned to follow her but found Rab in his way. "Give her some space, bro."

"I'm not sure what happened," Josh said.

"You probably have a good idea. We'll talk in a little while." She curled her nose. "Shower's open, you'd best take advantage of it."

"I'll need to get into my room afterward to get dressed."

"You get in the shower," Rab said. "I'll have Morgan out of the room by then. There is no way I'm letting the two of you occupy such a small space right now."

"Okay. Thanks, sis."

He walked up the stairs, placing a foot on each tread softly. As he did, he watched the top of the stairs to make sure Morgan didn't appear with his baseball bat. That she did not gave him some small hope he might live through the night.

He and Morgan definitely needed to talk, and soon.

It was already Friday. Rab had told him they were flying out Sunday – early.

Josh got into the shower, making sure he locked the door first, and continued to mull over Morgan's behavior.

Did she see him kissing Iris? That could be the only explanation. He doubted she'd be jealous of him simply working on a Mustang instead of Zinger.

He went through the motions of showering and shaving mechanically. A nick on his left cheek brought him back to reality and he continued with more care.

Josh rubbed the styptic pencil on the cut to stem the bleeding and finished his shave.

A knock sounded on the door. "Josh?" Rab called.

"Almost done here."

"Aunt Peggy is letting Morgan get dressed in her room. You can get dressed as soon as you're done, but make sure you're covered, okay?"

"I have my bathrobe," Josh said.

"By the way, we can't take the rental tonight. The inside is a mess. Whoever drives it would need a change of clothes."

"What happened to the car, anyway?"

"The short answer is – it got muddy. Real muddy," Rab said.

"We couldn't take the car anyway. We'll be going on the base, and it doesn't have a pass. I can't even take Old Blue. I'm sure Aunt Peggy has a plan to get us all there."

"That's good. Don't take too much longer. We're getting ready to go. Sally and Michael went ahead to talk with the chaplain," Rab said.

"I've got some equipment here. I'll see what I can do about the car in the morning. There won't be much else for me to do until it's time to get ready for the ceremony."

"I don't know about Morgan, but I'd appreciate it," Rab said. "I'm going to go check on her."

"Okay."

He put his shaving gear away, washed as much blood from the nick as he could, and then put his bathrobe on.

Peering out into the hall before leaving the bathroom, Josh went to his room and closed the door. All the pictures of him and Morgan were missing. The portrait she'd drawn of him had been taken down and turned to face the wall. That didn't bode well.

The door to his aunt and uncle's room had been closed when he left the bathroom, and he wondered if Morgan was still in there. He wondered if she'd calmed down some until he remembered Morgan didn't calm down easily.

He hoped he would have a chance to talk with her and sort this small matter out soon. Then they could go on to discussing the larger matter that they still loved each other.

Why should she be jealous anyway? It was just a kiss. Morgan was seeing someone else, and Josh was sure it was far less platonic than he would like to think.

Morgan may have seen him and Iris kiss, but she couldn't know what he was feeling. He would have to sort out those feelings for Iris later, if necessary. But could it wait until later? Should it wait until later?

What was that old expression? "A bird in the hand is worth two in the bush."

Should he just let Morgan go on with her life and choose to pursue a relationship with Iris? What if that didn't pan out?

If it didn't, it didn't. But wasn't that what he was facing with Morgan? They had been young and in love and had become lovers. Perhaps they had been too young. Perhaps their love had been an infatuation. In the end, it didn't matter. She had told him not to come home. That may not have been exactly how she'd said it, but the effect was just the same.

But he'd changed since then for the better. The long hours spent working and studying and his constant fatigue no longer existed. They had something before. Something good. Maybe all it would take was a small spark to ignite the flames of love again.

While Josh debated, he dressed. He chose a pair of khaki pants and a button-down shirt – green, of course. *May as well stack the deck in my favor.* It wasn't the same green shirt from years ago, but the color was close enough.

Someone knocked on the door.

"Josh, are you dressed?" Rab asked.

"You can come in," he replied.

She entered and examined his outfit. "You're not planning on going like that, are you?"

"I was until a second ago."

"Do you have a white shirt?"

"I do, but I wanted to wear the green one," Josh said. "For Morgan."

"Hand me your jacket and put the white shirt on."

Josh grumbled and handed her the gray sports coat. He pulled off the shirt and hung it back in the closet.

As he donned the white shirt, Rab closed the door.

"So, what happened today?" she asked.

Josh sighed. "Iris kissed me and, well, I sort of kissed her back."

"And Morgan saw this?"

"I don't know. I didn't see her at all today until I got home," Josh said.

"But you suspect she did?"

"Yeah. Karla said a green-eyed woman had come in to see me, but she didn't see her leave." He finished buttoning his shirt and tucked it into his pants.

"You two have the damnedest timing. You always manage to be in the wrong place at the wrong time and everything goes sideways," Rab said, shaking her head.

"So it seems. A few minutes earlier or a few minutes later and there would have been nothing to see," Josh said.

"You *are* going to talk to her, yes?" Rab handed him his jacket.

"I'll try." He slipped his arms into his jacket and turned so she could examine the effect.

"Don't make me drag you two together to talk *again* or I'm going to start charging to be your relationship counselor," Rab said.

"Honest, I'll try."

"It has to be tonight, or you may as well say goodbye to her."

"I'm too well aware," Josh said.

"Hmm. Put on a tie."

"I only have the black one from high school."

"It'll have to do," Rab said.

Josh took the tie off the hanger and tucked his bat out of sight while he was in the closet.

"Come on, Rab, we're leaving," Morgan called through the door.

"I'll be right there," Rab replied.

"Go on," Josh said. "I can handle it from here."

When Rab left the room, Morgan had already gone downstairs. Josh stepped across to the bathroom to check his tie, even though he was sure Rab would adjust it.

Satisfied, he hurried downstairs.

William met him. "I was just looking for you. You're riding with me."

"I'm ready."

When he reached William's SUV, another young Marine, Oscar, sat in the shotgun position. He was one of the groom's attendants, but he and Josh had never had a chance to speak.

While William drove to the base, Josh sat in silence. Tonight might not be his last chance to reconcile with Morgan, but it sure felt like it.

Chapter 19

In Which a Match is Made
Friday, August 14, 1998

"I'll be back in a minute," Morgan said to Rab as she got out of the back seat of the Hamptons' car.

Mr. Hampton had stopped to get gas on their way to the chapel and Morgan couldn't have been happier. Mrs. Hampton had also gone inside to freshen up, so Morgan took the opportunity to hurry away from the gas pumps and light up a smoke.

Yes, it was sad, but even in her head she could no longer refer to them as Aunt Peggy and Uncle Bill. She no longer felt like she belonged in Silverdale, and certainly did not feel like she was part of the family.

Damned wind. It took three tries to get her cigarette lit, and she only got in a couple of puffs before she saw the Hamptons coming out of the gas station.

Morgan stubbed out the cigarette and rushed back to the car, arriving at the same time as they did. A gust of wind blew up the hem of her dark blue silk dress and she had a disturbing Marilyn Monroe moment before wrangling the knee-length skirt back down.

Mr. Hampton chuckled and opened the car door for her. Still struggling with the dress, the shawl Mrs. Hampton had lent her slipped off her shoulders and nearly blew away. Mr. Hampton snatched it just in time, and gasped when he saw the bandages on her hands and arms that the wrap was supposed to be concealing.

"What happened to you?" he asked as she crawled painfully into the back seat of the car. Sitting, standing, and bending over hurt. Everywhere.

Thankfully, she had a few seconds before Mr. Hampton got in the driver's seat to recall the excuse she'd given his wife earlier that day.

"Car trouble," she told him.

Rab snorted and Morgan gave her the look.

"Were you taken to the hospital?" he asked, glancing in the rearview mirror, his face filled with concern.

"No, no. It's not that bad. Nurse Rab patched me up. Everything's fine now."

Mr. Hampton hesitated, then started the car and continued on to the navy base.

Morgan pulled a compact out of her purse and checked her reflection to see how the makeup was holding up. She never wore foundation, but Rab had dug some up to hide the scratches. It was definitely not her shade.

"I look orange," Morgan muttered.

"At least you don't look like a cat mauled you," Rab replied.

Morgan snapped the compact shut and snickered. "Sorry. Thanks for helping me."

"Of course. Are you ready to tell me what really happened yet?"

Morgan glanced at the Hamptons in the front seat. The radio was playing softly and they were engaged in a conversation of their own.

"There's literally nothing to tell," Morgan said. "I lost my temper and took it out on some . . . stuff. Terrible idea, I know. And believe me, I'm paying for it. But that's nothing new."

Rab stared out the window as she said, "Josh mentioned he might know what you were angry about."

Morgan sighed. So that was what the panicked look was about earlier. How would he have known she was there at the garage?

"What did he tell you?" Morgan asked.

"How about you tell me something for a change?"

"Fine. You obviously already know, but I went to visit your brother at work and saw him kissing another girl."

Rab turned from the window. "Why were you there?"

"That's a damned good question. Moment of insanity, I guess."

Rab rolled her eyes. "Okay. But explain one thing to me. Why does it matter that he was kissing someone?"

"It doesn't!" Morgan exclaimed loudly enough to attract the attention of the Hamptons. She smiled and waited until they looked away before continuing in a much lower voice, "It really, really doesn't matter. But now you know what happened and there's nothing more to talk about. I just want to go home."

The car pulled up to a gate and Mr. Hampton showed a card to the guard before they were allowed to proceed through.

Rab continued to eye Morgan as they drove to the chapel and parked. Morgan was first out of the car with the intention of fleeing further questions. She didn't get more than two steps away before she realized she didn't know where she was going. Rab was already at her side.

"This way," she said and steered Morgan toward the doors of the church. "But we're not done talking."

Morgan groaned but allowed Rab to lead the way.

"You say it doesn't matter, but I'm not buying it," Rab said. "Have you seen what you did to yourself?"

"I told you –"

"That it's not a big deal. Yeah, yeah, I heard. Here's what I'm getting. You went to see Josh and instead you saw . . . that. But did you give him a chance to explain? And why does he have to explain anything to you anyway? Do I have to remind you you're practically living with someone else? Someone you're thinking of marrying, no less?"

"No, you don't have to remind me," Morgan hissed. "I made a mistake, okay? I never should have been at that garage to begin with. But you know what? I'm actually happy I was there. It cleared up whatever was wrong with my head."

"Then why are you still mad?"

Morgan threw her hands in the air, no longer concerned about being quiet. "Because he came to the hospital, Rab. He told me he loved me. He –"

"So you do remember that."

"Yes. Are you happy now? I also found and read the note he left before he snatched it back. But why would he do that? And why would he go to all the trouble of turning his room into a shrine of the two of us? Why all the pretending? I was confused. I thought . . . it doesn't matter what I thought. I just don't understand why he'd do that stuff and then screw off and make out with some other girl!"

They had reached the door of the chapel and Rab pulled Morgan to the side.

"Look, I don't know what happened. I only know what the two of you think happened – and barely." Rab sighed. "Here are the facts. You are both hot and bothered and I am not on anyone's side. Not this time. But if you don't talk to each other – and by that I mean speak words that are honest – I think you'll end up being sorry you didn't."

"I told you, I'm already sorry. Sorry I came."

Morgan pushed past Rab and followed a couple into the church.

Against her will, her eyes scanned the crowd for Josh. He was standing with his back to her talking to a couple of guys – no floozy in sight. As if sensing her presence, he turned around.

Morgan quickly averted her gaze but saw him heading her way in her peripheral vision. She hightailed it toward a group of girls standing around Sally and inserted herself directly into the middle of them.

"Morgan, I'm so happy you made it. Are you sure you're feeling well enough?" Sally asked.

All eyes went to Morgan's bandages, but she simply pulled the shawl tighter to conceal them.

"Yep, all good."

"Okay. I don't know if you've met Heather or Iris yet, but girls, this is Morgan. And you remember . . ."

Morgan didn't hear Sally's reintroductions of the other women, whom Morgan had not remembered at all, because she was focused on keeping tabs on Josh. He'd been stopped by someone for a minute but was on his way toward her again.

Thankfully, a man dressed in a khaki uniform approached and introduced himself as the chaplain. He then instructed the women where they were to stand before the wedding would begin.

Once they were all in their places, the chaplain left and rounded up the groomsmen, including Josh.

Even as he gave them their directions, Morgan felt Josh's eyes glued to her. She stared at a spot on the wall and began planning her escape for when this was over.

Finally, the chaplain stepped up onto the platform.

"Thank you for coming, everyone . . ."

Morgan stifled a yawn and shifted uncomfortably as he droned on about the lovely ceremony they hoped to give Sally and Michael. Everyone else seemed to be listening intently – a side glance at Josh showed him to be the only other exception – and Morgan wondered if it would be rude to dig a painkiller out of her purse.

She forced her attention back to the chaplain when he began giving orders to the groomsmen. They were instructed to enter first and spread out to the right, followed by the groom. He showed each person where to stand and then returned to the bridesmaids.

They were given similar instructions, fanning out to the left instead of the right. Morgan was pleased when the placements resulted in much more room between her and Josh. Finally, something was going her way.

Next, Mr. Hampton escorted Sally to the end of the aisle. Morgan tuned out again as words were exchanged until he raised the fake veil and kissed Sally on the cheek before taking the seat by his wife.

It was kind of romantic when Sally stepped forward to take her future husband's arm. The look in their eyes was exactly what Morgan would expect to see from two people truly in love. Morgan wondered if she would ever look like that.

She needed to see Trevor. Not on Monday. Now. Watching the two of them up there, she missed him so much it hurt.

As they ran through most of the ceremony and their vows and all that, Morgan's emotional hurt was dulled by the physical pain from standing so long. How much longer was this going to go on for?

By the time it wrapped up, Morgan had decided that if she ever did get married, she would elope.

At last, Sally and Michael walked out of the church together and the chaplain addressed the rest of the wedding party. He told them when and how to follow the bride and groom, pairing the bridesmaids up with the groomsmen.

Oh hell, no.

Morgan stood rooted to the floor staring at Josh, who stood waiting with his arm out.

The chaplain chuckled and waved his hand in front of Morgan's face.

"Miss?"

Oh hell, no.

Morgan held her arm stiff as a board as Josh reached out to take it. She noticed the chaplain staring, along with most of the attendees not in the wedding party, so she plastered a smile on her face. She was sure it must be a grisly smile.

As they began to walk, Josh cut right to the chase.

"We need to talk," he whispered.

Morgan made her smile impossibly wider and kept her eyes straight ahead. She barely moved her mouth when she said, "Nope. In fact, we don't ever need to talk again."

"Were you at the garage today?"

"Why would you think I was at the garage?" She waved at Rab, who was sitting in the audience looking grim.

"Well, the receptionist said –"

"Oh, right. That was me. Sure, I remember now. I did stop by." Morgan turned to Josh. "You're supposed to be smiling. You look miserable."

"Listen, what you saw –"

"Was absolutely none of my business," she finished for him with the biggest smile yet as they arrived at the doors.

As soon as they passed through them, she forcibly detached his arm from hers and gave him the coldest glare she could muster before stalking off.

The mustering was not difficult at all.

Chapter 20

In Which Lips Lock Again
Friday, August 14, 1998

Josh stood frozen in place by Morgan's glacial glare. He wondered if he should go after her as others filed out of the chapel to enjoy the pleasant evening.

"There you are," Rab said as she appeared next to him.

"Yeah, I, uh . . ."

"Listen, we've been asked to stick around a few minutes. Sally and Michael are talking with the padre. They may want to run through the ceremony again."

"What happened?" Josh asked, still a bit stunned.

"Not sure. We'll know in a few minutes. I need to tell Morgan. Have you seen her?"

"No. She chewed my ass off, almost tore my arm off, and took off."

"So is that it? Is it over between you two?" Rab asked.

"No. It can't be. There's more I need to say."

"Then maybe you'd better go say it instead of standing here gaping like a fish out of water."

"Yeah, I should do that," Josh said.

Rab went to search for Morgan while Josh scanned the various knots of people. Iris stood talking with Heather. He lingered on her for a moment, marveling again at how beautiful she was. How had he never seen this before?

Hang on. Why am I pursuing Morgan when Iris wants to be with me?

The answer was simple. Because he owed it to himself, to Morgan, and what they once had. If Morgan wanted him back in Bathurst, he'd get there even if he had to walk across the whole damned continent.

He couldn't be thinking about Iris. Not until . . .

136

A flash of blue caught his eye, revealing Morgan's location to him. He strode over to the gazebo where she stood smoking.

As he approached, she noticed him and searched the area – possibly for an avenue of escape – but then stopped and faced him. When he reached the gazebo, she blew out a cloud of smoke and ground the cigarette into the butt can.

"What do you want, jerk?" Morgan asked.

"We're not done talking."

"Only because you're still flapping your lips, so shut the hell up and go away," Morgan said.

"I'll go away if you look me square in the eyes and tell me you don't love me."

Morgan lowered her head. "I don't love you, Josh."

"Not good enough, Morgan. I said look me in the eyes."

"I can't do that right now. Not when I'm angry."

"Then we need to talk," Josh said.

"You go first."

"Listen, I don't know how much you saw this morning, but that was the only time we've ever kissed." He chose not to say who started it. It wouldn't matter to Morgan.

"But you were kissing her. How could you be kissing her if you profess to still love me so much?"

"I do still love you. One kiss does not make Iris my girlfriend."

"So, what does it make her? A quickie? A one-night stand?" Morgan asked.

"Iris is not like that. She's a decent woman. What about you? Can you stand there and tell me your boyfriend has never kissed you?" He wasn't about to ask her if she was sleeping with him. He knew Morgan well enough to believe that she was, but really didn't want to know.

"At least he *is* a boyfriend. At least he shows up when he's supposed to and wants to do things other than lying around on the couch."

"You didn't answer my question," Josh said.

"It's a ridiculous question, but fine. Yes, I've kissed my boyfriend." Morgan rolled her eyes.

"Then, if we're not a couple, I should be able to kiss someone else, too."

"If we were a couple, how would I know it wouldn't happen again?" Morgan asked.

"You have my word of honor. As long as you're my girlfriend, fiancé, wife, soul mate, whatever, it'll never happen again. Not with Iris, not with Trixie, not with anyone."

Morgan frowned.

"I know you don't like me to use the word honor, but I still believe in personal honor. I believe it is stronger than saying, 'I promise' or 'I give you my word,'" Josh said.

"You just used a lot of words that I don't like. But wait, back up a bit. That was Iris? The same Iris I get to stand next to tomorrow?"

"Yes. It's hard to believe, but this is the first time I've ever seen her in a dress."

Morgan grunted an unintelligible reply.

"So why aren't we a couple, Morgan?" Josh asked. "I love you and I know you love me."

"Says you."

"You said as much in the hospital not two days ago."

"I was drugged," Morgan said and started digging into her purse.

"That only lowers your inhibition, like alcohol, so the real you came out."

"So you say."

"I have seen you drunk many times," Josh said.

"Wish I was drunk right now," Morgan muttered and stopped searching through her purse. Her eyes met his and narrowed. "You seem to be forgetting that it's your fault we're not together anymore."

"I beg to differ. I offered to come home. I asked if you wanted me to come home."

"To do what? To chain me to a stove with a baby on my hip?" Morgan asked.

"Is that how your mother was when you were growing up? She's not like that now. If I recall correctly, she works outside the home and has babysitters."

"Yeah, I was one of those babysitters. Look, children are noisy, messy, and demanding. They are really not for me."

"I could forgo having children if you wanted me to," Josh said, quietly.

"But you wouldn't be happy."

"With you, I would be happy."

"Maybe, but you came up with this bullshit demand," Morgan said. "You put it all on me. You were all 'answer me now or I'm going away.' What was I supposed to do? I made a snap decision for me, for us, for our future happiness."

"Well at least one of us found happiness. I accept part of the blame, but you didn't even ask for a few days so we could talk it over."

"I couldn't because you were pressuring me, Josh."

"I understand that now and want to make things right."

"What you did was just make things complicated."

"I still refuse to accept all the blame. You could have stayed and talked with me when I came to get my stuff from the apartment, but you didn't," Josh said.

"I had to work."

"And you couldn't get time off?"

"I was helping on an important case," Morgan said.

"In December? That's kind of a lame excuse."

"Fine. I probably could have made time, but I didn't want to see you packing up your crap. You didn't even stick around for Christmas."

"I figured my life in Bathurst was over," Josh said.

"So you just left. You're the one who didn't give us time to figure things out."

"Well, you're here and I'm here now. Let's figure this out, one way or the other."

"As I said, things are complicated. I'm with Trevor now," Morgan said.

"What does Trevor have that I don't?"

"Well, he has a good job, and it's only going to get better."

"I do too. You were with me when I was struggling to get there. It sounds like he'd already gone through his struggles when you met him," Josh said.

"He likes to go out and have fun," Morgan continued.

"I don't mind having fun, and now that I have a good job, I have the time and money to enjoy life a little bit."

"He's right upfront with what he's thinking," Morgan said.

"He's a lawyer, isn't he?"

"What's that got to do with anything? Yes, Trevor has passed the bar and is working on becoming a junior partner in the firm."

"The one you work at?" Josh asked.

"Yes. He's Shack's older brother."

Josh blinked hard. He remembered Trevor. *Cradle robbing bastard.*

He recovered and said, "A bit old for you, isn't he? Will you really be happy as a trophy wife?"

Josh saw the fury rising in her eyes. He must have struck a chord.

"Okay, okay, sorry I said that. But I can't see a lawyer ever coming right out and saying what they're thinking. They can't or they'd never win a case," Josh said.

"I know him better than you do," Morgan said. "He's very straightforward with me."

"Well, I believe in being tactful. So what else?"

"That's exactly what is wrong with you, Joshua Hampton," Morgan said. "You never just come out and say what you're really thinking. You hide behind that old-fashioned crap because you don't have the guts to actually do anything spur of the moment. You don't know what real passion is."

"That's not true. Okay, yes, I'm a bit old-fashioned, but you can count on me. I'm safe. I'm stable. I'm reliable."

"But you don't have an impulsive bone in your body."

"I do too. It's just that there's a time and place for impulsiveness," Josh said.

"Oh, bullshit. That's the whole point of it. It can't be scheduled, it just happens."

In an unprecedented show of spontaneity, Josh pulled Morgan into his arms and planted his lips on hers. She stiffened, but only for a moment. When she relaxed, he pressed himself closer to her, intensifying the kiss like it was their first ever – or perhaps their last ever. Either way, he was going to kiss her for all it was worth.

After what seemed like an eternity, they broke apart and stood breathlessly, face to face, still wrapped in a tangle of arms. Eyes flickered back and forth searching for meaning in each other's expressions.

"Let's skip the dinner and go get a hotel," Morgan whispered.

"Can't do that."

"Why not?"

"The simple fact is that I'm not about to have make-up sex with a woman who is another man's girlfriend."

Morgan pounded lightly on his chest. "Damn you and your honor. Damn you and your logic. And damn you for being right."

"One day, you'll thank me for it."

It felt so good to kiss Morgan again, the other kiss from this morning was forgotten. Josh took a chance and moved his lips close to hers again.

Morgan didn't pull away or resist. This kiss wasn't as hard as the other, but it was no less intense. It was like he'd never kissed this woman before, but at the same time it was so familiar and felt so right. Memories of long, cold nights spent cuddling and kissing flowed through his mind. His resolve weakened but didn't break.

"Ahem."

They broke apart as though they'd been caught kissing in a forbidden place, which was nonsense. Many kisses had likely happened here.

Rab stood there, eyes flicking between the two of them. "No second rehearsal. It's time to go."

"Can I ride with you, Josh?" Morgan asked.

"There might be room if you don't mind riding with a couple of Jarheads."

"They could be goons for all I care." She turned to Rab. "You don't mind, do you?"

"Hey, I traveled with you for eleven hours and we have another eleven to go. Just make sure you're presentable when we arrive at the restaurant," Rab said. She walked off toward the parking lot.

Josh offered Morgan his hand and she took it. They walked hand in hand to the parking lot.

William waved and motioned for them to hurry up. When they reached his vehicle, William said, "Way to go, Josh, connecting with a bridesmaid."

"This is Morgan. She's filling in for Brook."

"That Morgan?" his cousin asked.

"Yes, I'm 'that' Morgan. Can we go now? I'm suddenly very hungry."

"Climb in. Far be it from me to stand between a woman and a good meal," William said.

142

On the way to the restaurant, Josh wondered if they could make it a double wedding. Probably not for many reasons, but mostly because he was certain Morgan would rather just elope.

Maybe they could get a flight to Las Vegas after the wedding.

Chapter 21

In Which Morgan Might Have Made a Mistake
Friday, August 14, 1998

After William had so thoughtfully removed the hideous car seat from the back of his SUV, Morgan and Josh sat pressed together during the drive from the naval base to the steakhouse – not speaking but exchanging meaningful glances.

Actually, scratch the meaningful part. Morgan had no clue what she was thinking and therefore projecting, nor what she was seeing in Josh's eyes.

They'd been holding hands for most of the ride, but as Morgan's confusion grew so did her guilt. Just because Bathurst and Trevor were on the other side of the continent, it did not mean they had ceased to exist.

Morgan took her hand back with the excuse of checking her bandages and, instead of returning it to Josh, placed it on her lap.

"What *did* happen to you?" he asked with concern.

"Car trouble," Morgan said and then chuckled. "Actually, I don't think anyone's buying that. But it's a less embarrassing excuse than admitting I flipped my lid and did this to myself."

Josh raised a brow, but Morgan just shook her head and allowed herself the guilty little pleasure of leaning it against his shoulder for a minute.

When the car pulled into a parking spot at the steakhouse, Morgan was both relieved and saddened.

Relieved because she knew what she was doing – allowing herself to indulge in this very physical walk down memory lane – was wrong.

Saddened because it felt so good. This wasn't just some stranger. This was Josh. Her Josh.

But not anymore. She'd relinquished her claim on him when she'd told him not to come home. What's more, he'd left and she'd moved on.

So she'd thought.

"Angel?" Josh had gotten out of the vehicle and stood holding the door open for her.

Again, it felt so right and yet so wrong, but the smile came naturally to Morgan's face as she stepped out and Josh took her arm to lead her into the restaurant.

They joined the line of people filing into the private room reserved for the wedding party. When they entered, Morgan was met with yet another round of conflicting feelings.

The first one was a walloping crush of disappointment. The seating had been prearranged. There were three tables. Sally and her parents were sitting at one of them, and Morgan didn't need to see the "Brook" place card to know she'd be sitting at the table with the other bridesmaids instead of with the men.

The second emotion was something close to elation. As much as she wanted to totally sink into her "reunion" with Josh, she needed a damn break. Time to think. Also, apparently, time to talk. Rab walked by them, heading for the table Morgan would be sitting at.

Morgan smiled at Josh and gave his arm a gentle squeeze before following Rab. She didn't look back.

Morgan took her seat beside Rab and saw it was indeed the "Brook" seat. Good news, since it saved her the trouble of switching cards as she would have done if some other name had been there. She had to talk to Rab. Morgan's eyes went to the girl sitting directly across from her and her stomach churned.

So this was Iris. Sure, she'd seen her a couple of times, but not since she'd realized this was the woman Josh had been kissing. Iris stared back at her, not smiling, not frowning, just assessing.

Morgan was certain her eyes had narrowed and quickly averted her gaze.

"I'm so glad they put you at this table," she said to Rab.

"Me too." Rab turned to her and leaned close, speaking in a whisper. "What the hell was that?"

"I know. I nearly fell asleep. The ceremony tomorrow can't be any longer, can it?"

"That is not what I'm talking about and you know it."

Morgan sighed and ran a hand through her hair. A small laugh escaped when she saw Josh doing the same across the room. How many times had she seen him do that? Normally, he'd have to take his hat off first but –

"Morgan! This isn't funny," Rab said.

"I know. Believe me, I know. I don't know what happened. Honestly. We were outside arguing and the next thing I knew, we were kissing. But isn't that what you wanted? You told me I should talk to him."

"Right. I told you to talk to him, not make out with him."

Morgan groaned and put her face in her hands. "It was a mistake. It just happened so quickly."

"And the two of you riding together and holding hands on your walk to the car? Did that happen at the speed of light as well?"

"Rab, please don't." Morgan glanced across the table to make sure the other women weren't eavesdropping. Iris was staring off in the direction of the groomsmen's table. Well, good for her. She could look all she liked.

"Are you two back together then?" Rab asked.

"No!" Morgan's exclamation caught the attention of the table. She smiled a tight smile and shifted closer to Rab. "No. I'm so confused. I told you, it just happened. For once, he did something spontaneous. It really did take me by surprise and then . . . well, then it was like time had gone backward. I don't know what to do."

"You're going to have to do *something*. Did you two talk in the car?"

"No. Not really. Rab, I'm a mess. Just this afternoon I thought I hated him. I was wrong. I could never hate him. But I don't know if I still love him. I love Trevor. What am I supposed to do?"

"You need to pick one of them, Morgan."

"But how? This is exactly what happened before. I can't make a rational decision – certainly not one of this magnitude – under such pressure."

Rab shook her head.

"Don't do that," Morgan said. "You don't know what I'm feeling."

"Why don't you tell me then?"

"Because *I* don't know what I'm feeling. But I do know that kiss was a mistake." Morgan groaned. "You'll never believe what I did in between those kisses."

"Wait. *Kisses*?" Rab's eyes widened.

"Yeah. There was one big one that went on forever and it was nothing like any kiss we'd ever had before. It was . . . electric. Maybe because it was unexpected and forbidden and all that."

Rab's eyes narrowed.

"Right, right, the second one was different. It was more like they used to be. I felt so safe, and had I allowed myself to relax all the way, it would have been the sweetest thing in the world. But I couldn't because –" Morgan grimaced in anticipation of Rab's reaction to the next bit of information. "– in between the two kisses I suggested we skip dinner and get a hotel room."

"You have got to be kidding me!"

"Unfortunately, I'm not. But I didn't mean it. It just came out. I would never do that to Trevor. I think Josh took me seriously for a minute, but you know him. He wouldn't do that either."

Morgan's cell phone rang and she jumped. She held up a finger for Rab to wait as she dug it out of her purse and sighed. Trevor. She had promised to call him earlier that day. He must be worried about her. Even so, she couldn't bring herself to answer. She shut off the phone and turned back to Rab, her eyes pleading for help.

"Okay, here's my first bit of reworded advice," Rab said. "Talk to Josh. Don't yell, don't blame, don't suck face. Talk words that make sense."

"Should I do it now?"

"No, you should not do it now. This is Sally's dinner. And as much as I'd love to believe, I'm not so optimistic as to think the two of you could get through any sort of conversation without one of those three things happening."

Morgan couldn't help but laugh a little. The laugh was cut short when she checked her phone and saw that Trevor hadn't left a message. She stuffed the phone back into her purse and decided to deal with that later. Still, her stomach felt as if it were full of panicked butterflies. What was she doing? Was it worth the risk?

"Fine," she said to Rab. "But if I don't talk to him now, when am I going to?"

Rab chewed on her lip. "Not tonight. You need to ride home with me, not him, and sleep on this. At least now you know how he feels, right?"

Morgan nodded.

"But you don't have one stinking clue as to how you feel."

It wasn't phrased as a question, but Morgan nodded again.

"Thought so. I'm sure you'll get a chance to speak to him tomorrow, but you need to stop playing the blame game. You need to figure out your future and put the past to rest."

"You're right." Morgan sat back in her chair and rubbed her temples. "You make it sound so easy."

Rab's face softened and she said, "You know I was rooting for the two of you. I love you both. But I can't tell you what to do now. I do, however, have one final piece of advice for you."

"Shoot."

"Tonight's not the night, but when you do figure things out, it needs to be final. There's more than just one heart on the line here."

Morgan closed her eyes and drew in a deep breath. "You're right."

And she was. Pressure or no pressure, Morgan had to make a decision once and for all.

Josh was safe, comfortable, loyal, and they'd been through so much together.

Josh was also right here.

Morgan forced her mind to travel all the way back to Bathurst. It wasn't like she and Trevor were just in the hand-holding stage of their relationship. He wanted to marry her. Only a few days ago she thought she might want to marry him.

What was it about Josh that had made her practically forget about Trevor overnight? Was it just the memories? No. But there was no denying he had been a huge part of her life for years. What if she had made a terrible mistake by telling him not to come home?

Well, whether it was a mistake or not, it was done. That was the past, and Rab was right. She needed to get over the past and think about her future. Her future, up until today, had been Trevor.

Trevor was everything Josh wasn't. They'd been dating for months, but she still felt weak in the knees every time she saw him enter a room. He was confident and laid back – not prone to hysterics like herself – yet exciting at the same time.

They liked to do the same things. They had the same goals in life. Marriage to Trevor wouldn't be anything like the drudgery Morgan had previously associated with the rite. Their life would be filled with travel, passion, friends, and parties. It would also be child-free for the foreseeable future – perhaps forever – and no one's feelings would need to be sacrificed.

Morgan hadn't realized she still had her eyes closed until Rab nudged her from her thoughts. She opened her eyes and looked up into the face of a waiter.

"Drinks?" he asked.

"Oh, yes, please. Beer. No, wait. Vodka and cola."

The man nodded and turned to the next person.

"Wait. Make it a double."

He nodded again and Morgan turned back to Rab. As expected, she was giving Morgan a withering glare.

"What? You told me to relax and think." Morgan grinned. "But I just did a bunch of thinking, so it's time to do some of the relaxing. Can we please talk about something else for a while?"

They did drop the subject and Morgan tried her best to join Rab as she engaged in conversation with the rest of the table. It wasn't easy.

Morgan refused to address Iris and she seemed to be happy with this arrangement as well. As for the rest of them? The consensus was the peach-colored monstrosities that were the bridesmaids' gowns were a fabulous choice. Gag. Morgan hadn't seen any of the wedding decorations, but they sounded just as hideous and were equally adored by the other bridesmaids.

Morgan studied Rab for any sign of her true thoughts on these topics, but she was nothing but pleasant and composed when asked for her opinions.

Just like her brother.

Finally, the drinks arrived, and Morgan made sure to order another before the waiter left. Talk at the table had just turned to the women complimenting each other on their outfits, makeup, and hairdos.

Morgan tried – she really did – to take small sips from her drink. However, even small sips add up when one forgets to remove the glass from their lips in between. Her second drink arrived just in time. The waiter only needed to raise his eyebrows and Morgan nodded gratefully, confident a third would be on its way.

She gave up trying to keep her eyes off Josh and allowed her gaze to wander across the room.

He was deep in conversation with William, his face unreadable. She wondered what advice he might be getting from this man and if it would be more helpful than "sleep on it."

Chapter 22

In Which Josh Is Confused
Friday, August 14, 1998

Josh and Morgan had kissed. They had held hands. She had chosen to ride with him. It was wonderful, almost like old times. So why did Josh feel like something was off?

At least we're communicating.

There was a barrier between them, and Josh was afraid that barrier was 3,000 miles away. Was he going to have to travel to Bathurst, confront this Trevor, and fight for Morgan's favors?

Count ten paces, turn, and fire.

It didn't quite work that way anymore. Ultimately, the choice belonged to Morgan.

But still, he had made a start. He was further ahead than he had been this afternoon. He'd kissed Iris once and Morgan twice. In the category of lip locks, Morgan was ahead.

Josh had been disappointed when they arrived at the steakhouse, having hoped to sit with Morgan. Who arranged the seating anyway? He wondered if the reception would be more open. If he was lucky, the groomsmen could sit with their respective bridesmaids.

Maybe not. Molly would want to sit with her husband just as he'd want to sit with Morgan, if she was willing.

Who knew which way her emotional winds would be blowing tomorrow?

Tomorrow and tomorrow and tomorrow, the bard once said.

No, just the one tomorrow; that's all I get.

What more could he say? What more could he do? He had told her he loved her still. He had told her he was willing to live with her without marriage or children. He had even accepted the blame for the breakup. Well, half the blame anyway.

Would it take becoming a professional? Ezra had suggested he go back to school and get a degree in engineering. His boss was willing to let him work around his class schedule. But that would mean more long hours and Morgan wanted more hours from him. And the nearest school to Bathurst that offered engineering was back in Moncton.

He supposed he could attend the University of New Brunswick, like Rab, and become a nurse. But that would put him back at square one, and working as a nurse would not be conducive to the lifestyle Morgan sought. Josh wasn't sure he had the aptitude for it anyway.

He had done a lot to be able to provide a life for Morgan, but it hadn't been enough. It was impossible to instantly become years older with more life experience. And then be in a position to give her that lifestyle.

They had kissed and that was something. What's more, they'd decided that they had broken up, but the way they had done so could have been better. They seemed to agree that had they tried harder, they may not have broken up; but Josh had his doubts about that.

Josh wasn't sure what he could do. He supposed he'd just have to keep talking until he said something she would accept. Was there still hope? Maybe a shred, but Josh was clinging to it for all it was worth.

It might not be enough.

Realizing he'd completely zoned out, Josh focused his attention on the table where he, William, and Oscar were seated. He noticed an empty seat. The name card in front said "Fred."

Josh motioned to the empty spot. "Who's Fred? I didn't see him at the rehearsal."

"Fred Gaines," William said. "He's Brook's husband and he's not here for obvious reasons."

"How are they doing?" Josh asked.

"Last report is the baby is doing well and may get to go home with Brook and Fred as early as next week."

"I'm glad to hear that. Is anyone going to send flowers? I'd like to contribute."

"Mom sent some from the Hamptons, so you're covered," William said as the meals arrived.

Josh's steak was excellent. He couldn't help wondering if Morgan's was rare or how Iris liked her steak – if she even had steak.

"So, Sarge," Oscar said, "I saw you talking to the girl I get to escort tomorrow. Do you know her?"

"You mean Iris?" William asked. "Yeah, her dad and my dad are great friends. They've known each other since 'Nam. You wouldn't believe how stoked my dad was when he ran into Badger in the commissary one day. When he retired from the Marines, Badger decided to settle here and start a garage."

Josh suddenly became interested in their conversation, but he wasn't sure why.

"Her last name is Badger?"

"No, that's Gunny Brock's nickname from back in the day. Anyway, I saw Iris a lot going through school and at family outings. She's a sweet girl."

Josh silently agreed.

"Do you know if she's single?" Oscar asked.

"You did hear me say her dad's a retired gunny, didn't you?"

"You mentioned that. Do you think she might go out with me if I asked?"

Josh hoped Oscar would change the subject.

"Probably not. I think she's carrying a torch for someone," William said.

"I'm pretty sure she is," Josh said. He saw no reason to tell Oscar who it was.

Why am I being so defensive? They weren't dating, just working together. He wanted to attribute it to friendship among co-workers, but in his heart, he knew it was more than that.

In many basic ways, Iris was like Morgan. They were both intelligent and lived life to its fullest. They were also both attractive.

But in other ways, Iris was different from Morgan. She didn't smoke – even if she didn't smoke at work, he'd have smelled it on her. Although they didn't have many opportunities to socialize, he had never seen her drink to excess.

He didn't know whether Iris wanted children or not, but she had never spoken against it. Josh was sure he'd discover more similarities and differences if he got to know her better.

But she'd kissed him. More importantly, he had kissed her back. But what did that mean? He'd have to decide that soon.

For now, his focus was Morgan. Answering their questions would determine whether he could answer the question of Iris. But was that really fair to Iris?

Oscar's voice interrupted his thoughts. "Who's the dark-haired girl over there? I don't think I've seen her around before."

"That's my sister visiting from Canada and before you ask, she has a boyfriend," Josh said. He thought about adding that she dissected dicks in anatomy class but decided not to ruin dinner.

Once everyone had finished eating, the servers collected the dishes and continued to rotate in and out for those who still wanted drinks.

Sally and Michael were the first to leave. Sally went around the girls' table and spoke with each person there, giving each a hug and kiss.

Michael came to their table and Josh stood with the others.

"Well, Michael, enjoy your last night of freedom," William said and shook his hand.

"You don't scare me, Sarge," Michael said. "I'm marrying a terrific girl."

"You say that now," Oscar said as they shook. "Wait until she clamps on the old ball and chain tomorrow."

They laughed.

Josh shook Michael's hand next. "Don't know you very well, but I expect we'll be seeing more of you."

Sally had finished her rounds and caught up with him. "Get me home, dear. It's been a long day."

William and Oscar pointed fingers at Michael. He raised his hands in a gesture of defeat as he walked out with Sally.

Next, Uncle Bill and Aunt Peggy got up and motioned to Rab and Morgan it was time to leave. Josh stood and was going to offer to get Morgan back to the house, but Rab gave her head a slight shake warning him off.

Morgan stood and staggered a step until Rab helped her get her feet aligned. She managed to walk reasonably straight after that, but Rab was right at her elbow. She had probably done this many times for Morgan, just as he had when they were together.

Rab said a brief "good night" before escorting Morgan out of the restaurant. Morgan hadn't so much as looked his way.

Two steps forward and one step back.

"Sit down, cuz, and have another beer with us," William said. "We have the place until ten. Besides, we can't leave until my designated driver gets here."

"Your designated driver?"

"Molly. Since she wasn't a part of the wedding party, she asked to be excused from the rehearsal and dinner. She went shopping with a friend and should be here before too long."

156

"Good. I thought I'd have to drive you home," Josh said.

"I'm careful with how much I drink. A DUI would wreck my career, so I don't take chances."

Josh sat. "Okay, but if you don't mind, I'll have a Coke."

William shrugged. "Hey, to each their own, you know."

"Head call," Oscar said as he stood and left the table for the bathroom.

When Oscar left the banquet room, William leaned toward Josh. "You seem to have yourself a heap of girl problems, cuz."

"Is it that obvious?"

"Well, my sister does like to talk."

"The short of it is, I screwed up with Morgan and we broke up. I've got this one weekend to try to win her back," Josh said.

"Heck of a time to do that with the wedding and all."

"We don't always get to choose what life tosses at us. 'All we have to decide is what to do with the time that is given us.'"

"That's some pretty heavy philosophy there," William said.

"It's from *Lord of the Rings*, but it fits."

"You want my opinion?"

"I don't suppose it'll hurt," Josh said.

"As far as Morgan is concerned, I think that ship has sailed, and you're left standing on the pier."

"Why do you say that?"

"I hear things. Now suppose that Morgan hadn't come here this weekend but went off and married that dude back home. What would you do? Mope about her for the rest of your life?"

"No, I suppose I wouldn't. I'd eventually accept it and move on."

William leaned a bit closer, and Josh followed his example. William slanted his eyes to the girls' table. "Now

Iris there is a fine young woman and I hear tell she might actually like you. God only knows why."

"But I still love Morgan. Isn't that worth making a try?" Josh asked.

"Haven't you been trying since she got here?"

"As much as I could."

"And where's that gotten you?" William asked.

"I'm not sure. I felt we had a breakthrough tonight, but I don't know now."

"Listen, cuz, I'm not that much older than you and I don't claim to be an expert on love. But if Morgan gets on that plane Sunday without asking you to come back home, then you need to let her go."

"I'll keep it in mind."

William's phone chimed and he answered. After a moment, he lowered it and looked at Josh. "Do you think you're okay to drive? Molly has been delayed."

"Yeah, I'm good. I only had the one beer with dinner, and it's been way over an hour."

William put the phone back to his ear. "Josh can get us home, so just have Rosemary drop you off there."

He finished talking and hung up the phone before tossing Josh the keys. "As soon as Oscar gets back, we'll go."

Josh took the keys. "I'll go get the truck and a bit of fresh air."

"It's an SUV, not a truck," William said and laughed.

Josh just waved at him. He wasn't going to get into that debate again.

Outside the restaurant, the August air was still warm, and the parking lot had fewer cars in it. Still, Josh had to stop and search for the truck because he hadn't thought he'd need to remember where it was parked.

The yellow streetlights of the parking lot muted the colors of the vehicles parked there. They made William's dark green truck look black. The truck was much newer than

Old Blue, so Josh pushed the button on the fob and the truck flashed its lights at him.

A touch on his left arm caused him to turn and he found himself facing Iris.

"You looked nice today, Josh," Iris said.

"Well, I had a little help. Thanks," Josh stammered. "That's a lovely dress you have."

"You like it?" Iris asked and twirled. "I bought it special for tonight."

"Looks a lot better than coveralls."

Heather arrived next to Iris. "Well, I've got to go. See you tomorrow, partner."

"Tomorrow, yeah."

But maybe not the next day. And maybe never again after that.

The thought saddened him even though he wasn't sure why it should.

Chapter 23

In Which They Get a Clean Start
Saturday, August 15, 1998

Why on earth did the damned cot smell like Josh? Was his scent simply embedded in the walls of the room?

Morgan pried her eyes open and squinted at the vacant bed that Rab had already made. So much sunlight. She reached down and felt around on the ground for her phone. Only nine o'clock. Crap. She'd hoped to sleep right through the morning until she had to slap on a dress around noon.

Double crap. No missed calls. Trevor hadn't tried calling again and she had been in no condition to call him back last night. She briefly considered calling him now but cringed inwardly at the thought. She was not much better off this morning than she had been the night before.

First, she needed a shower. And coffee. And painkillers. And quite possibly a twelve-step program.

Morgan dragged herself into a sitting position on the cot, feeling as if she were ninety. The surgery aches would have been enough, but then she just had to go and beat the crap out of a pile of scrap metal. The hangover was the least of her complaints.

She leaned over to unzip her duffel bag and grabbed the first items of clothing she found. Ripped jeans and a white T-shirt. Her eyes went to the chiffon bridesmaid dress hanging on a hook by the closet, and suddenly the hangover was back in charge. She nearly threw up.

On the bright side, her hands and arms seemed to have healed enough that bandages were no longer required. She was fairly certain the damned makeup would be, though. Hopefully she'd be able to dig up a less-orange shade from one of the million women who would be traipsing through the house all day. She could already hear them laughing and chattering downstairs.

Deciding to make a run for the shower, she gathered her toiletry bag and leapt off the cot. Leaping was a terrible idea. Her right ankle twisted and she stumbled over her bag, bracing her fall with her arms. They might need some more bandages after all. Where was Rab when she needed her?

Morgan got up and brushed herself off. No, Rab wasn't here right now. But she was usually uncanny about being in the right place at the right time. At least when it came to Morgan.

Though the rehearsal dinner had become more tolerable and blessedly fuzzy as she'd continued to drink, she remembered that Rab had escorted her home, removed her bandages, and tended to her wounds again. She'd even tucked her in after the briefest fuss about who would be taking the cot.

The only comforting thought was that she hadn't had the chance to screw things up further by doing something stupid with Josh. It was bad enough as it was.

Morgan poked her head out the door, found the hall empty, and made a dash for the bathroom. Yep. The mirror confirmed her suspicions. Makeup would be required.

She turned on the shower and waited for the water to run hot, trying to determine the level of guilt she should be feeling.

It was just a kiss. Okay, two kisses, but they happened at the same time. So that only counted as one mistake. It hit Morgan that she would have to confess this slip-up to Trevor, and yeah, that cranked up the guilt.

She had promised to call him yesterday before the rehearsal and had forgotten. Then she'd ignored his phone call. She was still ignoring it.

Sometime today. She'd call him sometime today. And when she did, she would know what to say.

Morgan showered quickly, though the temptation to stand under the muscle-soothing, ache-removing water was hard to resist. The voices and giggling had moved up the stairs and the bathroom was about to be in high demand.

Next up: coffee. That would definitely involve talking to people, but she knew she couldn't avoid them forever. Especially Josh. She was surprised he hadn't been camped out in the hall waiting for her to emerge from his room.

Maybe she was making a big deal over nothing. Maybe he'd realized yesterday was a mistake, just as she had. Well, she was pretty sure it was a mistake, anyway. Definitely a bad thing.

The kitchen was quieter than the living room, but there were still people coming and going and shouting . . . what was with all the shouting? Happiness, she supposed.

Morgan managed to snag a cup of coffee without anyone paying her the slightest bit of attention and planted herself in a kitchen chair as close to the corner as she could get.

She yawned and wondered where Rab was. Probably upstairs helping with wedding junk. And there was still no sign of Josh. That was a good thing, right? Then why didn't it feel good? Maybe he had to work on weekends. Maybe she could avoid him for the rest of this wedding, except for the part when they had to walk down the aisle, and she could convince Rab to get a hotel room in Seattle for the night.

It made sense, really. They had to leave early enough without having to travel all the way from Silverdale. And Morgan could leave a note or something for Josh, explaining it was better this way. Sure, that was almost as lame as the phone call breakup, but at least he'd be left with something this time. He could read the note over and over again until it sunk in.

Now all she had to do was figure out what to write.

Morgan cringed at a loud whoop and an explosion of laughter from the living room. Enough was enough. She downed the rest of her coffee and hightailed it upstairs to grab those painkillers from her purse. She looked around the room and realized that even with the "redecorating" she'd done with the pictures, she couldn't hang out in there. So that only left outside.

Morgan trudged down the stairs and to the front door. Sunglasses. She'd need sunglasses. Well, those were outside in the rental car. All good. And it would be a great place to hang out and compose that letter to Josh.

The second she stepped onto the porch, her plans changed.

There was Josh, wearing – of all things – a green button-down shirt and jeans, toiling away at cleaning her car.

How he'd managed to get the car from wherever it had been parked with all the other cars lining the road to the driveway was beyond her.

Another thing that was completely unfathomable to her now was how she was supposed to just leave him. She couldn't. At least not like this. There was a reason her heart fluttered and a smile came unbidden to her face when she saw him. A reason her feet always seemed to take her in his direction whether she wanted them to or not. A reason a tear formed in her eye when she considered the possibility of never seeing him again.

Whatever those reasons were, she didn't have a clue. She wondered if she ever would.

Josh looked up and smiled when he saw her coming. Morgan forced her own smile to dim slightly. She had to be careful.

"You didn't have to do this," Morgan said as she approached the car to peer into the driver's side. "Holy crap. It's sparkling in there."

Josh set down the sponge where he was working on the outside of the passenger's side and chuckled. "Someone had to do it, and I doubted you would be up bright and early to tackle the job."

Morgan opened the door and leaned in, reaching across to the glove compartment to retrieve her sunglasses. Slowly, stifling a groan, she pulled herself back out. Morning stretches had not been on her to-do list for the day.

Sunglasses on, she released a sigh of relief and shut the door. Josh was moving around the front of the vehicle with a bucket and his sponge. Morgan headed toward the back, pretending to inspect his work.

"It looks good," she said. "I was just going to take the hit when I returned it and let them worry about it."

Josh shook his head and set the bucket down. "That's crazy. They would have charged you an arm and a leg."

Morgan shrugged. "It would have been worth it. Besides, I'm supposed to be on holidays." She hesitated before adding, "I think Rab and I might get a room in Seattle tonight."

Josh's head shot up from the car. "What for? You can have Sally's room here tonight. She won't be needing it anymore."

"It's just, we have to get up so early . . ."

Josh picked up the pail and started toward the back of the car, which he'd already cleaned. Morgan continued with her fake inspection, heading to the passenger's side.

"It's not that far," Josh said.

"I guess you're right. Besides, I don't think I'd get through the reception without a drink or two. I can't expect your sister to babysit me every night."

"Is that what she was doing last night? Babysitting you, or keeping you away from me?" Josh asked. "And how can you be thinking about drinking again already?"

Morgan laughed. Too loudly. He was on the move again, and so was she. "You're doing the stick-in-the-mud thing again," she said. "You still haven't learned to let your hair down, have you? Not that you have much hair left."

"I got it cut for the wedding. But you didn't answer my question."

"She didn't need to keep me away from you, Josh. I would have done that myself."

"*Merde!* Can we please stop this stupid dance?"

Morgan stopped walking and turned to face him, at a loss for words.

"Can we just sit and talk? Please?" he asked.

She nodded, resigned, and climbed onto the hood of the car, sitting cross-legged.

"Is that dry enough?" Josh asked as he came over to inspect it. Satisfied, he hefted himself onto the other side. "You're lucky I hadn't put the wax on yet."

"Wax? No way do you have to –"

Josh was laughing quietly, staring down the road.

"Ha, ha," Morgan said, but she couldn't keep from actually laughing a little herself.

They sat in comfortable silence for a while and Morgan clasped her hands on her lap to keep one from errantly reaching out to hold his, which was resting in the middle, slightly stretched toward her.

It was that instinct that cause her to start talking. The real words that needed to be said.

"We can't do that again."

Josh didn't turn her way, didn't move his hand, but he didn't ask what she was talking about either. He knew.

"Not the kissing," Morgan continued. "Not the hand-holding. Nothing." She paused and swallowed hard. "I don't know what Rab told you about Trevor, but I think you should know something . . . he asked my dad for my hand in marriage."

Now he looked at her, his eyes gone cold and distant. "Thought you didn't want to get married. I bet your dad couldn't wait to hand you over to Mr. Big Shot."

"Josh, it's not like that at all. Well, maybe my dad thinks like that, but not me. I haven't even decided what I'll say when he proposes, but I love him. And not because of the size of his paycheck. There are no words for how guilty I feel, betraying him like I did yesterday."

"You say you love him, and maybe you do, but I know you love me too."

"I don't think I ever stopped loving you," Morgan admitted. "How could I? It's just not that simple."

"I say it is. Who do you love more?"

"That's not a fair question. It's not something you can quantify. It's more about . . . actually, I have no idea. I can't think. I'm hungover."

"Lame excuse," Josh said.

"You're right. Sorry. I just . . . I need to go home, Josh. I need to see Trevor. And I need to think."

"You're just going to leave then?"

"I have to." Morgan threw her hands in the air and looked to the sky, exasperated. "It's clear there's still something between you and me, but I can't do anything before I – at the very least – tell Trevor what happened, and then figure out what that something that might be there is."

"And you expect me to just wait around while you figure all this out?"

"No, I don't. But I hope you will. It's not a small matter, and you should understand that. In fact, I'm not the only one who has stuff to figure out." She jabbed a finger in his direction.

"Say what now?" There was no mistaking the look of genuine confusion on his face.

Morgan sighed. "Iris."

"Hey, that was a new development. Brand new, literally, as of yesterday."

Morgan snickered and couldn't keep the smirk from her face. "It's probably not as new as you think. I mean this in the nicest way possible, but you are so clueless when it comes to girls, Josh."

His mouth twitched, fighting a smile. "Admittedly so," he conceded. "But I'm sure even I would have noticed . . . look, it doesn't matter. *We* are the issue right now."

"And like I said, *we* can't do anything about it today. Or tomorrow. Like it or not, we're going to have to get through this wedding for Sally's sake, with no funny business, and I have to be on a plane way too early tomorrow. If you want to give us a shot, it'll have to be long distance."

"That didn't work so well for us last time," Josh said.

"Well, it's the only option we have, okay?"

Josh nodded.

"Can we please just talk about something – anything – else for a minute?"

"Sure. How in the world did you get that car so dirty? Especially the inside. You would have to search hard to find that amount of mud."

Morgan grinned. "I kind of did. When I had that . . . car trouble, I was really hanging out at the junkyard practicing my karate skills."

"You mean the same junkyard where we found the part for Zinger?"

"That's the one." Morgan sighed, but it was a happy sigh. "I'll never forget that and how much it meant to me. Not only did you fix Zinger, but I didn't even have to remind you."

"Well, it would be hard to forget. Just like the drive you took us on through that city where he was damaged."

Morgan laughed. "That was a nightmare! I'll never forget those poor workers who had to jump out of the way as I ploughed through those traffic cones."

Josh was laughing too, but he sobered up quickly. "I'm just happy I was there that day. That was when . . ."

"Yeah. Kendra. Another thing I'll never forget. You were there for me when I needed someone the most. Getting over her death was one of the hardest things I've ever had to do."

"Well, you were there for me at the memorial when I was . . . working out stuff."

"Of course. But we had a lot of good times, too. Fun times. Remember when I finally convinced you to go to the bar and 'wiggle around some?'"

Morgan forgot all about the issues at hand as she and Josh sat laughing and reminiscing about the good times they'd shared, not once mentioning Trevor or Iris. The closest they came was when Shack's name came up.

"Poor Mel, and poor you as her friend, having to put up with that guy now," Josh said.

It didn't escape Morgan's attention that he'd purposely avoided referring to Shack as her boyfriend's brother.

"Ah, he's not that bad once you get used to him. Well, he still is, but he kinda grows on you. In a dumbass sort of way. And their kid's really cute. I mean, if you like that sorta thing."

A car pulled up and one of the bridesmaids – Heather, was it? – got out with a garment bag. She waved as she walked by.

They waved back and Morgan groaned softly. "I just know there's a whole lot of peach chiffon in that bag. I guess I should get in there."

Josh nodded and smiled a bit sadly as she uncrossed her legs and hopped off the hood. Without thinking, she turned to peck him on the cheek. She stopped herself just in time and pretended to stumble before waving and heading for the house.

Yeah, she was really going to have to watch that.

Chapter 24

In Which Josh and Morgan Walk Down the Aisle
Saturday, August 15, 1998

The Hampton house was organized chaos as the four young women got ready for the wedding ceremony. The living room had become the stage for final preparations. Sally stood in the center and the other bridesmaids each had a spot around her.

Aunt Peggy and a half-dozen other females assisted the women. Josh had met most of them during the past six weeks and knew the majority were Sally's cousins. His sister stood by and lent a hand where she could. Josh eyed Morgan as he passed, but she didn't acknowledge him. He figured she must be too busy.

Other than Uncle Bill, Josh was the only male in the house.

Josh and Uncle Bill were relegated to Josh's room to get dressed. Josh had taken a shower after he'd finished detailing the rental – a task he'd performed many times on Zinger. He didn't mind detailing cars, and he sometimes did it as a side gig, but he wasn't the scrub boy anymore. College and Ezra Brock ensured that he was not.

Josh's dark blue tuxedo jacket and royal blue pants were the same color as the Marine dress uniforms, but he did not have the red stripe on his pants. At least he wouldn't be alone in that aspect because Oscar hadn't earned his yet.

His uncle put on his dress uniform, which bore a slight cedar aroma. Josh recognized the Vietnam Service and the Purple Heart among the medals hanging on his uncle's uniform. Uncle Bill never spoke of his time "in-country" and Josh knew better than to ask.

"Aren't we getting ready a little early?" Josh asked instead.

"We need to allow time for any delays and want to get to the chapel about an hour before the ceremony," Uncle Bill said. "I'm guessing you haven't been part of many weddings."

"Yeah, exactly none."

"There's a whole lot of planning and coordination required. Fortunately, your Aunt Peggy can handle it."

"I have no idea what size wedding I'll have. If Morgan has her way, we'd be standing before a justice of the peace."

"So, you have won her heart back? Good for you."

"No, that was more speculation than anything," Josh said. "We're talking, which is good, but I doubt we'll get things resolved over the weekend."

"Long-distance relationships are hard. Your aunt and I are lucky we were already married when I went overseas. Even so, many a Marine has returned from deployment to an empty house and divorce papers."

"That's rough."

"Some couples can't handle the separation. I've always been thankful that your aunt is made of sterner stuff," Uncle Bill said and checked himself in the mirror.

"Josh? You ready?" William called from downstairs.

"Sounds like your ride is here," Uncle Bill said.

"How do I look?" Josh spread his arms for examination.

"You're a handsome young man," Uncle Bill said, "even if I'm somewhat biased."

"Thanks," Josh said as he left the room.

Oscar was waiting outside by William's Toyota. Both wore their dress uniforms. Molly sat in the shotgun seat and Oscar rode in the back with Josh.

When they arrived at the chapel, the photographer was studying the layout for the group shots that would be taken later. Michael had arrived with his parents and waved as he headed to the groom's room before the bride arrived.

Two floral vans sat in the parking lot with workers scurrying like bees to make the last adjustments to the arrangements. As the groomsmen reached the door to the chapel, the car with the bridesmaids arrived.

Josh paused to watch them get out of the car and walk to the chapel where William held the door for the girls. The men followed and the two groups separated to go to their respective rooms.

William checked his uniform and verified he had the ring in his pocket. Then he put a boutonniere on Josh's lapel. Because they wore their medals, the Marines wouldn't wear flowers. The Marines had also chosen not to wear their sabers.

Michael handed Josh a pair of white gloves. "Last minute change."

Josh shrugged and tugged on his gloves as the Marines tugged on theirs. Organ music drifted through the door as Uncle Bill stepped into the room. Josh felt like the odd man out, but at the same time was honored to stand among them.

"Is she here?" Michael asked his future father-in-law.

Uncle Bill laughed. "She is here and would be if she had to walk all the way. Relax, son, this is easier than boot camp."

William went to hand a pair of white gloves to his dad, but saw the senior Hampton already had a pair tucked in his belt.

"Your sister advised me of the change," Uncle Bill said. "She asked that the wedding party wear them so Morgan's scratches from her accident don't show."

The groom fidgeted while they waited for the guests to arrive and take their seats.

Finally, a young Marine serving as an usher opened the door. "Gentlemen, it's time."

Josh led the way and they lined up at the door. When the chaplain gave him the nod, Josh led the groomsmen in, because his position was the farthest away from the altar.

Walking slowly as they'd practiced, Josh spotted his sister on the bride's side. She'd chosen to wear a blue dress with a rose corsage. She was sitting next to a man, but Josh didn't pay much attention to him as he had to get to his position.

Michael stopped at the front pew and handed his hat to his mother.

As soon as Michael took his place at the foot of the dais, the bridesmaids made their entrance with Morgan in the lead. The long white gloves concealed any remaining scabs on her hands. She looked beautiful, soft, and oh, so feminine. Each bridesmaid carried a bouquet of red roses and peach carnations to match their dresses.

Behind her walked Iris, who shot him a quick glance and a smile before turning to take her place. Josh's heart skipped a beat as he marveled again at how beautiful she was and mentally chastised himself for never noticing before. For the second time in the past twenty-four hours, he wondered if he should end the apparently futile pursuit of Morgan.

Before Josh could entertain the thought anymore, Heather moved to the maid-of-honor's spot and Sally and her dad appeared in the doorway. The organist played the introductory chords to the wedding march and the guests stood to face the bride as she walked down the aisle to the front.

Sally wore a floor-length white satin gown with short puffed sleeves and a plunging neckline. An outer layer of white lace covered the dress and her lower arms. A crown of embroidered flowers held her veil in place. Her bouquet was red roses and white chrysanthemum.

Josh had never seen his cousin more radiant; her face glowed.

Sally stopped a pace from the dais and the chaplain asked, "Who gives this woman to be married to this man?"

Uncle Bill replied, "Her mother and I do."

He raised her veil and kissed her on the cheek. Then Sally stood next to Michael as Uncle Bill went to sit next to Aunt Peggy, who was already well into her box of tissues.

Josh wondered if his parents would even attend his wedding. At present, the prospect didn't look good, especially if Morgan was his bride.

Sally took the hand Michael offered and they stepped up on the dais to stand before the chaplain.

"Dearly beloved," the chaplain began, "we are gathered here today to witness the uniting of this man and this woman in the bonds of holy matrimony . . ."

As the ceremony continued, Josh half-listened for the keywords and tricky phrases that meant the ceremony was coming to an end. In the meantime, he allowed himself to enjoy the sight of Morgan and Iris standing across the chapel from him.

To him, that's where his future stood. *Two roads diverged in a wood, and I – I took the one less traveled by.*

But which road was the less traveled, the one to Morgan or the one to Iris? Robert Frost suggested in the poem that both appeared to be equally traveled.

Josh wasn't going to base his life on a poem. Nevertheless, on the road of life, he'd come to a fork in the road. The road on the right, as it were, he hadn't even been aware of a week ago, even if Iris had been in front of him practically since he and Morgan had broken up.

Josh's choice would be Morgan and had been Morgan since the day they'd left Bathurst together three years ago.

But he wasn't the only one who had a choice. Morgan had a choice as well. He hoped she'd choose him. Once Josh had believed she would. He wasn't so sure anymore.

As he gazed at Morgan, she made a small motion with her head toward the bride's side of the guests. Only Josh noticed it because everyone else was watching Sally and Michael exchange their vows.

After a second nod from Morgan, Josh slanted his eyes toward the guests. He scanned the crowd and again spotted Rab and the man sitting next to her. By sheer force of will, he avoided dropping his jaw and exclaiming, "*Merde*."

Rab was sitting with their father.

Josh examined the other guests on the bride's side and turned his head slightly to see the groom's side.

Josh's mother wasn't among the guests. That both puzzled and relieved him.

He wondered why she wasn't traveling with their father but was grateful she didn't seem to be present. Josh didn't need her interfering with his efforts to win Morgan back. He had no doubt the prospect of her as a mother-in-law was firmly on the negative side of the balance sheet.

Josh also wondered why their father was there. He'd never have expected to see his father near his estranged brother, Uncle Bill. They'd hardly spoken to each other since his father had left for Canada in protest of the Vietnam conflict.

"I now pronounce you husband and wife," the chaplain exclaimed. "You may kiss the bride."

Josh's attention returned to the dais. Sally and Michael broke their kiss and faced the guests hand in hand – husband and wife. A wave of happiness for Sally washed over Josh. He imagined standing before a preacher one day, but who would be standing next to him?

"Ladies and gentlemen, I present Mr. and Mrs. Sanderson," the chaplain said.

The organist began the exit march and the newlyweds stepped off the dais heading for the aisle. As they passed their attendants, each pair joined and followed behind, Josh and Morgan bringing up the rear.

As they'd agreed, they didn't speak as they departed the sanctuary. Morgan's grasp of his arm was barely perceptible, and she released it as soon as they were outside the chapel.

Michael and Sally had paused to wait for their parents. The couple left the chapel, closely trailed by the photographer. The newlyweds were kissing again, a bit more intensely than they had inside.

"If the wedding party and the parents would gather over at the gazebo, we can start getting the group photos," the photographer announced.

Morgan was already pulling off her gloves and making a beeline for the gazebo, probably for a smoke.

Josh searched the departing guests for his father. Once again, he had more questions than answers.

Chapter 25

In Which Morgan's Face Really, Really Hurts
Saturday, August 15, 1998

"Morgan, scoot closer?"

It was the second time the photographer had asked her to do this. She had already done it the first time. She was practically touching Josh. She scooted another half-inch, smile held firmly in place in hope that flash was about to go off.

"A little more?"

Oh, for – Morgan looped her arm through Josh's and felt her eyes begin to water. Her face hurt that much.

"Now if you could just tilt your head a bit – no, not away, toward him. There it is."

Finally. Click, click, click. He looked like he was going for another click, but Morgan was done. She was certain the smile had held up, but she was also willing to bet her eyes had turned murderous long ago.

Morgan walked off, heading in the direction of the reception. Most guests were driving, but it was just across a couple of parking lots and one road. Besides, Morgan needed some time alone – badly.

She pulled off her gloves and decided to have a smoke before making the phone call. She thought she heard someone calling her name but only quickened her pace. If they wanted more photos, they were out of luck. They already had enough. They'd been taking them for nearly half an hour. Everyone all together, just this group, just that group, then couples. It was inhumane.

At least that part was over and all she had to get through now was the reception. And as much as she wanted the day to be over, she really would have liked a bit more of a break between the wedding and reception. Her face was literally the most painful of all her injuries right now, and that was saying a lot.

Morgan's high heel dipped into a hole in the grass just before she reached the road and her ankle rolled slightly. The string of curses that followed was long. It hadn't even hurt that much – mostly startled her and threw her off balance.

But the curses had been bottled up for hours. And while this was not the most ideal place to let them loose – she wasn't the only one walking over to the hall – it was the best she was going to get for the foreseeable future.

It had all started on the ride from the Hamptons' house to the chapel. Morgan had never been much of a giggler – nor tolerant of bubbly, airheaded gigglers – but she'd done her best to appear cheerful. She'd even tried to participate in the conversation and excitement about the wedding.

She had not done a spectacular job of it.

The entire girl-chatter thing had been a challenge, but the clincher had been Iris. Even though Iris had been sitting directly in front of Morgan, that didn't stop her from constantly turning to smile at her.

And it was the strangest sort of smile. Morgan could not figure out if her eyes were saying "wishing you were dead" or if she was genuinely trying to be nice by including her. Morgan did manage to return the smiles, but hers were definitely of the former variety.

Perhaps she was simply biased, but Morgan thought Iris giggled a lot for a mechanic – for any human, really. And she was a suck up. No, the dresses were not lovely. No, not everyone was lucky to be here and looking forward to everything.

Fine. Morgan had to admit she was jealous. She couldn't stop replaying what she'd seen the other day at the garage every time she saw this woman. She had no claim on Josh – well, maybe she did, that's what they were supposed to be figuring out – but honestly, Iris's voice just annoyed her period. When she wasn't giggling, the tone of it was oddly low and grating.

By the time they arrived at the chapel and Morgan had thrown herself out of the vehicle, she had no more smiles to give. Until she was forced to for the wedding. And then the photos.

All in all, she had to admit that although it was not her style, the wedding had been nice. It would have been a lot nicer if it was about an hour or two shorter, but still.

The most surprising part of the ceremony had been when she'd noticed Josh's dad sitting in the audience. Weren't he and Josh's mother the main reasons Josh had chosen to leave Bathurst for good?

Morgan had spent more than her fair share of time after that discovery scouring the audience, looking for his mother. Her skin prickled at the thought of finding her there, but luckily Margaret was not in attendance.

Morgan chuckled to herself as she arrived at the reception hall and found a quiet corner in the parking lot by some trees. Actually, if Josh's mother had shown up, it might have solved one problem. She and Josh were trying to keep their distance tonight? That would have done it.

Morgan's laughter turned to a deep sigh as she pulled out her phone. There was no more putting it off. She had to call Trevor. She hadn't talked to him since Wednesday, after her anesthesia scare was over. She'd left him a message on Thursday saying she'd check in on Friday, but . . . no sense dwelling on that now.

It rang so many times, Morgan thought the call would go to voicemail. But no.

"Hello, my love."

Despite everything, Morgan felt herself relax at the sound of his voice. She really had needed to hear that. Even though her face was probably permanently damaged from smiling, she felt another one form.

"Hi. I miss you," she said.

"I was worried when I didn't hear from you yesterday. You're okay? No more complications?"

Morgan choked. "No more medical complications," she assured him, keeping her tone as light as possible. Because boy, there had been some other complications.

There was no way she was going to confess about the kiss over the phone, and certainly not about the maybe-feelings issue. She would have to tell him about the kiss eventually in person, but maybe the feelings thing would be resolved sooner rather than later and she wouldn't have to bring it up at all.

"I'm relieved to hear that," Trevor said. "Did I mention how much I miss you?"

"Not in detail, no," Morgan said. "But you can show me when I get home. God, this week has not gone according to plan at all. I didn't even get to talk to Damian. I only got to see him through a window at the hospital."

"That sucks."

"I get why, kind of. Compromised immunity and all. But Randy was . . ."

"Not much better than the last time you saw him?" Trevor guessed.

"Worse. I couldn't have felt less welcome at the hospital. But Damian's got the marrow, his procedure went well as far as I know, and at least I can be happy about that, right?"

"Of course. I'm proud of you for doing that, Morgan. What have you and Rab been up to since then?"

"Um . . . crazy thing, really. One of Sally's bridesmaids went and had her baby right in the middle of the shower, so I got roped into taking her place."

"Seriously? What sort of hideous dress are they making you wear?"

Morgan laughed. "Peach chiffon."

"Ouch."

"Yeah. So Rab and I have been staying with the Hamptons, what with the rehearsal dinner and all . . . that's why I missed your call last night."

There was silence on the other end for a minute. Then, "Are you at least managing to have some fun?"

If Morgan hadn't known him so well, she may have missed the slight strain in his voice. She thought hard about her answer. The most fun she'd had on this rotten trip had been during the few hours she and Josh sat on the hood of the rental car simply hanging out, joking around, and reminiscing. Not something she was about to proclaim to Trevor as the highlight of her vacation.

"No," she finally said. "This sucks. We haven't seen any of Seattle. We've been stuck in a house filled with estrogen, and squealing, and those peach chiffon things. Oh, wait. I did wind up with a free afternoon and made a detour to a junkyard. That was rewarding."

"Temper tantrum?"

"You bet. I've got some excellent scars in lieu of souvenirs. I'm telling you, you'll be impressed."

Trevor chuckled. "I have no doubt."

"Anyhow, my face hurts the most. Wedding pictures and stuff. Now I've just got to get through a reception, which shouldn't be too bad since they'll be serving medicine. But speaking of the reception, I need to get to it. I'll also need to work overtime for a month to pay off this phone bill."

"I'm sure we can arrange that," Trevor said, and she could feel his grin across the miles. "I really cannot wait until you get home."

"Me too," Morgan said, and meant it with all her heart.

"I'm sure you'll be tired after you get home tomorrow, so I'll probably have to wait until Monday to see you?"

"Yeah. Are you still using your dad's office next week?"

"I'm in it right now. Make sure to come straight here Monday morning?"

"Wild horses could not keep me away."

"Excellent. I love you."

"I love you."

Morgan hung up and allowed herself a moment to bask in the happy haze that always followed hearing his voice. Even though the number of guests entering the hall had slowed to a trickle, she also permitted herself one more smoke.

She saw Josh get out of an SUV with his buddies and shrank back under the cover of the trees. Why on earth did her mind reel back nearly three years ago to their first Christmas together? Not so much the day itself, but the gift Josh had bought her. It had been a pair of necklaces, each with one of their names inscribed on half a heart. She'd kept the one with his name, and he the one with hers.

She wondered if he still had his. She hadn't been able to make herself get rid of hers, though she obviously never wore it. The purpose of the gift had been to remind them that they would never be whole without each other. And even though her feelings continued to flail madly in one direction then another, that part still felt right. She couldn't imagine a world in which Josh didn't exist – in which he didn't have a place in her life, no matter how small.

But geez, even when they were together, sometimes he felt more like the older brother she'd never wanted than a lover. And thinking again of the few hours they'd been given on the hood of the car, when they were reminiscing, it was as if they had gone back in time. But their favorite memories had not been romantic ones. They'd been ones when they were just hanging out or fussing at each other.

The fact of the matter was, Morgan didn't know how to let him go. She didn't want to hand him over to – or even share him with – someone like Iris. She didn't want anyone to take her place in his heart.

Was that selfish, or was that love?

Better question: What should a romantic, possibly marital, relationship feel like?

What she had with Trevor was amazing. Her pulse still quickened at the mere thought of him. She was always excited to see him, as if every day were both their first and their last together. She was never, ever bored or miserable when he was around. They rarely bickered without it ending in a tickle fight or . . . something better.

What she'd had with Josh? Well, he made her feel like the most important person in the world. There were rarely any surprises from him – he was as predictable as an atomic clock – but that just meant he loved her and she was safe. He would literally do anything for her. If she told him she didn't want to fly home – which she really didn't – and asked him to drive her all the way across the continent in Old Blue, he would. Even if it meant possibly depositing her straight into the arms of another, he would do it in a heartbeat. Morgan had zero doubts about that.

So what was there to figure out? Maybe it wasn't a choice that needed to be made between Trevor and Josh. Maybe she was supposed to figure out what each of them meant to her – where they belonged in her life.

And Josh needed to figure that out too. The guy tended to get ideas planted into his head, and once there, they quickly cemented. Maybe he didn't love her like he thought he did. Maybe he was just confused. Again.

All Morgan knew was that in the end, this whole thing seemed to be up to her. And that wasn't fair.

Catching sight of Sally and Michael's car pulling up, Morgan knew it was time to get inside. She steeled herself for the sight of Iris. Worse yet, Josh and Iris sitting together, talking, maybe touching. She shouldn't care, but good luck telling her heart that.

When she entered and scanned the room, the first person she saw was Iris sitting with a couple of other women. Iris's attention, however, was focused on . . .

Josh, who was sitting with his dad and sister. Well, one out of two ain't bad.

As if he could sense Morgan's presence in any room, Josh looked up and waved. Rab did the same. To Morgan's surprise, so did their father. And they were all smiling. She had never seen that man smile before. She waved and smiled back, wincing at the smile-pain, then headed in the opposite direction.

A couple of young girls came up to her, eyeing her chiffon gown.

"You must be Morgan, Brook's replacement, right?"

"Yeah," Morgan said with another beyond-painful smile. "I'm sorry, you look familiar but . . ."

"No, we've never met," the shorter girl said. "I'm Rebecca, one of Sally's cousins. And this is my sister Claire."

"Hi," Claire said.

"That's why you look familiar," Morgan said. "You both look an awful lot like Sally."

"Yes. We get that a lot on this side of the family," Rebecca said. "Anyhow, it's nice to meet you. Sally's talked a lot about you over the years."

"Nice to meet you too. Hey, wait," Morgan said as they turned to leave. "Do you know where I'm supposed to go to buy drink tickets?"

"It's an open bar," Rebecca said, pointing to it.

Morgan smiled – it wasn't forced at all. Still hurt, though.

Chapter 26

In Which Old Wounds Are Healed
Saturday, August 15, 1998

By the time the photographer had finished taking group photos, most of the guests had driven or walked to the base's recreation complex. When Josh arrived, he'd scanned the room looking for Morgan. He hadn't seen her, even though the other bridesmaids were already there.

Iris had been standing with her father and mother. Ezra Brock had chosen to wear a charcoal gray suit rather than his uniform, but sported a Marine Corps pin on the lapel. His wife, Michiko, wore a royal blue, ankle-length dress with a chrysanthemum print.

Josh joined Rab and their father, who had already chosen a table near the edge of the room. That's when he'd spotted Morgan and waved to her. His sister – and surprisingly, his father – had done the same.

After pleasantries had been exchanged and Josh had taken his seat, silence settled over the table.

Although he didn't really want to ask, Josh had to know. "Did Mom come with you?"

"I'm traveling alone. Your mother . . . chose to stay home and take care of some important business."

"I'm glad you came to visit."

"I plan to do more than visit." His attention turned toward the bar. "I didn't know Miss Parker was going to be a member of the wedding party."

"It was a last-minute change. I can explain later. If Morgan is here, Sally and Michael must be about to arrive," Josh said as he stood. "I need to get to my table."

"I'd like to talk to you some more later, son," Josh's father said as he stood and offered his hand.

"We will," Josh said as they shook.

Finding his assigned seat, Josh sat between Morgan and Iris and across from Oscar. Morgan and Iris each had a drink in front of them. He was willing to bet that Morgan's drink was more intoxicating than Iris's.

"Ladies, Oscar. It looks like we'll be together a little longer," Josh said.

Oscar shrugged. "The company is pleasant enough."

"It seems like we've been together all day," Morgan said. "I didn't expect it to take this long."

"It's an honor to be a bridesmaid," Iris said and smiled gently.

"I sure wouldn't put anyone through this," Morgan replied. "Just me, my intended, and witnesses in front of a justice of the peace."

"This is nothing . . . it's Morgan, right?" Oscar said. "I've ridden in a hummer in a sweltering desert with five other grunts. Talk about a long day."

"Hah! I drove across two countries and back. Spent almost a whole month in a car," Morgan said, not mentioning that Josh had been with her.

Oscar raised his glass. "Fair enough."

After the caterers had distributed dinner, the group at the attendants' table continued small talk throughout the meal, with Iris and Josh carrying the conversation. Morgan limited her responses to a few words.

As the guests were finishing their meals, the servers distributed glasses of champagne to the adults and ginger ale to the younger guests. Morgan reached for hers immediately.

"Wait, that's for the toast," Josh said.

Morgan set it back on the table and scowled.

When everyone had something bubbly, William stood and tapped his glass with a fork. "Please join me in a toast for the bride and groom."

The guests fell silent.

"Michael and Sally, may your life be filled with love, joy, and happiness. Here's to you."

The guests clinked glasses and sipped their champagne.

"If the bride and groom will make their way to the dance floor, we'll get this place moving!" William said.

Michael and Sally walked hand in hand to the floor. The DJ played "You Are So Beautiful" by Joe Cocker. Josh watched the guests more than the dancers. Iris was smiling, but Morgan was busy tossing back her champagne.

"You going to finish yours, Josh?" Morgan asked after she'd emptied her glass.

"Probably not," he said.

"No sense letting it go to waste," Morgan said and picked up his glass. "This is pretty good stuff."

"You're welcome to mine, too," Iris offered.

The hall erupted in applause when Michael and Sally finished their dance and kissed.

"Okay, now everybody dance," the DJ announced as he chose a livelier tune.

Oscar stood and extended a hand to Iris. "Shall we?"

Iris accepted the offer and they headed to the dance floor. Josh glanced at Morgan, and she held up her hand.

"Later, then?" Josh asked.

"We'll see."

"Then I'm going to go mingle."

"If you hear of anyone leaving early, let me know," Morgan said.

"Good luck with that. The party is just starting."

Josh left the table and was searching for his father when Heather intercepted him. "Care to dance, Josh?"

"I don't know." He turned toward Morgan who was steadfastly ignoring him.

"It's just a dance, not a date," Heather said. "I don't think your girlfriend would mind. William is dancing with Molly, and I wanted to dance with some of the wedding party first."

"I'm not sure what Morgan minds or doesn't mind right now, but as long as you don't kiss me, it should be okay."

Heather laughed. "It'd take a lot more than one dance for us to kiss."

"I'll accept that," Josh said and offered her a hand.

When the dance ended, the DJ started a slower song and Josh offered to dance again. As they moved around the dance floor Josh asked, "How long have you known Iris?"

"What's your interest in Iris? I thought Morgan was your girlfriend."

"I don't really know what Morgan is or isn't right now."

"Don't you work with Iris?" Heather asked.

"I do, but I've seen a whole new side of her the past few days."

"You should ask Sally. She knows Iris better than I do. But from what I've seen, she's a sweet girl."

"I enjoy working with her," Josh said.

The dance ended. Before they separated, Heather gave Josh a peck on the cheek.

"I thought you said . . ."

"We danced more than once," Heather said and smiled as she began walking away. "Thank you for the dances."

"Wasn't your boyfriend able to attend today?"

Heather turned back and sighed. "No, he's out to sea."

"I'm sure you look forward to his return."

"I do," Heather said with a smile and motioned toward Sally. "Maybe it'll be my turn next."

Heather had barely stepped away when Sally met Josh on the dance floor. "Dance this next one with me, cuz?"

"It'll be an honor, Mrs. Sanderson," Josh said as the next song started.

"You know, as often as I used to doodle 'Sally Sanderson' on my notebooks, it's still going to take some time to get used to hearing that."

"I wish you and your husband all the happiness in the world."

"I wish I could offer you and Morgan the same," Sally said.

"What do you mean?"

"When you were here with Morgan three years ago, I could see the love in both your eyes as you looked at each other. This past week, I see the affection in your eyes when you look at Morgan, but it's no longer there in hers."

"It's that obvious?" Josh said.

"Sadly, yes. When she arrived, I was still rooting for you and Morgan, but not anymore."

"But I still love her."

"What do you want most for Morgan, Josh?" Sally asked.

"I want her to be happy."

"Do you love her enough to let her be with someone else if that's who she's happiest with?"

"I don't know if I can," Josh said.

"You're a Hampton, strong like my dad and brother. I know you can."

"On another subject, how well do you know Iris?"

"Well enough to know you caught her eye three years ago."

"What? I don't remember meeting her then."

"Do you remember when we had lunch at Osaka?" Sally asked.

"Yes, it was a pleasant lunch."

"Iris was the young woman who was our server. When I saw her again, she asked who you were and was saddened to learn you didn't live in the area."

"I had no idea," Josh said.

"I didn't think you would. You had eyes only for Morgan."

"I guess I did."

"Do me a favor?" Sally asked.

"Sure, what can I do for you?"

"Ask some of my cousins to dance? They're a bit shy."

"Sure, but which ones are your cousins?" Josh asked.

She laughed as the dance ended. "Any young woman with red hair is probably my cousin. Thanks for the dance, cuz."

"Thanks for the encouragement," he said.

Josh tried again to locate his father. He found him standing near the front table, talking with his brother, Uncle Bill.

Josh took a step toward them, but they weren't yelling or fighting, so he paused. He had to blink when he saw them shake hands and give each other a manly hug.

What's going on with my father?

He decided to find out when the brothers parted and his father made his way to the table where Rab sat. Josh followed.

"I'm glad you could join us. I was about to fill your sister in on what's happening. It'll save me from telling it twice," his father said.

"This I have to hear," Josh said. "What's with you and Uncle Bill?"

"I'll get to that. I need to tell you both what's going on with your mother and me."

"Is Mom okay?" Rab asked.

"Your mom is well. Last Monday, she got an offer to be vice president of a branch in Montreal. She accepted immediately and told me we were moving."

"You're moving to Montreal?" Josh was stunned.

"Your mother is moving to Montreal. I'm staying in Bathurst. As you can imagine, that didn't sit well with your mother."

Josh didn't have to imagine very hard.

"Why aren't you going with her, Dad?" Rab asked.

"About twenty years ago, when the bank offered your mother a position in Bathurst, we moved there from Toronto.

189

During the time we lived there, we bought a house, raised a family, and made friends. Bathurst is my home now, and I don't want to move."

"Long-distance relationships are hard to maintain, Father, trust me," Josh said.

"Which is why your mother and I are separating."

"You're getting divorced?" Rab asked with wide eyes, beating Josh to the question.

"I don't know if your mother would ever divorce me, but we'll have to see."

"So you'll be living in the house alone?" Josh said.

"No, your mother insists we sell the house. I've already found an apartment and will be moving into it shortly after I get back to Bathurst."

"Why did you come here, then?" Josh asked.

"I knew you would both be here. I figured I could talk to you, see my niece get married, and make peace with my brother."

"I'm happy you did, but why now?"

"In a big way, you are responsible, son. You had the courage to say no to your mother when she demanded that you break up with Morgan as a condition to getting a loan. You stood by what you believed in. In our many years of marriage, I never said no to your mother except for times when it didn't really matter. The change in you started a change in me. So here I am and let me say, I'm happier than I've been in years."

"When are you going back?" Josh asked.

"I'm leaving Wednesday morning."

Iris stepped to the table and placed a hand on Josh's shoulder. "Am I interrupting something?"

"Not at all, young lady. I think we're done for now," Josh's father said.

"May I have the next dance, Josh?" Iris asked.

Josh looked past her to where Morgan sat, alone and looking miserable.

"I'd like that," Josh said and rose from his chair.

It can't hurt.

They advanced to the dance floor and Josh took Iris into his arms as the DJ began another slow song. Josh noted the slow dances attracted more people to the dance floor and reasoned the DJ must have as well.

"I've had a chance to observe you and Morgan these past few days."

"I hope you're not going to tell me we don't belong together," Josh said. "Everyone else seems to be saying that."

"I am not going to say whether you should or shouldn't be together."

"What will you say, then?"

"I've seen your devotion to Morgan. It makes me want you all the more," Iris said. "May God forgive me for my covetousness."

"And may He forgive me my duplicity," Josh said. "I find myself drawn to you more and more each day." Iris felt so right in his arms as they moved in harmony over the dance floor.

"But you're not ready to let her go yet."

"We were lovers. I'm honor-bound to offer her the chance to marry me."

"Your sense of honor is strong. That appeals to my heritage," Iris said. "When she leaves tomorrow, will you know?"

"Probably not." He closed his eyes and lowered his head to rest lightly on hers.

"Then how much longer will this take?" Iris asked.

"I'm thinking about going to Bathurst to help my father move. I expect to get an answer there." He smiled a weak smile because he was afraid he already knew the answer. So, why go?

Because it's Morgan.

"How soon will that happen?" Iris persisted.

"My father leaves Wednesday and I'm going to see if I can travel with him. In either case, I plan to return Sunday," Josh said. "I'm going to owe your dad a lot of hours."

"*If* you return."

"Yes. I should have said if. Maybe I'm starting to believe what the others have been telling me."

"Can I ride with you to the airport?" Iris asked, changing the subject.

"That's a great idea. Then you can bring Old Blue back here."

"And pick you up when you return," Iris said with a note of hope in her voice.

The music ended and Josh pulled Iris in for a long, luxurious kiss.

She accepted the kiss willingly.

Now the kiss count was even.

"I hope Morgan didn't see that," Iris said breathlessly when their lips parted.

"Right about now, I'm not sure I care."

Chapter 27

In Which Blood is Spilled
Saturday, August 15, 1998

The second Morgan saw Iris and Josh heading out onto the dance floor together, she'd gritted her teeth and slipped out the door for a smoke.

And slipped was exactly what she did. Thankfully, she wasn't the only other guest in need of "fresh" air because some dude in a suit had saved her from a nasty fall. She needed another injury like she needed a hole in the head.

She'd giggled at the thought. What a stupid saying. Of course she needed a hole in her head. She needed five, to be precise. Everyone did. Two nose holes, two ear holes, and a mouth hole. Unless eye sockets counted as holes, then she'd need seven. But they were stuffed with eyeballs, so they probably didn't count.

Morgan vaguely remembered the man looking at her strangely as she stood there giggling, and she was almost certain she'd thanked him before stalking away – her amusement replaced with annoyance – muttering under her breath about the stupid high heels and unsafe floors.

It seemed like she just got her cigarette lit – damned wind – when she heard the announcement. That was another thing wearing on her last nerve; even though most of the music was crappy, none of it was loud enough. The same could not be said for that DJ's voice. She had no trouble making out his words even from outside. Cake cutting time?

Morgan tossed her cigarette in the direction of the ashtray and headed back in. If it were anything else, she would have stayed where she was, but cake cutting must surely mean an end to this madness.

Not that bad, not that bad, Morgan reminded herself as her eyes adjusted to the dim lighting inside. At least there were no balloons at this shindig . . . and cake cutting, right? They both lived happily ever after? The end?

Not quite. Morgan slumped back into the chair she'd vacated – wait, this wasn't her chair. There were different people sitting at the table. Oh, well. They didn't pay her any attention. All eyes were trained on the happy couple as Michael sliced the cake with – whoa, was that a ninja sword?

Whatever it was, it got the job done. But it finally dawned on Morgan that now that the cake had been cut, people would likely want to eat it.

She stifled a yawn and got up to head to the bar, seeing as how she'd lost her drink along with her table. Halfway there, a young man stopped her and asked her to dance. He looked vaguely familiar and his smile was enough to tell her they'd likely been introduced at some point over the last four weeks – or had it really been days? – since this wedding stuff started. Morgan declined, using the surgery-soreness excuse as she had been doing all night, and tottered around him.

After she got her drink, she tried to locate her table, but quickly decided the seating arrangements no longer mattered. Everyone appeared to be plopping themselves down wherever they wanted. Excellent news, because she would much prefer a table in some dark corner right about now. Even better, a table for one.

Morgan sank into this new and improved seat and eyed the crowd. Everyone looked so goddamned happy. Why was she the only one who was miserable?

Better question – why was she miserable at all? Her eyes sought out Josh and found him talking to his father and Rab again as they waited for the cake to be served. Sadly, she suspected she was feeling so wretched because Josh didn't appear to be suffering at all. Well, that wasn't very nice of her, was it?

But Morgan couldn't change they way she felt any more than she could change the way Josh felt. Her annoyance only grew as she pondered her situation. She was leaving tomorrow – in a mere handful of hours – and Josh was off making nice with everyone and ignoring her.

Josh. The guy who had professed his undying love and commitment so many times since she'd been here that she'd had to fight a gag or two. And there he was – at zero hour – partying with his friends. There was no denying it . . . something was just plain wrong with the guy.

But Morgan still couldn't help wondering if he was supposed to be *her* guy. She did not make a habit of running around kissing guys other than her boyfriend/possible fiancée, holding hands with them, and feeling feelings for them. There was no way she would risk her relationship with Trevor for just anyone. No. There was something special about Josh. Something that even now called to her. Something she didn't understand, for sure, but why didn't he look upset at all?

Maybe he was just putting on a brave face and making nice for Sally's wedding – like she should be doing – but if so, he was putting on a stellar performance.

Morgan knocked back half her drink – they were stingy with the portions – and eyed Josh some more. God willing, this night would soon be over. Acting or not, did he intend to just leave without talking to her at all? Sure, they had agreed to keep their distance to make sure there was no funny business, but this was a bit much. Didn't he realize she was flying home tonight?

Morgan hiccupped and mentally corrected herself. No, she was flying tomorrow. Tonight she just needed to get out of this building.

Regardless, she was leaving soon – all the way back across the continent – and what plans had they made? To figure shit out. Long-distance style. Yeah, right. Morgan knew exactly what would happen as soon as she set foot on that plane. Josh would be off traipsing around with that mechanic girl – no way was she not going to make a move on him. Back home, Morgan could probably expect the odd grunty phone call during which no meaningful words would be exchanged. Brilliant plan.

But really, who could blame Iris? No matter how you looked at it, Josh was a great guy. Honorable to the core. Sure, that could be supremely annoying at times – especially when he got some idiot idea stuck in his head that replayed on a loop – and he had a tendency to be stiff as hell in both general manners and the way he spoke, but wasn't that better than –

"May I have this dance?"

Morgan choked on her drink and looked up at the sound of Josh's voice, willing her eyes to focus. What did he do, warp across the room? She'd just seen him standing with his father.

"You okay?"

"Sure," Morgan said, hoping she was imagining the slur in her voice.

Josh helped her to her feet and took the drink from her hand, placing it on the table. She allowed him to lead her to the dance floor as another slow song began. Slow was good.

Morgan slid easily into his arms and leaned her head against his shoulder, both happy and sad. Maybe it was okay for this reception to last just a little longer. Because she had to face it; this was probably goodbye.

It was also probably for the best. They'd been granted a slice of time together that she hadn't been expecting. They had a walk down memory lane. It was nice. Soon she would leave, but that was likely as it should be too. At least this was closer to getting some closure than a nasty phone call.

Morgan realized she was practically dozing and had all but stopped moving. She straightened up and attempted to gain her composure.

"I didn't know you could dance so well," she said, ending with a choked sob. So much for composure.

"The slower stuff's easier," Josh said.

And that was the sad part. She couldn't recall ever dancing a slow dance with him. They had missed out on so much. They'd taken their relationship for granted time and time again and now . . .

"Josh, do you remember why we broke up?"

"Yes. You told me –"

"No. Not the damned phone call. The root problems. We didn't have what it takes."

"Well, that's what we're going to figure out now, isn't it?"

Morgan shook her head, but only briefly. It made the room spin.

"No. We couldn't make the long-distance thing work. And Moncton was a hell of a lot closer to Bathurst than Silverdale is. An opposite-coast relationship is definitely beyond our reach."

Morgan steeled herself and took a deep breath to clear her head. It was time to say goodbye.

Josh spoke before she had the chance. "If you wanted me there, I would pack up and leave this life behind today."

Morgan frowned. He was doing the same thing he'd done with that phone call – pressuring her and forcing her to make the decision.

Again, Josh beat her to the words. "But you don't have to say anything right now. You also don't have to worry about the opposite coasts, either."

He smiled down at her and Morgan's heart warmed. Whatever he said next didn't matter. She missed that smile. The way his eyes crinkled and his heart could so easily be seen in them. His eyes that were only for her.

"I'm sure you're wondering why my father is here."

Morgan nodded, not trusting herself to speak, but wondering what his father had to do with anything.

"Well, he and my mother are separating."

Morgan's eyes widened. *Good for him,* was her thought, but Josh didn't appear to be in a celebratory mood.

Still, he kept his smile as he continued, "It's a long story and probably what's best for them now, but something good will come of it."

Morgan had thought that part was good enough but raised a brow. She was really struggling with her words. And the spinning room.

"I'm planning on going back to Bathurst with him later this week. I'll help him get settled and . . . well, I'll be there for a bit."

"You're . . . coming to Bathurst?"

Josh sighed and pulled her closer so she could rest her head on his shoulder again. "Yes. We'll talk more about it tomorrow before you leave."

Morgan allowed herself to sink into his arms and close her eyes. She really needed some fresh air. This would do in the meantime.

Wait. No, it wouldn't. Her eyes popped open as she fully realized what he was saying.

Josh would be in Bathurst. Trevor would be in Bathurst. How would that work? What were they going to do? Swap her around every other night? Have a duel?

Morgan pulled away as the song ended and did her best to keep her expression neutral. Crazy thoughts continued to swirl. She definitely did not need another drink, yet at the same time that was the only thing she could imagine would help.

Josh was giving her one of his judge-y looks. She couldn't blame him. She knew she was still swaying even though there was no music.

"Yes, I had many drinks," Morgan admitted.

198

The DJ's voice flooded the hall again as the lights brightened and Morgan winced. She fought the urge to cover her ears and settled for squinting and letting her mind wander.

So, Josh in Bathurst. Well, there would be nothing wrong with hanging out together a bit. She had no intentions of doing anything romantic with him, but they could still . . . what could they do?

Whatever. That wasn't important now. At least she wouldn't have to leave him tomorrow all heartbroken with all these unanswered questions still up in the air.

That's what they could do in Bathurst, answer those questions.

But again, what about Trevor? She couldn't be with them both. And she still had to talk to him and confess what had happened here. Then there was the birthday party on Friday. The one where she fully expected him to –

Ah, hell. For tonight, Morgan decided to settle for feeling relief that she wouldn't have to deal with leaving Josh high and dry tomorrow. Selfish? For sure. But she could deal with the guilt in the morning. She'd clear a painful little place for it right next to the massive hangover she was sure to have. And the hip pain. And the arms. And the face trauma from smiling.

"Morgan?"

"Hmm?"

"You didn't hear any of that, did you?" Josh said. "They're leaving. We need to get outside."

"Right, right. All good things must come to an end, right?" Morgan hiccupped and tried to hide it with a cough. "Or in our case, a pause."

Josh stared at her blankly.

"'Cause you're coming to Bathurst, you see . . ." *Oh, God. Stop talking.*

Josh gave her a rather strained smile and led her by the elbow to join the other guests.

When they stepped outside, Morgan gasp-hiccupped. Shouldn't it be dark out here?

Oh. Someone had turned on a bunch of spotlights. Josh continued to lead her over to the side past a bunch of Marines lined up by the door, swords raised to create something of an arch.

Oh, she knew what this was. She'd seen it on TV once. It was an honor guard or something. Sure enough, after someone handed them some birdseed – which Morgan refused, there were no birds around – Sally and Michael came out of the church and the crowd began to yell. Oh, did they yell. Morgan cringed against Josh, who held her upright, as the couple entered the tunnel.

It took forever for them to get through the thing as they paused to kiss, and people threw seed, and Morgan fought to keep her dinner down.

At least the cool air was helping a bit because next thing Morgan knew, she was being herded into a group of women for the bouquet toss.

Deep breath. This for sure was the end of the festivities. Morgan nearly laughed as she was jostled about in the throng of eager women who wanted the coveted bouquet and the promise of being the next to be married. How much worse could this get?

Morgan would have slithered away if she hadn't been boxed in on every side. She didn't want the damned thing. She still had to decide if she ever wanted to get married at all.

And there it was, heading right for her. Jesus. The last thing she needed was to get her eye poked out by this wretched thing.

Morgan raised her hand, poised to flick the bouquet away, but then another hand appeared right in front of her face in the path of the incoming missile.

Sheer reflex caused her to elbow the owner of the hand in the side and grab at the bouquet.

The crowd cheered and yelled and . . . screamed?

The scream was coming from right beside her. Yeesh. Whoever she'd elbowed out of the way was sure being a baby about losing the prize.

Morgan looked down to see Iris crumpled on the ground, holding her face, blood flowing from between her fingers.

Well, shit. She hadn't elbowed anyone in the side at all.

Chapter 28

In Which Tea Is Served
Sunday, August 16, 1998

Josh hadn't seen Morgan since the accident the night before when he'd rushed to kneel by Iris. Morgan had apologized and departed the scene before Josh had the chance to say anything to her, which was probably a good thing.

When Josh had walked to the table to ask Morgan to dance, he had a notion to get down on one knee and propose when the song ended. But Morgan's less-than-sober condition and comments quickly squashed that notion. If he ever did propose, she'd have to be sober and he'd have to work up to it, not spring it on her. Still, those pesky notions of his . . .

Now Josh sat at the kitchen table, nursing a cup of coffee. He was going over last night's conversations and the things left unsaid.

Footfalls on the stairs alerted Josh the girls were leaving. They parked their suitcases by the front door and came into the kitchen. Morgan and Josh exchanged a look but didn't say anything. Morgan wore sunglasses and a pained expression.

"Are you sure you girls won't have any breakfast?" Aunt Peggy asked.

"Thank you, Aunty, but we decided to sleep in a little. Now we really need to get on the road," Rab said.

Aunt Peggy and Rab hugged. "It'll be quiet around here with everyone gone."

"Thank you so very much for letting us stay here, especially with all the wedding stuff going on," Rab said.

"Yes, thank you, Mrs. Hampton," Morgan said.

A brief frown flashed across Aunt Peggy's face.

"Drive safely and let us know when you get home," she said.

"But it'll be late, Aunty," Rab said.

"Late for you, but not for us, remember."

"I'm going to take our stuff to the car," Morgan said.

Josh jumped up from his seat. "I'll help you."

Morgan muttered something but let him take his sister's bags.

Outside, Josh asked, "Were you going to leave without saying goodbye?"

"I had kind of hoped. But didn't you say you were coming home?"

"Yes. I'll be flying into Bathurst on Wednesday, so I'll see you Thursday."

"And when will you be leaving again?" Morgan asked, setting down the bag she was carrying.

"If all goes right, I won't be. I'm buying a one-way ticket." Josh waited for her to open the trunk.

"Best make that a round trip. It'll save you some money."

"Are you saying there's no hope for us?" Josh asked as she unlocked the trunk.

"All I'm saying is if you return to Silverdink, you'll spend less buying a round trip ticket."

"A little extra money is no object."

"Oh, listen to you, Big Daddy Warbucks," Morgan said, dumping her bag in the trunk.

"I've told you my financial situation has changed. I can support a family now." Josh placed Rab's suitcase next to Morgan's.

Morgan's expression soured. "Okay, look, let's save that discussion for when we're on the other side of the continent. What day did you tell your boss you'll be back?"

"A week from tomorrow."

"Then you'll be back to your Iris," Morgan said as she slammed the trunk.

"She's not 'my' Iris."

"And I'm not 'your' Morgan."

"We're arguing again."

"We seem to be good at it," Morgan said. "Listen, tell 'not-your-Iris' that I'm really sorry about the nose. It was an accident."

"She knows, but I'll tell her when I see her again."

"Don't you work tomorrow?"

"I expect to, but whether she shows up is another matter," Josh said.

"Is she prone to not showing up?"

"No. But she might still be recovering from the accident."

"Where is Rab?" Morgan asked. "We need to get going."

Rab came out of the house carrying two paper lunch bags. "Aunty insisted on making some sandwiches."

In the doorway behind her, Aunt Peggy and Uncle Bill stood waving.

Josh side-hugged his sister. "See you in a few days, sis."

"You know you can't stay at the apartment with us, right?" Rab said.

"I didn't expect to. I'll stay at the hotel with Dad," Josh said, then turned to catch Morgan's eye. "Thursday?"

Rab blinked at him but only smiled.

"Not early," Morgan said. "I'll stop by with Rab later on."

Rab was already in the driver's seat. Josh knew Morgan wasn't a morning driver, especially after a night like last night.

He took a step toward Morgan but stopped when she shook her head.

She got into the car, and they were off to the airport.

Josh waved until they were out of sight.

Aunt Peggy had gone back inside, but Uncle Bill met Josh at the door. "I hate to say it, Josh, but I think you've lost that girl."

"I hope to prove you wrong."

"I hope you're making the right decision," Uncle Bill said.

"I think I am, but I'm going to go to the shop and think on it some," Josh said.

"Do you think Iris will be there?"

"I'm hoping she is."

***

Iris's brown Camry sat outside the bay doors when Josh arrived at the garage. Although the paint was fading, Iris kept it clean – inside and out. He parked next to her car.

After entering and relocking the front door, he called out, "Iris?"

Toshi stood at the entrance to the shop. Satisfied that Josh was not a burglar, he trotted back to his bed.

"I'm out in the shop," she replied.

Josh hadn't called to locate her. He'd just wanted to make her aware of his presence. He had no desire to have the business end of a large wrench applied to his skull.

Not planning to work right away, Josh sauntered into the bay without changing into coveralls. Iris was at a workbench scrubbing something he couldn't identify from where he stood. She set the brush down as he entered.

When Iris turned toward him, the bruise around her left eye stood out. Josh was happy to see that her nose wasn't taped up.

"I'm glad to see your nose isn't broken," Josh said.

"It still hurts, and I have to be careful to avoid bumping it," Iris said and examined his clothing. "Not planning to work?"

"I might check Old Blue over a bit later, but I mostly wanted to talk with you and hoped to find you here."

She pulled her nitrile gloves off and said, "I had hoped you would. Is she gone?"

"Yes. I left the house shortly after they left for the airport," Josh said.

"I can't say I'm sorry Morgan is gone, but your sister is a sweet girl – a lot like you in many ways. She's going to be a good nurse."

"Morgan is a unique person and, well, she'd have been better just as a guest at the wedding rather than a participant."

"Don't make excuses for her, Josh," Iris said. "She is an adult."

"She did ask me to convey her apology again for hitting you in the nose. She says it was an accident."

"I'll accept her apology – and forgive her – but I am not accepting that it was an accident."

"How do you mean?" Josh asked.

"Her lack of coordination and judgment was because she had chosen to drink too much. Therefore, her actions, although unintentional, were because of her choice."

"I kind of follow that," Josh said. "But let's not talk about Morgan."

"I agree," Iris said. "Wait here for ten minutes and then meet me at the break room."

Josh gave her a puzzled look.

"I prepared something, in case you decided to show up," she said. "Can you wait?"

"Sure, but I want to talk with you."

"We'll have a chance."

Josh waited in the repair bay for ten minutes. He idly examined the carburetor Iris had disassembled and spread out on the workbench. When he went to the break room, he was surprised by what he found.

Iris stood at the door to the break room in a pink kimono decorated with white lilies. A gold cross on a thin chain adorned her neck. She wore red lipstick and light blush on her cheeks.

"What's this about?" Josh asked.

"It would be my honor to perform the tea ceremony for you. Please remove your shoes before entering."

"What's the tea ceremony about?"

"It is an ancient Japanese ceremony of hospitality that honors the guest. The ceremony embodies the ideals of tranquility and respect, among others. I'll be glad to tell you more – another time. Please accept my offer."

"I'll be happy to," Josh said and kicked off his sneakers.

"When I bow to you, please bow in return," Iris said. "However you bow will suffice."

"Okay."

"Please enter," Iris said and bowed.

When Josh bowed in return, she entered first, and he followed. Iris had moved the hotplate to the table and placed the tea kettle on it. An ornate bowl sat in the middle of the table. Napkins, a whisk, a curved piece of bamboo, and a decorative metal canister sat to one side.

"Please be seated and we can begin."

As Josh sat, Iris turned on the hotplate.

"I am but an apprentice. This isn't a proper tearoom and I have had to improvise," Iris said. "For today, I have chosen function over form."

"Why are you doing this now?"

"Because you have been my partner and friend, I wished to honor you this way. This may be my last chance to do so," Iris said. "Now, while we wait for the water to boil, let us contemplate the floral arrangement."

Josh didn't recall ever seeing flowers in the breakroom.

She motioned to a vase on the counter next to the microwave. The simple gold vase contained a rose and the carnations from her bridesmaid's bouquet.

The rose stood in stark contrast to the carnations.

How different Morgan and Iris are.

Josh sat in quiet contemplation while sneaking peeks at Iris. She had arranged the flowers and seating so he could only see her right eye. Josh marveled at how serene she looked as she studied the floral arrangement.

The whistle of the tea kettle brought their attention back to the table. Iris turned off the burner and held her sleeve back with one hand while lifting the kettle with the other. She poured a small measure of water into the bowl and returned the kettle to the burner.

Josh didn't want to break the silence, so he watched attentively.

Iris opened a metal canister and removed three measures of green powder with the curved piece of bamboo. "This is green tea or *ocha*. You have perhaps had some at Osaka, but this is a bit stronger."

She set the scoop aside and closed the container.

"Now I will blend the *ocha*," Iris said. She picked up a bamboo whisk and blended the powder and water.

"Sorry to interrupt, but will we have a chance to talk?"

"*Hai*," Iris said with a gentle smile. "We'll have time to talk when we have finished the ceremony."

Josh wanted to watch her face but was fascinated with her hands as she moved with practice and precision.

Iris set the whisk on a napkin. With both hands, she offered the bowl to Josh and bowed. "As my guest, you must partake first. Please take a sip, rotate it a quarter turn, and pass it to me."

Josh bowed in return, took the bowl from her with both hands, and felt a thrill when their fingers touched. He marveled at this but chose to think on it later.

The liquid inside was green and frothy. He took a sip and found the liquid to be both hot and quite bitter. He rotated the bowl but held it.

"Now pass it to me, bowing as you do," Iris said.

"Are these instructions part of every ceremony?" Josh asked.

"Only for someone who has never experienced the ceremony." She accepted the bowl and took a larger sip than he did.

They repeated the cycle two more times before the bowl was empty, Iris having the last sip. She took a napkin and wiped the inside of the bowl dry before setting it aside.

Then she offered a plate of cookies to him with a bow. "Please have a sweet to offset the bitterness."

Josh bowed and took one. He discovered they were shortbread cookies from the vending machine.

"As I said, I had to improvise."

Josh waited until Iris had taken one before eating his. The sweetness of the cookie contrasted with the bitterness of the tea.

"To end the ceremony, I should like to recite a haiku I have composed for the occasion."

"Please," Josh said.

Closing her eyes, Iris said:

"Stone blocks bamboo shoot
Path chosen, growth continues
Old path cannot change"

She opened her eyes and they sat in silence with their gazes locked. Iris looked so tranquil.

"Thank you for allowing me this moment," Iris said and bowed.

"Thank you for honoring me. I am very moved," Josh said and bowed.

"We can speak freely now," Iris said.

"How often have you performed the tea ceremony?"

"Many times, for my mother as I learned, and later for my dad under her watchful eye."

"But never for friends?" Josh asked.

"You have the honor of being the first."

"I am indeed honored. We're like that shoot, aren't we?"

"Yes, once we have made a choice, we cannot go back and change the path."

"But we can change our choice, can't we?" Josh asked.

"That is true, but all that has passed between the two choices cannot be changed."

"I think I understand. If I had chosen to fly here instead of driving, Old Blue would still be in Bathurst. Then, even if I went back to drive here, I still wouldn't have had the truck here in between."

"Yes. Where we are in life is the result of a chain of choices. For example, if I had chosen to go back to North Carolina for college, I wouldn't have been here to meet you."

"And if I had chosen to stay in Canada to win Morgan back, I wouldn't have met you. Are you saying fate brought us together?" Josh asked.

"No. It was the choices we each made. When you chose to come to my assistance last night instead of escorting Morgan away, that's when I knew I loved you."

Josh sat quietly for a moment. He had gone to her side without a second thought. How could he not?

"I believe you love me as well," Iris said, "but your honor won't allow you to say it."

"You are a wonderful woman," Josh said. "And this week has uncovered feelings I have for you."

"The choice to come work for my dad is your rock. Like the shoot, you have grown past that and as a result, things have changed. Things like your truck being here, us meeting and working together, becoming accustomed to life in the States. But perhaps most importantly, Morgan meeting and becoming involved with another man. Going back to Bathurst may not be enough to reverse those changes."

"But you know I must try. If I return, I'd want to get to know you better."

"I know. I await your return. Now, let's give Old Blue a going over. I don't want it breaking down on the Tacoma Narrows bridge," Iris said, standing.

Josh shuddered at the thought as he stood. "I'll bring the truck in while you change back to my working partner."

"Sounds like a plan, partner." Iris smiled and headed for the locker room. As she did, she wiped her eyes.

Chapter 29

In Which Coffee is Served
Monday, August 17, 1998

Late to bed and early to rise. That sounded about right. Morgan did not feel healthy, wealthy, nor wise.

She thanked Rab for the ride and climbed out of Bob, steeling herself as she faced the building. It was only seven-thirty. Morgan had never been to work this early before. Since she often stayed late after work, no one seemed to mind that she usually breezed in a minute or two after eight, her designated starting time.

Truth be told, she'd considered doing the same thing this morning. But she couldn't put this off any longer.

Rab gave the horn a tap and Morgan spun around. The look on her friend's face asked the same question Morgan was asking herself. Why was she just standing there gazing at the building?

Morgan waved her off and headed up the walk. She heard Rab drive away just as she grabbed the handle of the front door.

"Dammit." It was locked and Morgan had broken a nail. Ah, well. It wasn't like she cared about manicures. She sucked on the finger, muttered a few choice curse words, and dug out her keys. The lights in the halls were still dim as she navigated them, heading for Trevor's father's office.

She stopped outside the door and raised her hand to knock but found she couldn't complete the action.

What was wrong with her? Why was she so nervous? The man she loved waited on the other side of this door. The man she was considering spending the rest of her life with.

He was also the man she had cheated on, and it was time to confess.

Morgan squeezed her eyes shut, drew in a breath, and forced her hand to rap on the door.

"It's open."

The sound of Trevor's voice was motivation enough to open the door. Everything else be damned – she'd missed him like crazy.

He was already on his feet and across the room by the time she entered and shut the door behind her.

The rest of the world ceased to exist as he swept her up in his arms, planted a kiss on her mouth, and then set her down only to continue that kiss more fervently.

Pressed up against the door, Morgan surrendered to the waves of pleasure washing over her. Now this was love. A moan escaped and Trevor pulled back.

"Did I hurt you?"

"No. Different kind of moan," Morgan said breathlessly.

Trevor grinned. "I would love to continue this, but I've got a meeting in fifteen minutes and I don't think that's quite enough time . . ."

"Not nearly enough," Morgan agreed and grinned back. "How many more days until you're set free again?"

"Fewer than five."

He kissed her deeply one more time, then headed over to the coffee maker.

Morgan's knees wobbled slightly as she recovered from the steamy welcome-home and followed.

Seriously, just the sight of him had been enough to make her swoon during the early days of their relationship. It was enough to make almost any girl swoon. Classically tall, dark, and handsome, he was six-two with a lean build, although he shared his brother's broad-shouldered physique.

He turned from the coffee pot and nodded toward the small table by the window.

Those eyes. They were the deepest brown imaginable, almost as dark as his hair, that lit up and sparkled whenever he was excited or passionate about something. Which was most of the time.

Morgan took a seat in one of the plush chairs. Trevor set the coffee mugs on the table and sat in the chair next to her, scooting it closer.

"I've never seen you so unshaven," Morgan commented, running her finger over the stubble on his face. "I like it."

"I've never seen you . . . are you wearing makeup?"

Morgan laughed. "A little bit. It doesn't do much to cover the scratches, does it?"

"Ah, my girl. You have so much to fill me in on."

Morgan swallowed nervously. "Sorry I didn't call very much. It was . . . well, you're right. I've got a lot to tell you."

"Let's start with what hurts the most."

My heart, Morgan thought, but didn't say it aloud. Instead, she filled him in on the highlights of her trip, focusing on Damian and the very, very long wedding, her various misadventures in the junkyard and bouquet sparring, as well as Zinger's status.

"He's still out at that garage? I'll find time to slip out and take you to pick him up," Trevor said.

"No. That's taken care of. Rab's going with me after work."

"All right. So back to this trip of yours. You have yet to tell me what brought on the junkyard wars."

Morgan began to sweat. Yes, it was about time to tell him the real stuff.

"But first drink your coffee," he said. "You look like you need it."

Grateful for a couple more seconds of respite, Morgan reached for her cup.

"No. That one's mine now."

He pushed a different mug toward her.

Despite everything, Morgan laughed. "This is perfect! When did you have time to get this?"

"I must admit to blatant abuse of the secretary pool, but I assure you they were adequately rewarded."

Morgan held her new coffee mug in her hands, smiling. It read – well, suffice to say the saying contained her favorite expletive and dissed Mondays.

She continued to smile as her eyes misted over. Years ago, when she'd been browsing the shops in the Pike's Place market, Morgan had realized she'd never owned a coffee mug of her own. She had decided then and there that when she did, it would not be lame.

Two years ago, for Christmas, Josh had had one specially made for her. He'd taken pictures of her late dog Chester and late best friend Kendra and had them laminated onto the mug along with swirly hearts.

Thoughtful. But Morgan had only tolerated it in Josh's presence. Who wanted to be sad and reminded of what they'd lost every morning at coffee time?

The search for a non-lame coffee mug had continued, but Morgan could never find the right one, so she'd settled for taking her own artwork – in this case a colorful geometric pattern – and putting it on a mug.

Acceptable. That mug now belonged to Trevor.

And her new mug? It was perfect. Thoughtful, much like the one Josh had given her, but not soul-tormenting.

And right there was the difference between Josh and Trevor. They both cared, but Trevor *got* her.

So there it was. The answer to a question she should not have been asking to begin with. Trevor was the one for her. Great news. She was enlightened. Now she could just cancel the whole confession thing, stay the hell away from Josh as she should have done in the first place, and live happily ever after.

"What's wrong?"

Morgan hadn't realized an actual tear had escaped as she continued to hold the mug and stare at it.

"You can have the other one back," Trevor said, sliding the old one over. "But it has cream in it. I only took it because I missed you, and I love you and the mug you made, and I thought you'd like this one . . ."

"I love it," Morgan said, setting the mug down. She couldn't lie to him, not even a lie of omission. He deserved better.

She wiped her eyes, turned to him, and took one last deep breath.

"I have something to tell you. I saw Josh. Well, you know that. But I did more than just see him. I . . . we . . . we kissed."

Trevor sat back in his chair and studied her for a moment. Morgan's heart pounded and threatened to burst from her chest. Why didn't he look mad?

"Did anything else happen?" Trevor asked calmly.

"Of course not! Well, there were two kisses. But in a row." Morgan narrowed her eyes as he continued to sit with a slightly sad half-smile on his face. "Aren't you angry? Don't you even care?"

"Of course I care." Trevor reached out and took one of her trembling hands. "I can't say I'm happy about it. I'm just not surprised."

"Well, I was!"

Trevor sighed. "Sweetheart, I've long suspected that the two of you needed closure."

Morgan barely kept her jaw from falling open. "Why would you think that?"

Trevor chuckled softly. "I don't think you realized how much you talked about him. Granted, you were usually ranting and raving about something when his name came up, but you've also spoken fondly of him. You two had a lot of good memories together."

Morgan looked down, feeling like shit. Not only had she betrayed Trevor by her actions in Silverdale, but she'd been doing things like this all along?

Trevor lifted her chin so she would look him in the eye. His smile was no longer sad. "Morgan, I understand. That's all they are, though – memories. It's okay to hold onto those. I have some of my own."

Morgan frowned. "But yours are just memories. I actually . . . I screwed up."

"I forgive you. We're not going to let something like that ruin what we have here, are we?"

"It's more than just that. You're likely right that I need closure or whatever, but we didn't get much of a chance when I was there. He's . . . he's coming to town in a few days."

"Coming here?"

"Yes. His parents are separating and he's coming to help his dad. But while he's here . . ."

Confusion flitted across Trevor's face. "Still going for that closure then?"

"I don't know. It's just I feel like I owe it to him to at least talk to him." Morgan sighed. "What do you think? Is this stupid? Should I just tell him I don't want to see him?"

"Do you want to see him?"

Morgan gulped. "I think so."

"Hey, I can't tell you want to think, or what to do for that matter," Trevor said, taking both her hands in his and leaning closer so their foreheads touched. "But I can tell you what I believe."

Morgan grasped his hands tightly and waited for him to continue.

"I don't believe you belong with him. I believe we belong together. But you need to realize that on your own." He sat back but continued to hold her hands. "So go, find out. But I will ask one favor of you."

Morgan nodded, willing her eyes not to leak any more tears.

"Let me know when you do figure it out. Because I have a question I'd like to ask you."

Morgan swallowed hard. "Is that the question I think you might like to ask on Friday?"

Trevor smiled warmly. "I love you so much that at times it hurts. In a good way. Just do me that favor and let me know when you've realized you feel the same way. Ah –" He held up his hand when Morgan opened her mouth to tell him she did. "Don't say it until you know you mean it."

He leaned forward again and kissed her. "It's you and me, girl. I have no doubts."

Morgan threw her arms around him. "Thank you. You're probably right. I just need closure. I promise I won't take any longer than necessary."

"I know." Trevor got up and pulled her along with him. "But make sure you do take the time you need."

Morgan nodded, kissed him once more, then turned to leave.

Trevor was confident, but not cocky. She knew she was incredibly lucky to have him and prayed to God she wouldn't mess this up. He was giving her the chance – willingly giving her the time and space – to figure out whether she was meant to be with him or some other guy.

However, Morgan knew he must be hurting a little. And he was certainly not going to propose marriage in the middle of her *figuring things out.* She also knew he wouldn't wait forever, nor would she ask him to.

"Morgan."

She stopped at the door and turned back.

"Don't forget your mug."

She laughed and took her new mug from him. He pulled her in for one last kiss before releasing her.

Morgan walked slowly down the hall to the office where her cubicle was located.

It felt so wrong leaving him like that. Normally, when he worked long hours, she'd spend a night or two at his place, letting herself in with her key, just so she could be there for the few hours he was home. Neither of them had even suggested such a thing today.

Dammit, Josh. What is it about you?

Well, she supposed that was exactly what they would find out.

She'd given Trevor the confession he deserved, and now she would give Josh the chance he deserved – possibly one that she deserved as well.

But there was no doubt about it. This would be their very last chance.

Chapter 30

In Which Josh Takes a Flight
Wednesday, August 19, 1998

Josh felt more comfortable crossing the Tacoma Narrows Bridge with each trip. Of course, he'd been the one driving and therefore felt more in control.

The morning in the Pacific Northwest was warm with the possibility of a rare hot day. Since Old Blue didn't have air conditioning, Josh and Iris rode with the windows down. She leaned against the door frame and the wind played with a few strands of hair that had come loose from her ponytail.

Josh had placed his Bathurst High School ball cap on the seat between them to avoid losing it out the window.

"You're not going to take the hat, are you?" Iris asked.

"I plan on it."

"I thought I convinced you to stop wearing a hat when going to see her."

"This isn't just an ordinary hat," Josh said. He touched the half-heart he wore on a chain beneath his shirt. "She gave me this hat on our first Christmas to replace the one I lost on our trip to Seattle."

"So, you're thinking the nostalgia of seeing you in this hat is going to tip things in your favor?"

"Hey, I have to use everything I can to get her back."

"I suppose I'm not really one to be giving you advice, since I have a vested interest in your return to Silverdale," Iris said.

"We have some time. Say what you want. Then I'll decide whether to use it or not."

"There has to be something more than memories. Love is a living, continuous emotion. It is one thing to love the memories you have, but it is more important to love the person."

"I understand what you're saying," Josh said. "If two people have shared a meaningful moment, but otherwise have no affection for each other, that's not a basis for love."

"Something like that, yes. As often as you have spoken of your time with Morgan, most of your stories center around the trip from your home to Seattle and back."

"Yes, it was crazy and fun, and we both learned a lot about ourselves on that trip," Josh said. "It changed our lives."

"Correct me if I'm wrong, but it was at the end of the trip that you two decided that you loved each other."

"You're not wrong. We declared our love for each other outside my parents' house at the end of the journey."

"But not everything was happily ever after," Iris said.

"No. Our troubles began practically as soon as we stepped into our respective homes. But we toughed it out and she moved in with me that Christmas."

"But your troubles didn't end there." It was a statement, not a question.

"No, even though we were living together, we hardly saw each other."

"It seems like you're basing your affection for her primarily on the one road trip," Iris said.

"Two, there and back, but it was more than that."

"Would you mind telling me why you love her?"

"I guess most of all, she's intelligent and attractive," Josh said.

"That describes hundreds of millions of women in the world. What else?"

"She helped me get through a low spot in my life."

"You mean when you couldn't join the Marines?"

"Yes, she came to get me from the station after they'd refused me," Josh said.

"What if you had made the trip to Silverdale alone like you had planned? Would you have gotten through the rejection without her?"

"Probably. Yeah, I'd have managed somehow."

"But you wouldn't have returned to Bathurst," Iris said.

"Not likely."

"So, you and I could have met three years ago, and no one would have been in the way."

"What are you saying?" Josh asked.

"Nothing, just thinking out loud. What else? There has to be something unique about her that has you enraptured."

"We were lovers. There's a special something between two people who are that intimate, you know?"

"No, I don't know," Iris explained. "I have never had a lover."

Josh spun his head toward her and gawked.

"*Baka!* Get your eyes on the road!"

Josh turned his attention back to traffic in time to avoid running off the road. "Are you saying . . ."

"Yes, Josh, I'm a virgin. You can say it. It's not a dirty word."

"How is that possible? I mean . . ."

Iris laughed. "How? By simply not having sex."

"That couldn't have been easy."

"Trust me, it wasn't and isn't. The peer pressure I faced during high school was terrible."

"Do you intend to save yourself for marriage?" Josh asked.

"Yes. Most people call me old-fashioned because of it, but it's my choice. If that's a problem for you, maybe you should stay in Canada," Iris said.

"It wouldn't be. I get called old-fashioned sometimes," Josh said. "When you called me *baka* just now, what was that about?"

"I had to get your attention fast. If I had said Joshua Éveriste Caleb Hampton, we'd be in Seattle by the time I finished."

"Or the back end of a truck. It's kind of funny, Morgan and I used to say that to each other mostly when we wanted to change the subject," Josh said.

"What, *baka*?"

"No. Eyes on the road."

"I guess I'll just have to tap your arm then. I don't want to remind you of her," Iris said.

"We're kind of talking about her."

"Sort of. We were more talking about why you love her. Except for the lovemaking part, we could easily be talking about me."

"Then let's talk about you. During the tea ceremony, you said you loved me. Is that true or was it just the moment?" Josh asked.

"I do love you, more than I am willing to admit."

"Why would that be?"

"Because I love you enough to give you space to figure out things between you and *her*. Then, if you don't come back, my heart won't be completely shattered," Iris said.

"I guess I'm guarding my heart too."

"I can't wait forever, though. If you don't ask me to come get you on Sunday, I'll know you won't be coming back."

"I'll know one way or the other before then," Josh said.

Iris pointed at a sign. "That's our exit."

"Do you want to park and come in with me?" Josh asked as he guided Old Blue off the interstate.

"No, I think it'll be best if I just said *sayonara* curbside at the terminal."

"As you wish," Josh said and felt a twinge of guilt. He'd often said that to Morgan when agreeing with her. Whether she'd known it or not, it was also a code for "I love you."

Did he mean it the same way with Iris?

223

He found a place to pull over to the curb. They got out of Old Blue and Iris came around to the driver's side while he pulled his dependable duffel out of the back.

When he handed her the keys, she looked into his eyes. "Kiss me, Josh. Either as a farewell, or a promise you'll be back. Just don't tell me which."

Josh dropped the duffel and gathered her into his arms. He kissed her long and deep, holding it until some other traveler honked his horn.

"Thank you," Iris said with tears in her eyes. "I guess I better go."

"Drive safely and I'll keep in touch."

He went around behind Old Blue and watched Iris drive away, knowing he had left his ball cap on the seat – intentionally.

Josh stood looking for the Air Canada sign. With only a duffel bag, he figured he didn't need a skycap.

"That wasn't Miss Parker," a familiar voice said.

Josh turned to the source of the voice. His father stood there with a carry-on bag and his ticket envelope.

"No, that was Iris," Josh said. "We work at the same place."

"I know I've lived in Canada for a while, but I don't remember saying goodbye to co-workers in the States quite that intimately."

"It's a bit of a story. I need to pick up my ticket. I can fill you in later."

His father picked up a suitcase. "I need to check this in anyway."

They walked together to the Air Canada ticket counter, chatting amiably about his father's surprise visit. After getting coffee, they found the departure gate and took some seats.

As they settled, his father said, "Tell me more about this Iris."

"Her dad owns the garage and is one of Uncle Bill's best friends," Josh said.

"Does she know what she's doing, or is her father just amusing her?"

"Her mechanic skills are as good as mine, maybe even better."

"How much older or younger than you is she?" his father asked.

"She's only a few months younger. Her birthday is in March," Josh said.

"How long have you been working together?"

"Since I started working at Brock's garage."

"Is Iris your girlfriend now or something more?" his father asked.

"Neither, really. It was only this past week that she let me know she had feelings for me, and I'm finding I have feelings for her. But I still have to settle things with Morgan."

"Are you still carrying a torch for Miss Parker? Because, and I hate to be the one to break it to you, she's not carrying one for you."

"Rab let me know she's seeing someone in Bathurst," Josh said.

"Not just someone, but the oldest son of Franklin Shackleford. That's some competition you're facing. Add to that the fact that you're here and he's there."

"I know, but I have to try."

"Didn't she dump you about a year ago?" his father asked.

"She didn't actually dump me. We broke up last December, but it was probably as much my fault as it was hers."

"Then why are you still pursuing her?"

"I'm sure you know we were lovers," Josh said.

"You never really came out and told me, but when a couple shares an apartment, they aren't just good friends. That only happens on TV."

"I'm sure a TV show would have had a nicer apartment."

"So now I know for sure. At least you had the good sense not to get her pregnant like the other Shackleford boy did to that one girl," his father said.

"Even though I didn't get her pregnant, I should offer to marry her."

"How's that supposed to work if she's been sleeping with the Shackleford boy?"

"I don't know that she has been," Josh said.

"Did you ask Mary? They share the apartment. Your sister would know."

"I haven't, because I'd rather not know with any certainty."

"For the sake of argument, let's assume Miss Parker has been sleeping with Mr. Shackleford's son."

Josh remained silent. He really didn't want to hear it, but he told his father he would listen to what he had to say.

"So, if you both have had her as a lover, who has the greater claim?" his father continued. "Even if you could fight it out, Miss Parker wouldn't be obligated to accept the winner."

"I'm not sure how that works. I just know I need to talk to her and figure these things out," Josh said.

"Times have changed since your grandparents grew up. I had notions like yours once, and may have made a mistake."

"What do you mean?"

"Sometime after I arrived in Canada, I drifted to a community of ex-pats who lived in Toronto. There I met a college freshman," his father said.

"My mother."

"Yes. Well, we were both young and soon became lovers. When she became pregnant, I married her."

226

"Wait, wait. That doesn't add up. You were married several years before I was born," Josh said.

"You're right. You weren't her first pregnancy."

"What happened to the child?"

"Unfortunately, your mother miscarried. We went through a rough time of sorrow and blame after that," his father said.

"I'm sorry to hear that."

"If we hadn't married, we'd have gone our separate ways after she lost the baby."

"Then Rab and I would never have been born," Josh said.

"No, and although your mother and I don't usually agree about most things, you and your sister are the bright spots in our marriage."

"Then why separate now?"

"Because you're both adults now. It's no secret that your mother was the main breadwinner of the household. When she wouldn't help you get a loan for college, I disagreed, but wasn't in a position to do anything. Besides, Mary was still at home at that time," his father said.

"Did you charge her rent when she turned eighteen?"

"No, but only because she was still in high school. Then she left home at the end of her junior year."

"So, what's different between you and Mom now?" Josh asked.

"The difference is that I won't have to pay part of the mortgage since we're selling the house. I'm making enough to live modestly in a small apartment. Any equity from the house I can use for other things, like helping pay for Mary's tuition."

"I'm sure Rab will appreciate that."

"Anyway, the point I'm trying to make is don't ask her to marry you just because you've been lovers. I won't say that was good or bad. But you aren't lovers now, so only ask her to marry you if you genuinely love each other or you may regret it years from now."

An Air Canada employee announced, "Flight 249 is now boarding for Winnipeg and Montreal."

Josh and his father stood.

"Well, I'm still going with you to Bathurst," Josh said.

"Son, we've had some rough years. I don't know if our relationship will ever be the same, but this is a good start. I appreciate the company and the help."

"I may also go talk to my mother and see if we can patch things up."

"Don't go as my advocate. We have made our choice," his father said.

"I won't. That's for you and Mom to work out."

"I'm going to give you some advice, son. What you do with it is up to you."

"Sure, Dad, I'll hear you out," Josh said.

His father paused and smiled at Josh. "Let Morgan go. Visit Bathurst and say a proper goodbye, then go home to Iris."

"I have a feeling that's how it's going to turn out," Josh said, his heart aching at the thought.

Chapter 31

In Which Morgan is Sick of the Guilt
Thursday, August 20, 1998

Even though it was Thursday, Morgan happily accepted her Monday coffee mug from Trevor with a heartfelt thank you.

"You know you have to wash that sometime, right?" he said.

Morgan laughed. "I do wash it. I just happen to love it."

"Well, I'm happy that you do. I knew you wanted a 'non-crappy' mug, but I hadn't realized how imperative it was."

"It was a long time coming, is all. It's perfect." Morgan took a sip and set the mug down, leaning closer to Trevor. "Miss your dad's office yet?" she asked in a whisper.

Whenever Trevor's father went out of town, Trevor used his office not only because it was bigger and fancier than his own, but because, in his words, he could hear himself think there. Sure, everyone knew where he was "hiding out," but few chose to bother him unless it was absolutely necessary.

Now, back in his own office, there were half a dozen people entering and exiting at any given time and Morgan couldn't blame him for his hideout penchant.

Trevor chuckled. "It's not that bad. Especially now. We're way ahead of our projected goal on this case. If we do much more preparing, we'll just start mucking things up."

"So, you're completely off this weekend then?" Morgan asked.

"Not completely. We'll need to do some reviewing before court starts on Monday, but it won't be anything like the last few weeks. Have I mentioned how much I appreciate your patience?"

Trevor scooted his chair over and kissed her. Just a peck. Which was normal. They didn't make a habit of making out in front of the office staff.

But ever since Monday, the chaste pecks had become a thing outside of the office as well. Not that they'd spent much time out of the office together at all . . .

"What's wrong, sweetheart? Did I use up all my patience points?"

Morgan forced a smile. "Of course not. I was just thinking of something else."

What she'd been thinking about was her guilt and her own terrible behavior. He hadn't been neglecting her at all. She'd been avoiding him.

Trevor excused himself to speak to an associate who was about to leave. Morgan checked her watch and realized she should be leaving herself. She'd stopped by for a quick coffee after work before heading to her parents' house. She hadn't seen them at all since she returned from Washington.

Truth be told, Morgan hadn't seen a lot of anyone since she'd been back.

As much as she'd wanted to, she hadn't felt right showing up at Trevor's like she used to, letting herself into his oceanside condo and making herself at home to surprise him when he got off work.

She hadn't been doing any of the things she used to do – no going to the café, and her talks with Rab were brief and superficial.

Last night was a prime example of her aberrant behavior. She knew Trevor wouldn't be burning the midnight oil, but what had she done? She'd gone straight home after work and locked herself in her room with the excuse of cleaning.

Of course, cleaning actually meant pulling everything back out from her keepsake trunk and pawing through the stuff, reliving memories.

To anyone who didn't know her, Morgan was sure people would think she was depressed. Morgan hated to admit, even to herself, that she'd spent the past week avoiding her life and everyone in it because she knew Josh was coming. She wasn't depressed; she was in limbo.

Josh and his father had arrived late the night before and Rab had gone to see them at their hotel. Morgan had declined crashing the family time, but she'd spent the night thinking of them nonetheless.

Today, after seeing her parents, Morgan would pick Rab up from work and finally, finally, go to see Josh herself. In her purse, she had placed the half-heart necklace with his name on it. She had no idea what she was going to do with it. Give it back to him? No, that would probably be too bitchy. But what was she supposed to do with it now? She couldn't throw it away. She didn't feel right keeping it any longer. And she certainly wasn't about to wear it. It was haunting her.

"Sweetie?"

"Hmm?" Trevor was back and sitting beside her. She'd totally missed his arrival.

"I said it looks like we'll be breaking early tonight. Around nine."

"Oh . . . that's good."

Morgan saw the flash of disappointment cross his face before he composed himself and got up to take their cups to the coffee area. She didn't blame him. A proper girlfriend – the old Morgan – would have jumped at the chance to make plans with him for the evening.

"More coffee?" Trevor asked.

"No," she said, standing. "I'm going to see my parents and then pick Rab up from work at eight."

Morgan hurried over to give Trevor another fit-for-public kiss before he had the chance to ask what she and Rab would be doing.

His smile was weak as he turned to wash out her mug. Because he knew. He was just too goddamned . . . perfect to say anything about it.

But Trevor being Trevor, he bounced back immediately. The charming, confident grin Morgan loved so much was back in place as he wrapped his arms around her and kissed the top of her head.

"Call me later if you get bored. I'll probably stay here and get some more paperwork out of the way after everyone leaves. In silence." He nodded to the other employees still sifting through papers and chattering.

"I love you, you know," Morgan said.

"Of course. And you know I love you. Now get outta here."

Morgan took the out and hurried to grab her purse before she could change her mind. This was a good way to leave things for the evening.

But she couldn't *keep* leaving things this way. She was already having serious doubts about this whole Josh business. So far, she'd done nothing but mess up her life since he'd been back in it. And he really wasn't back in it at all. What was she thinking, screwing around with stuff like this? Just two weeks ago, she'd been over Josh. And since she'd returned to Bathurst and regained her senses, she had no doubt she and Trevor belonged together. They wanted the same things in life and she really did love him.

But what had she been doing since her return? Hiding. She'd been stuck in this stupid limbo, and it was beyond ridiculous already.

Was hanging out with Josh worth risking what she had with Trevor? Was she just being an idiot? Sadly, Morgan suspected the answers to these questions were no and yes respectively.

Whatever happened tonight, it had to end. For Trevor's sake. For her sake. Even for Josh's sake.

Morgan took one last peek over her shoulder at Trevor. He was deep in conversation with one of the associates. He didn't seem worried or jealous of Josh, but no matter how you looked at it, Morgan was choosing Josh over him tonight. And that just wasn't right.

Regardless, she'd come this far and she was going to see it through.

The drive to her parents' house was a quick one. It would have been a lot quicker if she hadn't been pulled over and given another speeding ticket. Morgan had only sighed and tossed it in the glovebox with the others.

The reception she received when she arrived at the house was as expected. Her dad gave her a stern talking to about the whole anesthesia thing and told her how worried they'd all been, ending with a heartfelt bear hug. Her mom had cried, then hugged her, then cried some more – but the last batch was happy tears. Morgan prayed with all her heart that this was finally the menopause hormones and not a sign that another wee one was on the way.

Morgan had interrupted Matthew in the middle of trying to give Mary a haircut in the kitchen. Excellent news for Mary, who had been sitting happily in her highchair waiting to play hairdresser. Terrible news for Morgan, who had to listen to Matthew's wails as the scissors were taken away and he was sent to his room.

Finally, peace reigned. Morgan's dad had gone into his office and Matthew had stopped screaming from his jail cell. Morgan and her mom settled in the living room with cups of coffee and Mary, who sat happily on the floor playing quietly with her blocks. Oh, how Morgan wished Mary had been the older one instead of Matthew. She wouldn't have minded babysitting her at all.

"So . . . isn't Trevor having that birthday party for you two tomorrow night?"

Morgan set down her cup with trembling hands. She did not need any more coffee today.

"Yes. His case is going better than expected, so that's still on."

"Are you . . . looking forward to it?"

Morgan sighed. "Mom, I know what he might have planned. Actually, he might as well have come right out and said he wants to propose tomorrow. It's just there's some stuff I haven't told you about my trip."

"What? Something else went wrong?"

"Not health stuff," Morgan assured her. "Josh stuff."

"Oh."

"Yes, oh. It seems he's not over me. At all."

"And you?" her mom asked nervously.

"Me?" Morgan chuckled mirthlessly. "I have no clue. I screwed up. I kissed him. And now he's here. I'm going to see him tonight."

Her mom's eyes widened.

"It's not like that," Morgan said. "Well, not exactly. He didn't come to Bathurst just for me. He's helping his dad out with some stuff. But we agreed that we do have things to talk about . . . or figure out or whatever."

"Does Trevor know?"

"Yes. And that's the worst part. He's been nothing but pleasant about it, taking it all in stride as usual. I feel like shit."

"Oh, my dear." Morgan's mom patted her on the knee. "Young love is not a simple thing, is it?"

"That's putting it lightly. But it's also kind of inaccurate. I'm not that young anymore. I'm a grownup. I shouldn't be running around like a fool, messing things up like this. I just don't know what to do. I think, mostly, that Josh and I just need closure. But then I get to thinking about what we once had. And then . . . well, I think I just stop thinking. What would you do?"

Her mom laughed loudly enough to startle Mary. "Sorry, sweetheart," she said to the little girl, who smiled and returned to her blocks. Then she turned back to Morgan. "I can't tell you what to do. But I can tell you that 'foolish' matters of the heart are not exclusive to young people. Love is complicated. And it has confused many a person many a decade older than you."

"But you like Josh," Morgan said.

"Of course. He's a wonderful young man. Serious, devoted, and not hard on the eyes."

Morgan had to laugh.

"But I like Trevor too," her mom said. "In fact, I remember thinking when you first started seeing him that he was much better suited for you. Also not hard on the eyes."

"Please stop wiggling your eyebrows, Mom." Morgan wiped a tear of laughter, then quickly sobered. "Okay, you can't tell me what to do. I get it. But can you give me some advice?"

Her mom smiled and sighed. "That I can do. Don't shortchange yourself, Morgan. But don't rush into anything either. With that said, I can tell this has been bothering you for a while."

Morgan nodded.

"Go see Josh. But don't let memories or even his feelings weigh on your decision. You'll know the answer. You probably already do."

Morgan raised a brow. "Doesn't really feel that way. But I know what you're going to say next. I can't keep leading both of them on. I need to make a choice, and soon."

"You sure do."

Morgan closed her eyes and felt a headache coming on. It was obvious, but she hadn't wanted to hear it said out loud.

"Honey." Morgan opened her eyes at the sound of her mom's voice. "Just remember, you don't owe anyone anything other than your true feelings."

"And I'll figure those out . . . or already know them, right?"

"It sounds more complicated than it is."

"Here's hoping."

Morgan hugged her mom and Mary, asked for her farewells be passed on to her dad and Matthew, then left.

There were no cop cars in sight as she sped to Burger Barn to pick up Rab. Which was good, because she was already waiting outside.

"Sorry I'm late," Morgan said as Rab got in.

"No problem." Rab fastened her seat belt then gave Morgan a strange look. "You sure you want to do this?"

Morgan turned to her, caught off guard. They hadn't talked about her and Josh at all since arriving home. "You don't think I should?"

"No. I just want to make sure you don't feel obligated."

"What do you know that I don't know?" Morgan asked, crossing her arms.

"Nothing. I swear. It's just . . ."

"Just what?"

"Don't be angry," Rab said. "You know I love you and you know I love my brother. It simply seems that the spark I remember you two having is no longer there."

"There's nothing simple about any of this," Morgan muttered as she pulled out of the lot and headed for the hotel. "But I think you might be right."

"You want to go home?"

"No. At the very least, I need to see him. Family time in a hotel should be a good and weird place to do that, right?" Morgan said sarcastically.

Rab didn't say anything, but Morgan kept thinking aloud.

"Actually, maybe it is that simple. Maybe that's all I need to do. We'll hang out for a bit and I'll find a way to discourage him from pursuing this any further. It's gone on for too long."

Morgan glanced at Rab, who shrugged.

The rest of the drive and the trip up in the hotel elevator were spent in silence. Morgan barely noticed the lack of words as her thoughts raced ahead. That really was the answer: hang out for a while then take off. For good.

She exited the elevator, confident in her plan, and knowing she loved Trevor.

Rab knocked on the door and Josh opened it.

And there was the problem. She loved Josh too. How could she not love him? He was Josh, for crying out loud. And he was here, standing right in front of her. He did come home after all.

Josh smiled somewhat nervously and ushered them inside.

Morgan managed to greet his father and accept *yet another* cup of coffee while her thoughts stumbled all over each other.

Sure, she loved Josh. She also loved Rab. And her parents. And Trevor. So what kind of love was it that she felt for Josh? If it was indeed romantic love, was it enough? Was it real? And was this really his home anymore?

Morgan's hands shook so badly she dropped her coffee cup.

Josh's hand shot out to grab it before it hit the floor. "We have decaf, if you'd prefer."

Morgan refrained from asking to raid the minibar and agreed to the decaf.

Chapter 32

In Which Zinger Plays a Part
Thursday, August 20, 1998

When Josh had opened the hotel door, the first thing – the only thing – he saw was Morgan.

She was wearing the purple blouse. Could it be the same one she'd bought years ago on their return trip from Seattle? The one he'd convinced her to buy after she'd lost her original one in the theft? Well, if it wasn't the exact same one, it was close enough to make his heart pound. It was also close enough to make him wonder if she'd chosen it on purpose to make him remember the good times.

Josh had chosen his outfit with that intent. He was glad he'd put on his green button-down shirt, but wondered if it had been a mistake to leave the hat behind.

Josh's pulse had continued to race as he stood in the doorway admiring Morgan. Then he noticed Rab, who was standing right beside her, wave impatiently. He'd managed to pull his attention from Morgan and nervously say, "Please come in."

Had his dad and Rab not been there, Josh would have arranged to meet Morgan in the lobby. It would not do for them to be alone in a hotel room alone.

The funny thing was, they had never been together in a hotel room since their return to Bathurst three years ago. They had never made it back to Montreal to go to the museum again as he'd semi-promised Morgan. They'd never left town together at all, despite her hints to do so – perhaps visit a romantic little bed and breakfast. They had rarely left the apartment. It was little wonder Morgan found him boring.

Maybe he should have taken a weekend off and spent it in a hotel with her – even if it was in Bathurst – then never

238

leave the room and make love as often as they could. He quickly pushed the thoughts away. There was no time for a cold shower right now.

After Josh had given Morgan a cup of decaf coffee – she seemed to be as nervous as he felt – they all sat down at the room's tiny table.

"It's good to see you again, Miss Parker," Josh's father said.

"It's, uh, nice to see you too, Mr. Hampton," Morgan replied.

"Since I've been making amends, let me apologize for not being nicer to you while you were dating my son. I offer no excuse."

"I accept your apology," Morgan said.

"How is your family?" Josh asked.

"They're doing well. Matthew is growing like a weed and Mary is an absolute little angel. I stopped and saw them before picking up Rab at work," Morgan said.

"Bob was low on gas, so Morgan was nice enough to drive me to work," Rab said.

"I doubt I'll get to see your parents on this visit," Josh said. "Please give them my regards when you see them again."

"Mom and Dad said to thank you and your sister for being there for me at the hospital," Morgan said.

"I believe you two have some things to talk about?" Josh's father said. "I have arranged with Margaret to get another load from the house. I can take Rab with me."

"We can't stay here," Josh said, eyeing Morgan and hoping she would agree. He was thankful that his father didn't ask why. He was sure Rab knew they shouldn't be alone together in a hotel room. And he didn't want Morgan to have to explain that to Trevor.

"I agree," Rab said. "But you two have things to sort out. Why don't you go somewhere where you can talk – even if that's sitting in Zinger out in the parking lot."

Josh and Morgan agreed and prepared to leave. They bumped into each other as they tried to reach the door first.

After a nervous laugh, Morgan let Josh open the door for her.

As they left, Josh caught his sister shaking her head as she gathered her purse.

Rab caught up with them as they reached the elevator, and they rode down to the first floor in silence.

"No fighting, you two," Rab said as they left the elevator.

"I'll try to get your brother back in one piece," Morgan said with a laugh. She picked up her pace and headed to Zinger.

When Josh reached Zinger, he waited by the door, mildly surprised it was actually locked.

"That's right, you don't have a key," Morgan said.

"I returned it to you last December," Josh said.

"You returned it to Rab," Morgan said. She got in and unlocked his door. "It feels weird having to unlock the door for you again."

Josh sat in the car and strapped in, noting the back seat was cluttered, as usual. At least the passenger side floor was clean, but he suspected that was more Rab's doing than Morgan's.

"So where to, eh? We're not going to talk it out in Zinger, in spite of what my sister suggested."

"I'm not sure," Morgan said. "Do you have any suggestions?"

"Let's do this: drive around town some so I can see the place. Then when we spot somewhere to sit and talk, we can do it, like maybe Youghall Beach Park."

"Maybe not. I don't have a swimsuit with me," Morgan said.

"At least it would be nice and open, and we could talk."

"You forget that summer is almost over. The beach is liable to be crowded."

"Well, start driving anyway. We'll figure something out," Josh said.

Morgan started the car, left the parking lot of the hotel, and headed south.

"Thank you for wearing the purple blouse for me," Josh said as they approached the bridge.

"This is not 'the' purple blouse," Morgan said. "Yes, it's a blouse, but I just happen to like purple and it's what I tossed on this morning."

Josh was disappointed by that but didn't let it show. When Morgan didn't offer any more conversation, he let his mind drift back to the call he had made the night before.

When he and his dad had arrived at the hotel, Josh called Iris to let her know they had arrived. He wasn't surprised at how glad she had been to hear his voice, but he was surprised at how hearing her voice lifted his spirits after the long, weary day they'd had. He resolved that, if he flew back to SeaTac, he would dig into his reserve and fly first class.

Of course, it had been late in Bathurst, and he couldn't talk long. But before he hung up, Iris made him promise to call as soon as he knew his return flight number.

He felt Iris was being presumptuous but promised her anyway. It couldn't hurt. If things worked out with Morgan, he could simply not call her, and she would know.

No, I couldn't do that. I would have to tell her.

Josh wondered what he would do about Old Blue. He supposed he could just give the truck to Iris. Or maybe he could convince Morgan to fly with him to Seattle and they could drive Old Blue back.

"You're a bit quiet," Morgan said.

"I was just thinking of last night."

"Rough trip?"

"We had a lot of turbulence flying into Moncton. Then it must have taken us a half-hour to get our bags," Josh said. "It was after midnight when we got to the hotel. Rab only stopped by for a few minutes."

"Ugh, turbulence. If I never fly again, it will be too soon," Morgan said.

Well, so much for that idea. He might just have to sacrifice Old Blue for her love. It would be hard, but Morgan was worth it.

"Did you and your dad drive from the airport together?"

"Yes. We're getting along okay. I slept some and then drove some while he napped," Josh said.

"Like father like son," Morgan said.

Josh ran his hand over Zinger's dash. "I suppose. I spent more than a few hours sleeping right here."

"And snoring."

"Goes with the territory," Josh said. "I bet you still can't sleep in a car."

"That's a safe bet."

Across the bridge, Morgan turned onto King Avenue. Josh wondered if she planned to take him to her parents' house, but they drove past their street.

Not far from there stood Bathurst High School. Seeing the building brought back many memories of school days, not all of them pleasant.

Although Morgan had been in his graduating class, he'd hardly paid any attention to her. He hadn't even known her name. When he thought about it, he realized that Trevor would have graduated high school while he and Morgan were still in elementary school.

Why was she even dating a guy that old?

Shortly after that, they passed Dumaresq Street, where Old Blue's engine had given out. If it hadn't, the trip to Seattle with Morgan would never have happened. He doubted she would have tried to go by herself.

"The town has changed some since I left," Josh said.

"I haven't really noticed."

"Remember back on the road home, how we talked about not being able to go home again?"

"Vaguely," Morgan said, stealing a glance at him.

"It doesn't seem changed to you because the changes have been happening around you. But I've been gone for eight months."

"Longer, really, when you count your time at college."

"I don't count that because I came home almost every weekend," Josh said.

"It was less often than you think."

"Perhaps." Josh wasn't going to argue the point. "But it was often enough to see the changes happening."

Bathurst really didn't feel like home to him anymore, not even with Morgan there. There was a time when he felt at home whenever he was with her.

Have we really changed that much?

They passed the office building for Franklin Shackleford, Esq., Attorney at Law. Josh wondered if she had done that intentionally but didn't ask. He remembered keeping a lot of thoughts to himself when he was around Morgan.

"Did you know Cal's Garage moved?" Morgan asked.

"He mentioned that business had picked up enough for him to move to a better place."

They lapsed into silence again.

Josh had driven back and forth on King Avenue for years. But after being on the streets in the States, the road seemed narrower now.

When they reached Highway 11, Morgan turned north and hit the gas pedal as she merged with traffic.

"Having flashbacks of Montana?" Josh asked.

"God, let's not talk about Montana. That was a really bad time for us."

"Let me ask you this. If you hadn't had your wallet stolen, would you have kept on driving past Butte?"

"Yeah, probably," Morgan said. "I was really, really angry at you. I probably would have gotten to Washington before I turned around and drove back to find you."

"By then I would have been at a hotel in Butte and not on the highway – or in jail."

"Jail?"

"Yeah. Didn't I ever tell you that the sheriff stopped and told me I couldn't walk on the highway?" Josh asked.

"Must have slipped your mind."

"I guess I was just so happy to find you at the bus station the next day it was no longer important."

"But if I had driven on, we wouldn't be sitting here today," Morgan said.

"You're right. I don't think we would be."

So many of the things that had brought them together had fallen into place one after another. His truck blowing an engine, Shack convincing him to go to Cindy's party, and Morgan's drunken declaration. Then the loss of her wallet at Bismarck, her parents refusing to send her more money, and him finding her at the bus station in Butte.

And most significantly, his failure to enlist in the Marines. If any of those things hadn't happened or had gone the other way, the chain of events would have been broken. He would be far away from Bathurst, and she would be here, doing who knows what.

At St. Anne Street, Morgan exited the highway and drove back toward the northern part of Bathurst.

"Some of the better places to eat are up here," Morgan said.

"I suppose I could go for a bite."

"Not a burger place. A proper restaurant. I can cover you if you're short on cash."

"No, I'm good," Josh said. "I've told you my finances are in good shape. I'll pay for your meal."

Morgan grimaced. "I think it would be better if we each paid for our own meal."

"Whatever you prefer."

Why hadn't he said, "As you wish"? Just a few days ago, he would have.

"Here we go," Morgan said, and they pulled into the parking lot of a gastropub.

"I don't think I've ever eaten here," Josh said.

"I've been here several times with . . . yeah, several times. And the best part is they have beer, wine, and cocktails."

Josh was sure she had stopped herself from saying the name of his rival. He suddenly didn't want to go in but couldn't think of a good reason to refuse.

He would just have to keep Morgan's focus on the two of them.

Josh got out of Zinger and started to go around the car to open the door for her. But she was already inside and had probably ordered her first drink.

Josh sighed and followed. The door was closed by the time he reached it, and he felt his chances of resolution had closed with it.

Chapter 33

In Which Someone Figures it Out
Thursday, August 20, 1998

"You coming?" Morgan asked as she held the second set of doors to the restaurant open for Josh.

"I was locking the car," Josh said eyeing the doors, probably wondering how to turn the tables and be the one holding them open for her.

Morgan didn't budge and Josh had no choice but to scoot through.

"Ah, how I didn't miss that," Morgan said, only half-joking. "You're lucky I didn't leave my key in the car."

"You seriously haven't learned to lock the doors? Zinger was locked at the hotel," Josh noted.

"I lock them sometimes. It's just not necessary to do so all the time. In fact, it's often smarter to leave them unlocked if you don't have anything important in the car. A thief will smash your window just to walk off with a handful of change."

"There's more than a handful of change in there."

Morgan held up a hand as they approached the hostess station. "It's just junk in the back seat. And please don't start with that either. My car is messy, not dirty; remember?"

"How could I forget?"

They grinned at each other and Morgan relaxed. They were supposed to be talking, not fighting.

"Miss Parker, it's good to see you."

"Hi, Tanya," Morgan said to the hostess. "Pretty busy in here for a weeknight, isn't it?"

"Yes, end of summer and all. Who's your friend?"

"Um," Morgan glanced back at Josh, "he's just visiting from out of town."

"Welcome," Tanya said to Josh, who moved up to stand beside Morgan.

"Thanks," Josh said somewhat bitterly.

"Anyway," Tanya said as she gathered the menus, "your regular table is open. Would you like to sit there?"

"No!" Morgan exclaimed loudly then checked herself. She laughed nervously and lowered her voice. "I don't think my, uh, friend would be comfortable sitting so close to the bar."

Tanya smiled and led the way to a table in the middle of the restaurant. "Will this be all right?"

"Perfect. Thank you," Morgan said, reaching for her chair.

Another hand beat her to it.

Tanya placed the menus on the table as Morgan took her seat.

"I'll take it from here. Thanks," she said before Josh could try pushing it in for her.

He chuckled and glanced at the chair closer to Morgan before taking the one on the opposite side of the table for four.

"Looks like some things never change," he said. "You still hate that?"

"Actually, I don't," Morgan said. "It's just not . . . appropriate here."

Josh raised a brow but didn't pursue the topic. Thankfully, their server arrived to take their drink orders.

"Your regular?" he asked Morgan.

"Yes, please, Joey." She refrained from asking for a double for two reasons: she really didn't feel like listening to Josh's alcohol-is-bad spiel, and she didn't want him having to drive.

"And you, sir?"

"Cola will be fine."

Morgan rolled her eyes as Joey departed. "I'm not getting drunk tonight. You could have a beer, you know."

Josh shrugged. "I'm fine."

Morgan just shook her head and opened her menu. Josh did the same.

"So, your dad is a lot different than I remember," Morgan said as she put her menu down. She already knew what she would order.

"He has changed a lot since I last talked to him. I couldn't believe it when he showed up at Sally's wedding."

"Yeah, I was surprised too," Morgan said. "I wasn't sure if you knew he was coming or not."

"Nope. He took both me and Rab by surprise."

"And your uncle? I thought they hadn't talked for years."

"They hadn't. You heard him at the hotel, he's making up for lost time. Funny, a lot of the changes he's made, and is still making, are because of me."

"You?" Morgan said, surprised. "I thought you'd hardly spoken to him for years."

"I hadn't," Josh said. "But that was partly my mother's fault. It's a long story, but when I stood up to her and refused to break up with you to gain their financial support for schooling . . ."

The drinks arrived and Morgan took a healthy gulp.

"Are you ready to order?"

"I am," Morgan said. "House burger with fries, please."

Josh looked disappointed. "I would have thought you'd have the steak."

"Why would you think that?"

"I just remember how much you liked your steak . . . you know, extra rare."

"Well, I'm not that hungry today. Are you going to order?"

Josh ordered the steak, medium rare, with a side salad. Just before the server left, Morgan held up her nearly empty drink and he winked.

"I thought you weren't getting drunk," Josh said.

"I'm not. It's legal to drive after having one or two drinks, you know."

"It may be legal, but it's not smart."

Morgan bit back a scathing retort and said, "So, do you think you'll go see your mother while you're in town?"

"That depends. I'm not sure she's in the best of moods right now. But if I end up staying longer . . ."

Josh didn't come right out and say it was up to Morgan how long he would be staying, and Morgan refused to acknowledge it. But the implication was there.

Morgan finished her drink as they studied each other in silence. It was like a standoff. For the life of her, Morgan could not figure out what the hell they were doing here. So she asked him.

"What are we supposed to be doing here?"

Josh blinked. "Honestly, I'm not sure. We keep saying we need to figure things out, but really, what is there to figure out?"

He leaned across the table and extended his hand to her. Morgan averted her eyes, pretending not to see it, although it was frightfully obvious. She waited until he pulled it back before looking at him again.

"I kind of get what you're saying. I mean, we probably know the answers to everything, but we're just confused."

"I'm not confused," Josh said.

His eyes were so intense. Morgan had to look away again, lest they burn a hole right through her. The server arrived with her second drink and their meals. Morgan hadn't realized she'd muttered her thanks to the lord above aloud until she heard Josh scoff.

"I was thirsty," Morgan said.

"Sure," Josh said, carving viciously into his steak.

They ate in silence for a few minutes before Josh set down his knife with more force than necessary.

"Well, are you happy with this new guy?"

Morgan shifted her fries around the plate. "Of course I'm happy. But I don't want to talk about Trevor with you."

"Fine," Josh said, in a tone that implied anything but. "So why did you say those things to me when you were in the hospital?"

Morgan sighed. "Because I was on drugs. Lots of drugs that weren't agreeing with me. You know that."

"Fine," Josh said again, undeterred. "Then what about the kiss?"

Morgan stabbed her fork into her untouched burger and left it there. "*You* kissed *me*, remember?"

"Sure. The first time. Then you kissed me back and suggested we go to a hotel. You weren't under the influence of anything except tobacco then."

"Oh, for Chrissake. I wasn't serious."

Josh gave her the look.

"Okay, maybe for a second," Morgan admitted. "But I wouldn't actually have done such a thing. You took me by surprise, Josh. For once in your life . . ."

His eyes narrowed and he stood. "You want spontaneity? I'll give you spontaneity." He walked around the table and began to kneel down.

Morgan's hand shot out and grabbed his arm. "Don't you dare," she hissed.

Josh stopped where he was, leaning over, but didn't back away.

"Get back in your chair," Morgan said. "Now."

For a second, it looked like he was going to dive in for a kiss, but he noticed her balled fist and retreated to his seat.

"Why the hell would you do that?" Morgan asked, surveying the restaurant to make sure he hadn't attracted too much attention. "People know me here. Dammit."

Tanya, the hostess, was on her way over. Morgan gulped back the rest of her drink.

"Is everything all right here?" Tanya asked.

"All right? Of course. My . . . cousin here was just being funny. Oh, would you mind telling Joey to bring me another drink?"

"Sure thing," Tanya said and left.

Josh shot Morgan daggers.

"Is it marriage in general you're opposed to, or just me?" he asked.

"Just you!" Morgan threw her hands in the air. "You don't know how to do anything right. Back when I wanted – *needed* – you to care, you couldn't stay awake long enough to do so. Now . . . I have no idea what you're doing. In what world was that appropriate?"

Josh shook his head in lieu of an answer. "But don't you remember the good times? On the road, in Zinger?"

"Sure," Morgan said. "It was the summer of '95. We had fun. That was it. Everything went to shit as soon as we got back to Bathurst."

"So you're blaming me," Josh said, resigned.

"Actually, I'm not," Morgan said. She couldn't stand seeing him so despondent. "No one's really to blame. We just didn't enjoy doing the same things. We still don't. And our life goals? Not even close. I know you said you'd sacrifice having kids and stuff if I didn't want to, but you shouldn't have to sacrifice something that's so important to you."

"I can change?" Josh said, though it was phrased as a question.

"Listen to yourself. You can't change the way you feel. And listen to me," she continued before he could argue further. "I care about you, Josh. A lot. But not in the way that you're thinking – or the way I was thinking for a minute. We had a walk down memory lane last week; that's all. And we both know we broke up shittily –"

"But did we?" Josh interrupted. "Did we really break up at all?"

The server arrived with Morgan's drink, and she took the moment to phrase her next words as nicely as possible.

"We did break up, Josh. And we'd already drifted apart long before that phone call."

Josh leaned back and seemed to chew on her words as their meals sat forgotten.

"Tell me you're not here just because of me," Morgan said, hoping to give him an easy out. "You're helping your dad out and that's it, right?"

Josh shook his head.

Morgan sighed deeply. "Then what is it? What do you want?"

"I want you back, Morgan. I'll do anything. I'm here to stay, if you'll have me."

"So it's all up to me again," Morgan said, exasperated.

"Well, yes," Josh said. "I've already made up my mind."

"Why would you even want me back? All we did was fight. I feel like we're fighting right now."

"Why? Because I owe it to you, Angel."

Morgan grabbed her drink. "Owe me? What do you think you owe me?"

"Well, we lived together. You know that's not something we – I – take lightly. I feel obligated to see this through, to offer to marry you."

The drink Morgan had just taken a sip of flew out her nose as she snorted. Josh jumped up when she bent over choking, but a man from the next table beat him to offering assistance. Morgan saw the wait staff heading over through watering eyes.

Once everyone had been assured that Morgan was not in need of the Heimlich maneuver, she put her head in her hands and began to laugh.

"What's so funny?" Josh asked.

"Let me see if I've got this straight. We slept together and you . . . *feel obligated to marry me?*" Morgan laughed so hard her sides threatened to split.

"Well, yes," Josh said. "I know I should have asked your father's permission first, but I doubt he'd be willing to grant it to me. I still don't know what you're finding so funny about this."

"My God," Morgan said, dabbing her eyes. "You really are serious. Are you sure that's just cola? You sound like a crazy person."

"You make me feel like a crazy person!" Josh rubbed his eyes hard. "You make me feel like a lot of things I'd rather not be. Half the time I feel like your caretaker, the other half I spend bending over backwards to make you happy – to make a life for us – and this is the thanks I get?"

"Oh, stop it," Morgan said.

"What? You know what I'm saying is true –"

"No. Literally. Just stop it." She waved for the check. "We should leave."

Josh sighed. "Fine. I'll drive."

Morgan didn't argue, even though she'd had less than three drinks. When the check came, she put enough money in the billfold to cover her meal and the tip.

"I'll wait outside."

Morgan left Josh to settle the rest of the bill and exited the restaurant. Damn. She'd run out of smokes. She hadn't bought any since she'd returned from her trip to Seattle. She hadn't had the urge for one since then.

Josh wasn't far behind, and Morgan let herself in the passenger seat of Zinger before tossing him the keys.

They drove back to the hotel in absolute silence until Morgan asked that he park the car in front of the hotel and send Rab down when she was ready.

He nodded in response and Morgan could hardly keep herself from crying as she watched him walk away, head down, shoulders slumped.

But holy hell. Perhaps there had been a point to this evening after all. She remembered exactly why they had broken up and exactly why they needed to stay broken up.

So then why did it feel as if her heart had broken in two?

Because she still cared about him.

Well, that was a problem for another day. She'd figure out how to explain her feelings to him – nicely. She'd prepare a speech beforehand if necessary.

But in the meantime, it was about time she made one guy happy.

Morgan took out her cell phone and dialed.

"Trevor? Are we still on for that party tomorrow?"

Chapter 34

In Which Josh Makes the Rounds
Friday, August 21, 1998

The click of the door lock woke Josh up. It took a second for him to realize he was in a hotel room.

"What time is it, Angel?" Josh asked.

"It's almost ten, son," his dad said. "But I'm hardly an angel."

"Oh," Josh said, crestfallen. "I guess I slept in." He had been dreaming of Morgan. Or was it Iris?

"Rough night?"

The events of the previous night came crashing back into his mind as he fully woke up.

"Let's say it didn't go as well as I hoped."

"You were out pretty late with Miss Parker," his dad said.

"I was out late, but Morgan brought me back here early."

"But you didn't come back to the room except to pick up your sister until after I was asleep."

"I needed to do some thinking, so I walked out to the seashore for a while," Josh said.

"It was really dark last night, wasn't it?"

"Yeah, looking out to sea was amazing. There were billions of stars above the darkened water, and the lights of the houses along the shore weren't enough to dim the stars."

"And what did you two figure out?" his dad asked.

"I'm afraid she has decided I'm not the one for her. I have not decided the same about her."

"Rab suggested that if you haven't decided before tonight, things will be decided for you. But, from the way you're talking, that decision may have happened last night."

"Well, it started pleasantly enough, but when we got to the restaurant, the staff seemed to know her well and she lied

255

to them about who I was like she didn't want them to know I was her boyfriend."

"Emphasis on the 'was,'" his dad said. "I thought you broke up last year."

"I thought we had and now I'm sure we did. I'm trying to get it unbroken."

"Well, the apartment is set up enough that I can move in and stop paying for a hotel room. You're welcome to use the couch."

"No offense, Dad," Josh said, "but I think I'll splurge and stay at the hotel at least through tomorrow night. But I'll be around to help during the day."

"I understand and appreciate the help."

"I plan to go see Mom today."

"She's your mother, you should go see her, but don't go on my behalf," his dad said. "Unlike you, we know what we want."

"Okay, but can I have the room for a few minutes? I need to make a call."

"Just as long as you come down and take over the room by eleven. I'll be in the lobby."

"I shouldn't be too long," Josh said.

His dad nodded and left the room.

Josh dialed Iris's number.

"*Mushi, mushi*," Iris answered with a yawn.

"Hey, Iris, how are you?"

"Josh, my God, are you okay?"

It was so good to hear her voice and to know that she genuinely cared for him.

"Yeah. I got back to the hotel late last night, so I decided not to call," Josh said.

"So you decided to wake me up instead?"

"I guess it is still early there. Sorry."

"So what's going on?" Iris asked.

"I think I really just wanted to hear your voice."

"If that's the case, I'll forgive you for calling so early. How are things with your dad?"

"He's moving out of the hotel today. I'll probably stay here tonight and tomorrow night," Josh said.

"And after that?"

"If I need to, I can stay at his place."

"Your calls make me think you won't need to," Iris said.

"Morgan and I had a chance to sit down and talk last night and it didn't go very well."

"But you're still not convinced, are you?"

"When I told her I wanted to marry her she laughed – had a noser even," Josh said.

"That sounds bad. I'm sorry you had to go through that, but I can't say I'm sorry she's rejecting you."

"She dropped me off at the hotel without making any plans to meet again. She's working today, so I'm going to see what the day brings."

"Whatever happens, Josh, remember I love you," Iris said.

"And I miss you and Washington."

"Hold that in your heart and come back to me."

"I better let you get back to sleep. I'll call tonight," Josh said.

"Remember, I'm here for you."

"Always."

Another phrase I've used to say "I love you." Is my subconscious trying to tell me something?

Iris hung up and Josh sat there staring at the phone for several minutes. Hearing her voice warmed his heart and strengthened his resolve to face the day.

Bringing his mind back to Bathurst and the present, Josh took a quick shower, got dressed, and went to the lobby to take possession of the room.

After Josh went to his dad's new apartment and helped him unpack, he borrowed the car to go out. He drove to the

Burger Barn and let Rab know he was free for the afternoon, arranging to meet later at the café. Then Josh located Cal's new garage. Somehow, he had missed seeing it when they drove down King Avenue the night before. The new location was around the corner from the previous place.

As he pulled into the parking lot, he imagined what Old Blue would have looked like sitting there. But, while the place was newer, it didn't have as much parking space for vehicles awaiting repair. Brian, the young man Cal had hired to replace Josh when he left three years ago, was outside detailing a car.

When he went inside, a very pregnant Robin waddled around the counter. "Josh, it's so good to see you."

"Look at you," Josh said.

Robin laughed. "Yeah, you missed a lot."

"I guess I must have. I seem to remember seeing an invitation to the wedding, but I couldn't get away."

Cal entered the office and offered his hand to Josh. "I didn't expect to see you back anytime soon."

"I wasn't expecting to come back for a while, but my dad needed some help," Josh said.

"Are you going to be staying?"

"I thought I might be, but I'm not so sure now."

"Listen, Josh, business has picked up, as you can see, and another grandchild will be here soon," Cal said motioning to Robin, who had sat back down. "So, I'm looking to hire an experienced mechanic to help out. I'd love to hire you if you're interested."

"I'd be lying if I said it wasn't tempting, but I have a good position back in Washington. But if I decide to stay, I'll certainly take you up on that."

"How soon will you know?"

"I'll let you know by Monday."

"Fair enough. I need to get back to this job, but it was good to see you."

They shook hands again and Josh wished Robin well before heading back to the car.

It was getting close to the time for Rab to get off work, so Josh drove around the town for a few minutes before arriving at the café.

Josh paused at the door and scanned the interior for Morgan. He didn't expect to see her, but she had been there so often, either working or hanging out, it had become a habit to look for her.

Morgan was not there, but Shack sat among the few patrons in the café. Josh thought about waiting outside for Rab, but Shack had spotted him.

"Hey dumbass, I heard you were in town. Come on over and sit down."

Josh could hardly refuse the invitation without insulting Shack. He let the door close behind him and plopped down in a seat. A toddler looked up from her coloring and waved at him.

"Kayla has gotten bigger since I last saw her," Josh said.

"Isn't she a little cutie?" Shack said.

"Good thing she gets her looks from me," Mel said as she arrived to take Josh's order. "What would you like?"

"I'll have coffee with two sugars."

"Coming right up." Mel ruffled her daughter's hair before she left.

"So why haven't you married Mel?" Josh asked quietly.

"Other than the fact that she has no desire to marry me, why should I marry her?"

"Because you are this child's father," Josh said, dumbfounded.

The bells on the door rang as Rab entered the café. She waved at Josh as she went to the counter to get her own beverage. Shack had said something, but all Josh caught was "go back."

"What was that?" Josh asked, turning back to him.

"I said, you need to get into your time machine and go back to the '50s. That sort of thinking went out decades ago, dumbass."

"But shouldn't your daughter have a daddy?"

"She has a daddy," Shack said and turned to Kayla. "Where's your daddy, baby girl?"

Kayla turned to the counter and pointed at Mel. "Daddy!"

Rab and Mel came over and sat down. Mel set Josh's coffee in front of him.

Shack shrugged. "She'll learn."

"He's right. She'll learn. But I'm in no hurry to teach her," Mel said and pointed to Shack. "Who's that, honey?"

"Shack," the toddler replied.

Mel smiled.

"You need to lighten up, dude," Shack said, addressing Josh. "You sound like my old man."

"What do you mean?"

"Robert, you need to get serious about life," Shack said in a deeper voice. "Robert, you should marry that girl and make an honest woman of her."

"He's not entirely wrong," Rab said. "You do need to prepare for the future."

"I'm going to be an NHL superstar. In a few years, I'll be rolling in the money."

"Dude, every boy has that dream the first time he picks up a hockey stick. In the States, it's basketball, but the principle is the same," Josh said.

"Well, I do have an athletic scholarship," Shack said.

"What do you think of the arrangement, Mel?" Josh asked.

"The jock and I have an amiable relationship. Shack sees his daughter every day when he's home from school, and he provides child support – without a court order."

"Even my mom has warmed up to her granddaughter," Shack said. "But if the old man wants a Shackleford to carry on his legacy, Trevor will have to provide one. Speaking of Trevor, he's having a big party tonight. You should come since you're in town. Everyone will be there."

"I've heard that line before."

"And if you hadn't listened to me the last time I said it, you wouldn't have gone to Seattle, right?" Shack said.

"I don't think you should go, Josh," Rab said, shooting a look at Shack. "There will probably just be a lot of drinking and I know how that makes you uncomfortable."

"But it's Trevor's birthday," Shack said. "There will be cake and lots of food, too. You know what our parties are like."

Josh looked at his sister, who was looking at him with narrowed eyes.

"Maybe. No promises," Josh said.

"Well, I suppose you and your father can spend the evening watching baseball," Shack said with a grin.

"Or I could catch up on some sleep. I did say maybe."

"So how have the States been treating you?" Rab asked.

Josh silently thanked his sister for changing the subject. He had understood her warning. It was a birthday party for Trevor. Morgan was sure to be there. *With him.* He should stay away.

Mel left the table to take care of more customers and Josh regaled Shack with the glories of life in Washington. He avoided any mention of Iris, even though everything he talked about reminded him of her.

When Josh finished his coffee, he got up. "I'm going to go to see Mom," he told Rab.

"I'll be here for a bit longer, but I need to go and get ready for the party soon."

Josh said farewell to Mel and Shack, then drove off to the house where he had spent his youth.

After he parked in Old Blue's spot, he sat looking at the door and wondered if he really wanted to face his mother. She had disliked Morgan from the first time they met and refused to help him get a school loan unless he broke up with her. He could have said he had broken up with her, but that would have been a lie. He had many faults, but being a liar wasn't among them.

He got out of the car and went to the door. Although his dad's key ring had a house key on it, he knocked.

"You have a key, just open the damned door," a muffled voice called from inside.

"It's me, Mom. Josh."

The door opened.

"I saw the car pull in and I thought it was your father. Did he send you?" his mother asked in French.

"No, I came on my own," Josh replied. "I don't need to get involved in your fight."

"I don't suppose you're going to speak to me in French," she continued in the same language.

"I'm an American now. We speak English."

"And you have completely forgotten your heritage," she said, switching to English. "What do you want?"

He decided not to get into a discussion about his heritage. "I'd like to look in my room and see if there's anything I want."

"You won't find anything. When you turned against me, I cleaned the room out to use as a home office. You could try the pawnshop on King Avenue. They may still have some of your stuff."

"Can I come in, or are we just going to stand here and talk?"

She said nothing but left the door open and walked to the kitchen.

Josh closed the door and followed her. When he arrived, his mother was at her usual seat at the kitchen table.

He sat without being invited. "I'd just like to know why you refused to help me get a loan, Mom."

"I was trying to be a parent and doing it for your own good."

"Because of that, I may have lost Morgan," Josh said.

"So, in the end, the result was the same, but you chose the hard way and gained a lot of heartache for it. Was playing house with her worth it?"

"I happen to love Morgan, Mom."

"Apparently the feeling was not mutual. You may have been in it for the emotion, but she was in it for the pleasure," his mother said. "Tell me, how long did you know her before she lured you into bed?"

"I won't answer that."

"Well, you had no more than left Bathurst before Miss Parker was sleeping with someone else."

"You don't know that," Josh said.

"You're right, I don't. But believe it or not, I do still speak with Mary and got that impression."

"Rab wouldn't gossip like that."

"No, she never accused Morgan of such, but said enough that I could put two and two together," his mother said.

"Why are you judging me by a different standard? You and dad were sleeping together before you were married."

"Did your father tell you that?" his mother asked. "Never mind, he must have. Yes, it's true. I was young and foolish and have regretted it for over twenty years now."

"So you regret having Rab and me?"

"I didn't say that. You are my children, but don't seem to want to be."

"You married dad because you were pregnant," Josh said.

"I did."

"Would you have married him if you hadn't gotten pregnant?"

"Maybe. I don't know. I think we would have drifted apart back then," his mother said. "That is what I was trying to spare you from."

"I was an adult. You should have let me make my own decisions."

"You were only nineteen and not fully mature. And it was your decision to go to Seattle rather than come back home."

"Uncle Bill found an excellent job for me," Josh said.

"But it cost you your relationship with Miss Parker," his mother said without emotion.

"It was a mutual thing."

"Is that why you are back home, to try to win her back?"

"Mostly. We talked when she came out to Sally's wedding."

"And you decided to chase that tail back here. Are there no young women in Seattle?"

"There are, but they are not Morgan," Josh said.

"Which might be good for you. Have you won her back?"

"Not yet. I'm not sure I can."

"I know you didn't ask for it, but here's some advice. You've wasted almost a year pining for a woman who no longer wants you. Go back home to Seattle. Find a girl that will love you as much as you love her."

"If I do, it will be my choice and not because of your advice."

"The end result will be the same. You will be happier and so will I."

"From your point of view."

"We all filter our feelings from our own points of view."

"You may not believe it, Mom, but I do love you. Whether you feel like you need it or not, I forgive you."

"Joshua Éveriste Caleb Hampton, you are a stubborn young man and infuriating at times. But you are my son, and I love you."

"When you get settled in Montreal, you can let me know where you are through Uncle Bill," Josh said.

"I will do that."

When Josh left his old home to go back to his dad's place, some of the weight on his soul had been lifted.

Chapter 35

In Which the Good Times Roll
Friday, August 21, 1998

"You are going to be late for your own birthday party."

Morgan turned from her makeup mirror to find Rab standing in the doorway, hands on her hips.

"Do you realize how many times you've said that already? It doesn't start until eight," Morgan said.

"And now it's quarter to eight. If we got in the car right now and floored it, we would just make it on time."

"Yeesh, you're right." Morgan quickly wiped off her lipstick and applied her regular lip gloss, then hopped off her bed. "We can make it in plenty of time if you let me drive. I know how to floor it."

"I'm familiar with the concept, but I don't have a glove box full of speeding tickets. And don't even think I'm letting you drive the crap out of Bob like that. Just quit playing with your face and let's go."

"I'm done. I have no idea why I always fiddle with this makeup stuff. It never works out. Just let me grab my purse."

"Turn the makeup mirror off," Rab said. "It'll light your bed on fire."

Morgan flashed her friend a sheepish grin, turned off the light on the mirror, and stuffed her phone into the wallet on a string that had been her purse for years.

"I can't believe you still use that thing," Rab said as she shifted her own adult-sized bag on her shoulder. "There's no room for anything in there."

"I've got what I need. I can't stand those big purses; they look like diaper bags. No offense," she added.

"None taken," Rab said. "As usual."

"Wait." Morgan paused at the floor-length mirror beside the door and examined her outfit – a shiny pink, sleeveless tank top with a white silk skirt that landed just above her knees. "Do you think I'm overdressed?"

Rab snorted. "The only time I've ever seen you overdressed was at the wedding. It's good to see you out of those ripped jeans."

Morgan wrinkled her nose. "The peach chiffon, hey? I knew you were lying when you told Sally you liked it."

"I was being polite," Rab said, "but yeah, it was gruesome."

"What if I'm the only one wearing a skirt?" Morgan asked, eyeing Rab's outfit of black pants and a light-weight blue sweater. "Maybe I should change. Maybe I should have tried putting my hair up . . ."

"Oh, no you don't." Rab grabbed Morgan's arm and propelled her toward the door. "Time's up. Besides, it's half your party too – your night to shine."

"Shoes!" Morgan declared. "I need shoes. You can't expect me to wear sneakers with this."

Rab sighed and released her arm as Morgan dashed back into her room. After a few moments she emerged in a pair of low-heeled strappy sandals.

"Good?" she asked.

"Perfect," Rab said and opened the door. "Your chariot awaits."

It was almost eight by the time they were in Bob and heading to the Shackleford residence.

"Thanks for waiting for me," Morgan said. "And for driving. Trevor would have picked me up, but I know he was busy with the party plans."

"No problem."

Morgan studied Rab as she drove, grateful to have such a friend. "Actually, thanks for a lot of things. You're so much like your brother, you know."

Rab's eyes widened and she risked a glance at Morgan. "In a good way, I hope?"

Morgan laughed. "Yes, in a good way. As much as I know we're not meant to be together romantically, he's a terrific guy. I suppose I don't have to tell you that, but I kind of feel like I need to tell *him* that at some point."

"So, what happened with you two last night? Josh didn't say much except that it definitely did not go well."

Morgan cringed and rubbed her eyes hard as the events of the previous night replayed in her head. "Oh, Rab. It could not have gone any worse. He literally tried to propose to me in the restaurant."

"He did not."

"Oh, but he did. He was almost down on bended knee, and I nearly had to break his arm to get him back in his seat."

"Shit."

"Shit indeed. And can you imagine the reason he thought he should propose to me? I won't make you guess – he said he felt obligated to offer to marry me because we'd slept together."

"Damn. That does sound like my brother."

"Still, despite his old-old-old-fashioned ways and the fact he has a few loose screws, I feel sad that he'll no longer be in my life."

"Does he know you've made this decision?"

"Oh, he must. I told you last night couldn't have gone any worse." Morgan thought for a second then added, "Actually, I'll probably still need to talk to him to make sure it's clear. He does have a way of holding on to crazy ideas."

Rab considered that for a minute before saying, "I'm not sure how crazy his idea really is. You can't deny he loves you."

"Honestly, I can. Don't you remember the grudge he held against your dad for most of his life? He had himself convinced the man was a draft dodger and had brought dishonor on the family by not serving in the war. There was such a simple explanation behind it all, but Josh wouldn't – or couldn't – listen to it until he'd made a pilgrimage across the continent and back." Morgan shook her head. "No. I don't believe he loves me like he thinks he does. He just doesn't know how to let go."

"You've let go?" Rab said.

"Yes. No. I mean, not completely. As much as he irritates the living *merde* out of me, I still care about him and I would never want to hurt him." Morgan sighed. "However, I suspect I have and will continue to hurt him until I can make him understand how I truly feel. I'll just have to worry about that another day. Not tonight."

"You think tonight is really the night for you and Trevor?"

Morgan bit her lip and smiled. "Absolutely. Of course, it was originally supposed to be a surprise, but then they had to let some cats out of the bag. My mom gave me the first heads up because she wanted me to have time to think it over. But Trevor had to not-so-subtly hint at it because of the whole Josh thing . . . he wouldn't propose in the middle of all that."

"He knows about Josh then?"

"Yes. And he couldn't have been more understanding. I'm a really lucky girl."

Rab smiled and pulled onto the Shacklefords' street. "Yes, I think you are."

"Holy crap, how late are we?" Morgan asked as she noticed all the cars lining the road by the house.

"Just a few minutes, but we'll have to hoof it some."

They parked a few houses down and started walking.

"How do you think he's going to do it?" Rab asked.

"Oh, that part's still a surprise. Maybe he'll wait until dark and we'll steal outside for a romantic proposal under the stars. Looks like it's going to be another clear night. Or maybe he'll wait until much later when we're back at his place. Yeah, wouldn't the ocean view be dreamy?"

Rab laughed. "I take it from the dreamy look on your face you've decided to say yes?"

"If he does ask tonight, and I hope he does . . . I do want to say yes."

The two girls squealed and hugged each other as they walked up the sidewalk to the house where Trevor himself was waiting at the open door.

"Get lost?" he asked with a grin.

Morgan's smile grew as wide as it could, and she ran the remaining feet straight into his arms. He picked her up and twirled her around, then set her down for a proper kiss that soon had her blood racing hot through her veins.

"Sorry I'm late," she breathed when they broke apart.

"I have never, ever, known you to be early. I'm not complaining."

"Just one of the things I love about you."

Rab smiled and waved as she followed the people streaming into the back of the house where the stairs to the basement were. Morgan waved back and snuggled deeper into Trevor's arms.

"It feels like I haven't seen you in forever," she said.

"I know. It's been way too long. Work doesn't count. Then there was your trip and all . . . let's not waste another minute."

After one last kiss, they headed for the basement to join the others.

"Wow!"

Morgan couldn't believe how different the basement looked. Even though Trevor had his own place, they often hung out here at the Shackleford "mansion." Really, it was just a large house in the area of Morgan's and Mel's parents' homes, but the basement had been designed for the

Shackleford boys – pool table, bar, big screen TV, all the perks.

Tonight, the lighting was positively surreal. It looked more like a golden mist hovering over them with strings of violet lights hung on the walls. Morgan didn't dare imagine where the lights came from or the cost. The decorations were minimal – simple banners placed sporadically declaring the "Balloon-free Birthday Celebration for Trevor and Morgan."

In the middle of the room was a gigantic circular table that held stacks of presents which grew as guests continued to arrive and deposit their packages. Narrow tables filled with hot and cold food, beverages, and sweets lined the walls.

"You like?" Trevor asked as he wrapped his arms around her from behind, resting his head on hers.

"I love."

Morgan turned to kiss him again – she could never get enough of kissing him – just as Shack walked by and yelled, "Get a room!"

Trevor chuckled and whispered to Morgan, "Soon. In the meantime, how about some drinks and mingling?"

"If I must," Morgan said cheerily.

Truthfully, Morgan didn't mind at all as they went from group to group, greeting Trevor's colleagues and friends and whoever Shack had invited. It was a motley group to be sure, but no one seemed to mind. That was the beauty of Trevor and all his endeavors. He did everything with such confidence and grace it was as if he was incapable of failing.

The basement was soon filled to capacity, and the party overflowed back up the stairs and out into the backyard. Morgan offered to help Trevor with setting up additional tables and seating, but he told her to go ahead and enjoy herself. He and a group of his cronies took off to handle the situation, which they'd already prepared for in the event of too many guests.

Morgan wandered around accepting birthday wishes and sampling the food in between drinks. She wasn't surprised to see Mel deliver a playful smack to Shack's head, but she was surprised to find her doing so while sitting on his lap.

Half of Morgan's drink sloshed out of her glass, and she caught it just before it fell from her hand, when she saw Mel deliver another smack to Shack. It wasn't a hand to the head, it was lips to lips!

It was impossible to move anywhere quickly in this crowd, but Morgan attempted a dash anyway. The lip lock was over by the time she arrived, but Mel was still sitting on Shack's lap with her arm slung over his shoulders.

"Who's got Kayla tonight?" Morgan asked, because they were the only words she could come up with.

Mel blinked up at her. Yeah, she was half in the bag.

"Grams and Gramps." She giggled and then clarified, "The ones that don't live here."

"Uh huh. You look . . . cozy."

Mel just grinned and then turned her attention to the table in front of her, picking up and putting down empty beer bottles as she searched for a full one.

"Hoo boy."

Morgan turned to find Rab standing beside her.

"I know, hey?" Morgan said. "I guess Mel was long overdue for a night out."

"I wonder what they're going to name the next kid," Rab said.

Morgan laughed and felt her purse vibrating. She pulled out her cell phone and saw it was an unknown number. No sense answering it in here. It was too loud. She let the call go to voicemail and went to shove it back in her purse but stopped. The necklace was still in there. The half-heart that had Josh's name engraved on it.

272

For just a second, Morgan's own heart broke yet again at the sight of the metal one mashed, forgotten, and all alone in the bottom of her bag.

She had really wanted to give it back to Josh the night before. She wasn't sure why she wanted him to have it so badly – maybe just for her own selfish closure – but it felt like something she had to do.

Morgan stuffed the phone back in her purse and willed herself to forget about it. She could always send it with Rab if she and Josh didn't get the opportunity to speak again. A slightly unsettling thought, but they very well might not. Surely, even he could tell from their time together the night before that they were undeniably over.

Josh would go back to Washington. And he'd probably eventually figure out that Iris was a girl. One who obviously liked him.

Morgan still found it difficult to picture them together – to imagine being replaced by the woman. But really, from the very little she'd seen of Iris, Morgan suspected she'd be good for Josh. She might even make him happy, which Morgan had failed to do. That's what Josh needed. Someone proper and tame.

Morgan forced her thoughts from bitter and jealous to happy and hopeful for the two of them. She had to face the fact that she might have to learn to live in a world without Josh. Because when push came to shove, it was Trevor who was her future.

As if merely the thought of Trevor summoned him, he was there next to her. Morgan leaned into him and knew she could never be happier than she was right now.

Chapter 36

In Which Josh Changes His Mind
Friday, August 21, 1998

Josh stared at the clock on the nightstand between the beds. It was after nine and the minutes were flipping over one by one on the ancient device. He wanted to call Iris, but it was only four there. Quitting time wasn't for another hour. She would still be working . . .

And wondering if she'll ever see me again.

Now, he believed she would.

Josh got up and went to the balcony door. Sliding it open, he stepped out into the evening air. Even though it was late summer, the sun was still up.

He had lost Morgan. The inevitability of it crashed upon his soul like relentless waves battering the coast nearby.

As he stepped back inside, another minute flipped over.

He went into the bathroom to get water. He supposed he could have called room service for something to drink, but he just wanted to have a sip of water.

His reflection startled him; forlorn was written all over his face.

"So," he asked his reflection, "is this the end?"

He lifted his hands to the level of his ears and made speaking motions with them.

"Are you going to allow her to get away with that *merde*, boy?" asked the hand representing a devil at his left ear.

"You aren't *allowing* her to do anything. She's a grown woman, she has made her choice. It's time you made yours," the angel hand said.

"I can't say I blame her. Were you listening to what he said? 'I feel obligated to marry you because we had sex.' Really, Josh?" Devil Hand said in a mocking tone. "Did you

274

tell her that on your first Christmas together? Hell no, or she would have walked out the door and you'd have been taking a cold shower."

"He allowed his lust to overrule common sense," Angel Hand said. "He has since realized his mistake and was trying to correct it."

"Josh, my boy, you need to go to that party. You need to tell her to come back here with you and remind her why she loves you so much."

"You know she won't do that," Angel Hand said. "She has a boyfriend."

"Pfft. Okay, so go and beat the ever-living *merde* out of the bum and then bring her back here," Devil Hand said. "I'll put my money on mechanic muscles over limp lawyer limbs any day."

"You said it right there – lawyer," Angel Hand said. "He would sue Josh down to his boxers and have him arrested for indecent exposure. Josh would never be free again."

"So, what's your suggestion, pretty boy?" Devil Hand asked. "That he sits here and feels sorry for himself in a cold shower then goes to bed?"

"He should stay here, book a flight back *home* to Washington, and give Iris a call," Angel Hand said. "But he's not going to listen to common sense. So, what you should do, Joshua, is go to the party, get to Morgan, and apologize. Tell her you weren't thinking straight. Tell her you want to marry her because you love her, totally and completely. Tell her you'll make her happier than anyone else can."

"I liked the idea of coming back here for wild make-up sex better," Devil Hand said, "but that might get the same result."

"What happens afterward is up to Morgan and Joshua," Angel Hand said. "But you better get going – now."

Josh balled his fists, shutting off any further commentary, and thrust them in the air. "Yeah, yeah. I'll do that."

"Eye of the Tiger" was running through his mind as he grabbed the green button-down shirt. He stared at it then tossed it into the bathroom wastebasket, choosing a blue shirt instead.

Having decided, Josh pulled the phone book out of the nightstand drawer. He flipped to the back to locate a cab company. He called Friendly Cab, who told him a driver would be there in about ten minutes.

Josh steeled his resolve and slipped the half-heart necklace over his head before going down to wait for the cab.

When it arrived, Josh climbed into the back and directed the cabby to take him to the Shackleford house.

"Lot of folks heading to that address tonight," the driver said.

"I guess cabs will be busy after the party too."

"Sure. I bet some folks just didn't want to hassle with the parking."

"I might need a ride back to the hotel. How late do you run?" Josh asked.

"We run twenty-four-seven. Just call the dispatcher."

At the Shackleford home, Josh paid the driver and gave a generous tip. Signs at the main entrance directed partygoers to go around back.

At least some things don't change.

Bob sat like the big orange bug he was named for among the luxury automobiles parked on the grounds and down the street. The subcompact did not look like it belonged. Josh felt out of place here, much like he had the first time he'd driven Bob to Morgan's place.

That day, he had decided to stay, for Morgan, instead of driving away. The same motive pushed him forward now.

The night air was warm and there was no moon. The decorators had hung colored paper lanterns around the patio out back. A dozen people stood smoking and joking and sipping beer from the long-neck bottles they held.

276

A quick scan did not locate Morgan, as he had hoped. Talking to her outside would have been much easier with fewer people and less noise.

The outside door leading into the basement stood open at the bottom of the stairs. Josh faced them, took a deep breath, and plunged into the chaos.

During the years of his friendship with Shack, he had been to several parties at the Shackleford home. But the decorations in the room far exceeded anything he had experienced before. Two impressions came to his mind. Something big was going on, and the feeling that he clearly didn't belong here was reinforced.

If it wasn't for Morgan, he would have turned around and walked away. Across from where he entered hung a huge banner proclaiming the "Balloon-free Birthday Celebration for Trevor and Morgan."

Trevor and Morgan. Do I need any more evidence?

Apparently, the answer was yes, because he pushed on into the crowd. The main lights were dim and purple decorative lights hung around the periphery of the room. Somehow, he didn't think that was Trevor's favorite color.

Beneath the banner, a fountain splashed punch. Red plastic cups filled with the liquid lined the table. The punch was, of course, purple, and doubtless spiked. Someone had gone all out for Morgan.

What did Josh have to offer her? A ball cap, a green button-down shirt, neither of which he had worn, and a few good memories.

Now wait a minute. Love can't be measured in material things.

Josh pushed on through the crowd – mostly residents of Bathurst, but very few of whom he recognized. Had he been gone that long? This was where he grew up, but it was becoming less and less his home with each passing minute.

The big-screen TV in the main room had Baywatch playing. Josh ignored it and headed for the room with the home theater at the far end of the basement. Inside, five guests watched the Toronto Blue Jays playing the Los Angeles Angels. Morgan wouldn't be watching the game. Still, he scanned for her face by the flickering light of the projection.

Ordinarily, Josh would have watched the game, but he was on a mission and the clock was ticking. Leaving the theater, he spotted her at the far side of the main room. Morgan stood next to a dark-haired man, who was clearly taller than her – and Josh. The man could only be Trevor. She didn't show any sign of having seen Josh.

Josh had never really seen his rival much growing up. By the time he and Shack had become friends, Trevor was off to college and law school. He was no longer the skinny older brother of his friend. Josh doubted those limbs were as limp as Devil Hand had led him to believe.

He froze in place, watching the two of them. It was like watching a good romance movie without the sound. Their body language spoke more than words could say.

It's clear now; they're in love.

He should have listened to Angel Hand and stayed at the hotel.

But then Trevor held up a finger and said something to Morgan. She nodded and began moving to the center of the room as Trevor stepped away. Morgan was having difficulty getting through the crowd.

This is it! This is my last chance.

Josh began to weave and dodge his way through the crowd on a path that took him toward her.

"Hey, down in front! You're blocking C.J.'s boobs!" The voice was Shack's.

"Sorry, I'll be out of your way in a second," Josh said.

"Dumbass! You did come." Shack jumped out of the chair, holding onto the remote and his beer, but summarily dumping Mel onto the floor.

"Hey, dumbass, you could have warned me," Mel said wiping the beer off her blouse.

"Sorry, babe. I'd have caught you, but my hands were full," Shack said.

Mel got off the floor and took the chair that Shack had vacated. "Good luck getting your seat back, ya big jock."

Shack laughed and caught Josh before he could get away. "Come on buddy, let me introduce you to some girls."

"No thanks, dude. I came to talk to Morgan," Josh said.

Shack tossed the remote to Mel. "Hang on to this for me, okay, babe?"

He didn't wait for her to reply. Guiding Josh with the now empty hand, he said, "That girl over there, the blond in the pink shirt, is Jennifer. She's a bit older than you, but that means she's more experienced, if you know what I mean."

"No, really, Shack. I need to talk to Morgan," Josh said.

"I think Morg . . . an is around somewhere. What about Felicia? She's that dark-haired girl over by the fountain. She just turned eighteen and I hear she's a wildcat. She'd probably wear you out."

"I saw Morgan over there with your brother."

"Hah! What a dumbass. I thought he had taste in women. At least you were smart enough to dump her," Shack said.

"Really, I just want to talk to Morgan before it's too late."

"Too late for what? What about that black-haired girl over there in the black slacks? She goes to college here but has a boyfriend at a college somewhere else. She ain't interested in me, but maybe you could convince her to forget that other guy."

"Dumbass, that's my sister. We were sitting with you at the café this afternoon," Josh said.

"Oh, right," Shack said and chuckled nervously. "Sorry. I'm just trying to help you out."

"You could help me by being like Gretzky and get me in position."

"Ah, got you. Hold on a second and I'll play center, even though I normally play the wings." He turned to hand his bottle of beer to Mel.

Josh took the opportunity to escape his attention and move toward Morgan.

Too many things began to happen at once.

Someone raised the lights, and the DJ said, "Let's make some room in the center for Trevor and Morgan." The catering staff circulated through the crowd with flutes of champagne. People moved away from the center, making the crowds that much denser.

Trevor's parents and Morgan's parents entered the basement – with Trevor.

Morgan's eyes locked onto Josh's. Her eyes went wide and she started toward him.

Trevor said above the crowd, "Morgan, darling, meet me in the center, I have a special surprise for you."

Morgan paused as Rab reached Josh's side and put a hand on his shoulder.

"Josh, no. It's too late. Let the events run their course," Rab said.

Josh stopped and stood with his arm around his sister. His heart was about to break, and he needed Rab's strength.

Chapter 37

In Which There is More Than One Kind of Love
Friday, August 21, 1998

It wasn't supposed to happen like this.

Morgan stood frozen in the center of the room by the pool table, her eyes wide and glued to Josh. What in the world was he doing here? Rab stood beside him, her hand on his shoulder, expression unreadable.

Josh's expression wasn't unreadable. Morgan was sure it mirrored her own. Shock. Fear. The knowledge that heartbreak was only seconds away.

Morgan pulled her eyes from Josh and Rab and turned in Trevor's direction. Faces blurred, but she caught a glimpse of her parents standing by the basement entrance. Trevor's parents too.

There was no denying what was about to happen. There was no fleeing either. Her heart pounded so hard she knew she would pass out.

Morgan averted her gaze from everyone to stare at the floor. And then time froze.

They say that just before a person dies, their life flashes before their eyes. Morgan wasn't dying, but her life as she knew it was about to change one way or the other.

Morgan was back at another party, feeling quite out of place and drunk, having just announced her plans of driving to Seattle to the entire crowd after an ill-fated song ending. A guy in a baseball cap had come over and asked to drive to Seattle with her. She had never been so embarrassed in her life.

Then Morgan was at Cal's garage, where she was to pick up this Joshua Hampton fellow – a virtual stranger she had somehow ended up agreeing to cross the continent with. The sight of his dingy gray socks hanging out the window of his broken-down truck had been forever seared into her mind.

The flashes continued, merging into one big collage. Josh checking Zinger's oil. Josh snoozing in the passenger seat as she drove. The freedom of the open road. Getting lost on their very first day into the trip. Josh feeding her fries as she drove and accidentally sticking one up her nose.

Morgan and Josh bickering. Morgan and Josh laughing and joking around. Morgan realizing what a truly good person he was. So serious, steadfast, and loyal. He was there when she had her breakdown over her late friend Kendra. He was there when she crashed her car. She was there when he visited the Quebec Vietnam Memorial, and then after his dreams were crushed when he was disqualified from joining the Marines.

They had made it to Seattle. Together. Their celebration had been short – a hug and some cheering on the side of the road. But then there was the ferry ride. The visit to the Space Needle. The trip home. Their first Christmas together.

And then nothing.

Josh was gone.

Morgan was sitting in the office she worked in. It was the day she first laid eyes on Trevor. He walked into the room and surveyed everyone in it, his eyes landing on her. With that one look he'd claimed her as his own, and she him.

Their connection was magnetic. There was no hemming and hawing or decisions to be made – it just was.

Morgan was in Trevor's office on the leather sofa, having stayed late after their shifts. They were working on some legal document or another – heads or hands touching more often than not.

Morgan and Trevor were out at their favorite restaurant, sometimes surrounded by friends, other times alone. Drinks and merriment were never in short supply.

Then they were at his place, curled up on the couch. Nights in with him were a treat, not a chore. A movie was chosen and played in the background while they talked and talked and talked. If they ever saw the ending of a movie, Morgan couldn't recall.

Morgan stood on the balcony of Trevor's condo, wearing one of his shirts, looking out at the ocean. He came up behind her and wrapped his arms around her.

Talk of the future was never scary or annoying. It was exciting. Morgan couldn't wait to live her life with Trevor.

She hadn't realized she'd closed her eyes, but they suddenly popped open and she was back in the basement of the Shackleford house.

She knew what she wanted. But why-oh-why did this have to go down here and now?

Trevor was right in front of her. He took her hand and smiled that slightly crooked smile – the one reserved only for her. It always would be. Looking into his eyes, so confident, so full of life and love for her, Morgan relaxed enough that she could hear the slight murmur of the crowd. Her vision cleared and she glanced toward the stairs as Trevor slowly bent down to rest on one knee.

His parents stood there with their arms around each other, beaming. Her dad's smile outshone them all. Morgan's mom's smile was a bit tremulous and her eyes glistened.

Trevor squeezed her hand and she only had eyes for him as he opened the ring box and cleared his throat.

"The first time I saw you, I knew we belonged together. You shine brighter than any woman I've ever met. Your zest for life, your creative soul, and your beauty both inside and out are beyond compare."

Morgan's eyes prickled, tears building.

"Morgan Parker, will you please marry me and make me the happiest man alive?"

She choked on a sob. She wanted to – needed to – say yes.

But she couldn't. She could never hurt Josh like this. She had no choice but to mutter an apology and pray for Trevor's understanding.

The crowd had gone completely silent as Morgan took a deep breath that echoed across the room and prepared to say the words.

Just before she did, her gaze slid over to Josh.

His eyes were also shimmering, but he was smiling. And that was no fake smile. Slightly wistful, but mostly happy. For her. He nodded ever so slightly, and the breath Morgan had been holding exploded.

"Yes!" Tears blinded her as she turned back to Trevor. "Yes, I will marry you!"

The room burst into applause and shouts of congratulations. Trevor barely had time to slip the ring onto her finger and kiss her before they were overwhelmed with well-wishers.

The champagned flowed. Hugs, kisses, claps on the back all blurred together. Morgan's mother was sobbing by the time she made her way to them. Morgan hugged her fiercely and shed more tears of her own.

Her dad held her so tightly she thought he'd never let go. "Congratulations, my girl."

"Thanks, Dad."

The room quieted a bit as her future in-laws raised their glasses in a toast; the happy couple kissed, then chaos resumed.

Morgan felt like the luckiest girl alive.

Throughout everything, Morgan and Trevor remained with hands clasped, occasionally stealing secret looks at each other.

Then Mel attacked her and captured her in an awkward bear hug.

"Man, I can't believe how drunk I am. Did this really happen?"

"Yes." Morgan laughed. "I'll tell you all about it tomorrow."

Shack turned from pounding on his brother's back and looked at Morgan like he'd just realized who Trevor had proposed to.

"Damn. You're going to be my sister-in-law," he said.

"Damn. You're going to be in for a world of pain," Morgan replied.

Shack threw his hands in the air. "Come on then." He pulled her in for a hug and planted a kiss on the top of her head.

"Thanks for not trying to feel me up," Morgan said, shocked at this rare display of affection.

"Nothing to feel up," Shack said, grinning.

"You ass," Morgan said and laughed.

Shack ducked to avoid her punch and there stood Josh.

"Hi," Morgan said.

"Hi," Josh said. "Congratulations." He turned to Trevor, who was watching the exchange. "To both of you."

"Thanks, man," Trevor said, and extended his hand.

Josh shook it then addressed Morgan. "May I kiss the bride-to-be?"

"Of course," Morgan said.

Josh leaned in and pecked her cheek. Before he pulled away, he whispered, "I am very happy for you, Morgan."

Morgan beamed and tears filled her eyes once more. "Thank you. So much."

Rab was next in line. Morgan had never, ever seen her cry before. Which only made her own tears cascade over again.

They laughed and hugged, and Rab once again begged Morgan not to name their first child Mary. Morgan once again promised, denying all culpability for her parents' choice of the name for her sister.

The lights dimmed and the party music resumed as hoards of people continued to approach them with congratulations and best wishes.

Morgan caught sight of Josh heading toward the exit. She handed Trevor her champagne glass and whispered in his ear, "I've got to say goodbye."

He smiled and kissed her. "I know. Hurry. He's getting away."

Morgan kissed him once more for good measure then took off after Josh.

It was impossible to make any sort of decent progress through the throngs of people. Frustrated, Morgan slipped off her sandals that kept tripping her up and resorted to elbowing her way through – keeping in mind that some people were shorter than others and their faces were sometimes where she expected their sides to be. She didn't want to repeat the wedding gaffe.

Finally, she burst out of the basement and into the backyard. She scanned all directions and her heart plummeted.

"Josh!" she yelled into the night as she ran around to the front of the house, sandals in hand, bare feet slipping on the grass.

"I'm right here."

And so he was. Morgan skidded to a halt and caught her breath.

"You're leaving?" she asked.

"Yep. Just waiting for a cab."

"No. I mean, you're leaving Bathurst, aren't you?"

Josh nodded.

"Are you really okay with what happened?"

"I really am," he said and gave a low chuckle. "You know, we could have saved ourselves a lot of trouble if I'd have just seen you two together like that earlier."

"Like what?"

"You'd have to be blind to not see how much you love each other. That's real love."

"Josh . . ."

"No. It's okay," he said. "We should have known from the start. We had to work too hard at . . . everything. You're where you belong now."

"And where do you belong?" Morgan asked.

"I think you probably knew that before I did."

"Iris?"

"Yes. I only hope she'll have me after all this."

"She will if she has any common sense at all," Morgan said.

A cab pulled up and honked its horn.

"That's probably for me," Josh said.

"Wait." Morgan slid her phone out of her purse and took the necklace with his name on it from the bottom. "Take this."

"What for?" he asked.

"Because," Morgan said, "we're not through."

Josh's eyebrows flew to the top of his head and she laughed.

"Hear me out," she said. "This wasn't a wasted trip. I don't think we belong together as a couple, but I don't think it was just closure that we needed, either."

She took his hand and put the necklace into it, closing his fist around it. "For the life of me, I couldn't figure out when I stopped loving you. And that's because I never did. It's just a different sort of love than I'd thought it was."

"So you're saying you want to be friends?" Josh said a bit sarcastically.

"More than friends," Morgan said sternly. "I can't picture my life without you in it somewhere."

Josh thought for a moment then smiled. "I agree." He reached under his shirt and produced the other half of the necklace that had Morgan's name on it. Pulling the chain over his head, he handed it to her and said, "What now?"

Morgan looked down at the necklace and smiled. "Now we keep in touch." She jerked her head up and gave him a sharp look. "And I don't mean a stinking card at Christmas or something like that. I really mean it, Josh. You're important to me."

"And you to me." He grinned. "How about I do you one better? I'll keep in touch with Shack too. That way I can make sure this Trevor guy is treating you right."

Morgan laughed. "You'd be better off talking to Rab if you want the real story. I tell you, Shack's growing on me, but he's definitely a few cards short of a deck."

Josh laughed too. "Agreed." He glanced at the cab. "I do need to get going."

Morgan threw her arms, shoes and all, around Josh and hugged him hard. "I wish you all the happiness in the world."

"Right back at you."

Josh pulled away and walked off into the night.

Morgan sighed happily, knowing she'd see him again – knowing he wasn't leaving her. He was just leaving.

She watched until the cab disappeared, then headed back inside to her future.

Chapter 38

In Which Josh Takes a Different Road
Sunday, August 23, 1998

The Air Canada 747 descended toward SeaTac Airport. From the first-class section, Josh watched the lights of the Settle metropolitan area glitter below. The interstate gleamed like a ribbon of Sunday night traffic. Out in the Sound, a ferry moved its load of passengers and vehicles toward distant Bremerton. Josh's anticipation grew.

Iris should already be at the airport.

As the airplane touched down, Josh was glad to be back on the ground. He decided he wasn't a fan of air travel, but realized that times were changing and he would likely need to fly more often in the future.

When they reached the terminal and started to deplane, Josh pulled his duffel from the overhead compartment. He hadn't checked it so he wouldn't have to wait for baggage at the airport.

Unfortunately, arriving passengers had to clear customs. But with nothing to declare and an American passport, the wait was minimal.

Iris was waiting for him at the arrival concourse. She was wearing black culottes and a white blouse with a floral print. As soon as he saw her, Josh picked up his pace and when their eyes met, she hurried to him and wrapped him in an embrace.

There was no hesitation. Their lips met for a passionate kiss. They stood for an extended moment as weary passengers parted around them as though they were a rock in a stream.

When they finally came up for air, Iris said, "Welcome home. I missed you so much."

"I missed you, too," Josh said. "Come on, let's get out of traffic."

Josh took her hand with his free hand, and they left the concourse.

"Did you really miss me?" Iris asked.

"I called you every day," Josh said.

"Did you bring home any extra bags?"

Josh hefted his duffel. "Nope. Just the one I took."

"Good. I'm parked this way," Iris said and pointed with her free hand.

They crossed the sky bridge to the parking garage and took the escalator up to the level where she had parked Old Blue.

Iris offered Josh the keys.

"Are you good to drive?" Josh asked. "I managed to sleep some on the flight, but it has been a long day."

When Iris unlocked his door, Josh made a mental note to get her a set of keys to Old Blue. He climbed into the truck on the passenger side and picked up the Bathurst High School ballcap. Josh tucked it behind the seat. He wanted nothing between him and Iris.

Iris navigated the ramps of the garage and paid for parking before heading to the interstate.

"Let's take the ferry home," Josh said.

"Taking the interstate is faster," Iris said. "You're not going to let that bridge spook you just because it's dark, are you?"

"Nothing like that. Taking the ferry will give us some time to talk and there is something I want to do."

"I've got you covered."

"If I doze off, just let me snooze," Josh said.

Once they merged with traffic on Interstate 5, Iris asked, "What did you want to tell me?"

"I'll start with apologizing for leaving you the way I did."

"Did you get that matter resolved?"

Josh merely nodded his head. Although they had talked since Friday, they had avoided the subject of Morgan. He felt that returning to Silverdale should be answer enough.

"Then don't be sorry you went," Iris said. "I hated to take the risk, but I knew you needed to go. A lack of resolution could have overshadowed any relationship we tried."

"You're right."

"There is an old saying, 'If you love someone, set them free. If they come back to you, then they are yours.'"

"And if they don't?" Josh asked.

"Then they were never meant to be," Iris said, "but you came back. That's enough for me."

"I can accept that," Josh said and nodded off to sleep.

***

A bump woke Josh up.

"Where are we?" he asked and looked around.

"We just boarded the ferry," Iris said.

"How long was I asleep?"

"Counting the wait for the ferry, about an hour and a half."

"You should have woken me when we got here," Josh said. "How much was the fare?"

"You were sleeping so soundly I didn't want to wake you. I covered it."

"You shouldn't have to pay to give me a ride home."

"You can pay me back by taking me to dinner at Osaka tomorrow night," Iris said. "Including all the sushi and sashimi I want."

"Sounds like a bargain to me," Josh said. The food could get expensive, but a night with Iris was worth it.

"The bad news is, we missed the last ferry to Bremerton," Iris said.

"Is there good news?"

"We are on the last ferry to Bainbridge Island, and we have a front-row seat."

Josh saw that Old Blue was parked close to the safety chain at the front end of the ferry.

"You could have turned around and taken the highway back," he said.

"I could have, but you wanted to ride the ferry and I dozed a little while we were waiting. We can probably nap some more during the ride."

"Come with me. I want to go up to the balcony," Josh said as he got out of the truck, taking the Bathurst High School cap with him.

Iris got out of the truck and tugged on a Mariners hoodie she grabbed from the back of the seat.

They climbed the stairs to the passenger deck and went out to one of the aft balconies. Below them, the boarding ramp was lifted, and dockworkers cast off the lines.

With a surge of engines, the ferry pulled away from the dock, leaving a luminescent wake.

Josh offered Iris his arm. They huddled together by the side rail, watching the lights of Seattle recede.

When the Space Needle became visible, Josh raised the cap and looked at it. "Well, it's time for you to go."

With that, he flung the hat overboard like a Frisbee.

"What did you do that for?" Iris asked.

"It represented many things and many connections. But mostly my connection to Bathurst and . . . her."

"But did you have to throw it away?"

"It is fitting that it goes this way – to join its brother at the bottom of the Sound," Josh said. "I love this area, I love my new life, and . . ."

"And?"

"And I love you. I have almost since I first met you, but I just couldn't see it."

"I'm so happy you finally did."

"I have one more offering for the deep," Josh said.

He dug into his pocket where he had put the half-heart and chain. He was going to toss it into the Sound too, but stopped. Morgan had returned this as a reminder of their special friendship. While he had yet to figure out what that exactly meant, now was not the time to dwell on it.

Instead, he removed a loonie he had left from his visit. With a sidearm swing, he tossed the coin toward the cap, which had already sunk out of sight. "Forsaking all others."

"What was that?" Iris asked.

"I said 'forsaking all others.'"

"That's a line from wedding vows."

"You're right," Josh said and smiled at her.

"What are you trying to say?" Iris turned and faced him with hope and confusion competing for the right of expression.

"It means I've put any notion of being with Morgan behind me. I have been far too foolish when my future has been right in front of me for a long time."

"Josh . . ."

He raised a finger to his lips. "Shh. Let me finish."

She looked down at him, her eyes shimmering. Hope and happiness were clearly winning.

"I know we talked about getting to know each other better, but we've worked side by side for almost a year. I think it's high time we started doing things as a couple and talking about the future. Our future, if you agree?"

"Yes, oh yes, oh yes!" Iris said and wrapped her arms around him.

Josh leaned in for a kiss. They remained entwined and Iris buried her face in his shoulder. Happy tears dampened his jacket.

This is true love.

Josh stood there holding her, the scent of her hair mingling with the salty tang of the air. He reflected on the winding road that had brought him here, to this woman, to this moment. Some events were unlikely, and some events were inevitable, but every event and every choice had brought him to this woman who, he believed, would be the love of his life.

Josh had a glimpse of what the future could be when she performed the tea ceremony – for him. For the first time in many years, Josh was fully at peace.

After climbing back down the narrow stairs, they walked hand in hand back to Old Blue and their future – together.

Epilogue

Tuesday, December 25, 2012

The Hampton house sat on a spacious lot on the edge of Silverdale, Washington. On this particular Christmas afternoon, the green-shingled bungalow was covered with a thin layer of white.

Large flakes continued to fall as a black SUV navigated the mostly deserted streets and pulled into the driveway next to a silver sedan and an ancient pickup named Old Blue.

Inside, the living room curtain was pulled open at the sound of the vehicle's arrival.

"They're here!" shouted twelve-year-old Bobby.

His father came from the kitchen where he and his wife were tending to Christmas dinner.

"That can't be them," Josh said. "It's too early."

"It is them! Uncle Trevor's getting presents out of the back and Aunt Morgan's almost at the door."

Iris entered the living room and slid an arm around her husband's waist. "Open the door then, Bobby."

Iris kissed Josh and winked, then went down the hall to let their ten-year-old daughter Miko know her unofficial aunt and uncle had arrived.

Josh joined his son at the door as Morgan entered in a whirlwind, brushing snow off her hair and jacket.

"Bobby!"

The young boy flew into her arms for a hug. Morgan tried to pick him up, but grunted and abandoned the attempt.

"Either you've grown a lot in the last year, or I'm just getting too old for this."

"I grew two inches," Bobby declared proudly.

"Come in," Josh said, making room for Morgan to remove her shoes. "I can't believe you're early. I don't remember the last time you were ever . . . not late."

Morgan laughed. "Surprised me too. Especially with this weather. But everything went smoothly at the airport for once."

Josh held the door open for Trevor, who was laden down with gifts.

"I like the rental," Josh said. "How does it drive?"

"It's all right," Trevor said, handing a stack of presents to Josh. "Better than a car in this weather, that's for sure."

"I can't remember the last time it snowed here for Christmas," Morgan said.

"Four years ago," Josh said.

"That's right," Trevor said. "But this has been mostly rain since we left the airport. It just turned to flakes when we came into Silverdale. It's very, very white back home in Toronto."

"It started snowing half an hour ago. Miko and I want to go make snowmen," Bobby said as Trevor snatched him up for a hug.

"Well, I'm not sure you'll have enough for snowmen, but you never know."

Trevor set the boy down, and Iris and Miko entered from the hall. Unlike her older brother, Miko hovered behind her mother and peered out at their guests.

Iris ushered her forward. "Why don't you go say hi and help with those presents?"

Outgoing Miko was not, but helpful she was. With a task to be completed, she approached Aunt Morgan and Uncle Trevor, received her hugs, then set to helping her brother arrange the gifts under the tree.

"I'll be back," Trevor said.

Josh raised a brow. "Just getting the overnight bags?" he asked.

Trevor's guilty look was the only reply Josh needed. "Hang on. I'll get my coat and help. And you," he said, wagging a finger at Morgan, "will get your talking-to later."

Morgan laughed and held up a hand. "Oh, shush. We have no kids to spoil, so you have to share yours. Besides, Trevor's the one with the paying job. You can give him heck about the presents while you're out there and save me the headache."

"You're the shopper," Trevor said and ducked out the door, avoiding Morgan's whack.

Iris only sighed and shook her head, yet she was chuckling.

"I simply love your kimonos," Morgan said as she removed her coat to reveal her outfit of jeans and a Christmas sweater. "They look so cozy yet fashionable."

"Thank you," Iris said. "It's a family tradition, and you two have missed out on it for too long. Perhaps Santa will fix that this year."

Morgan grinned and joined the kids at the tree where they were shaking presents.

Josh and Trevor came in through the front door, arms loaded with more presents, just as two little fluff balls came slinking around the corner from the hall.

"What's this?" Morgan said. "Cats?"

"Yes. The newest additions to our family. The black one is Ochi and the orange one is Obi."

"Oh, they're so cuddly," Morgan squealed as Obi brushed against her and she stroked the cat's fur. "No trouble with your asthma, Josh?"

"Nope. It hasn't been a problem . . . well, ever, really. Certainly not since I tried to enlist."

"I don't see any luggage there," Iris said.

Josh narrowed his eyes at Morgan. "It seems we need to make one more trip outside yet."

Morgan stuck her tongue out at him and returned to petting the cat as the men left to retrieve the rest of the cargo. She looked up at Iris once they'd left.

"You don't really mind, do you? It's mostly little stuff, but I just can't help myself."

Iris smiled. "It is a bit much, but it makes the children happy. We'll work on it next year."

Morgan grinned.

Once the packages were all inside, including the all-important overnight bags, Morgan and Trevor were shown to their room and given a chance to freshen up before presents.

The children were given permission to start opening theirs and had made decent progress by the time they returned.

"Children, thank your aunt and uncle, Miko in Japanese and Bobby in French," Josh said.

"*Domo arigato*," Miko said with a bow.

"*Merde*," Bobby said.

Morgan burst out laughing.

"I believe the word you're looking for is '*merci*,' son," Josh said.

"But you say it all the time, Dad," Bobby said.

"But not when I'm thanking someone."

"Oh, then *merci*, Aunt Morgan and Uncle Trevor."

"You are very welcome, kids," Morgan said. Turning to Iris, she asked, "Can we help in the kitchen?"

Josh laughed. "You can help by staying out of the kitchen."

"Hey, I've gotten better over the years. Not great, but better . . ."

"Keep her out of the kitchen," Trevor said.

Morgan punched him in the arm. "We like eating out," she said in her defense.

"Dinner is nearly ready," Iris said. "It can sit while we open presents."

Morgan and Trevor had brought hostess gifts of crackers, cheese, dainties, and wine in lieu of wrapped gifts for the adults, but they each received a gift to open.

"It's so pretty," Morgan cooed as she lifted her kimono from the tissue paper. Violet with dainty embroidered birds.

Trevor's was dark blue with a chrysanthemum. "I think we'll need to freshen up again before we do much more."

"Agreed," Morgan said. "Thank you," she said to Iris and Josh.

Once they were all clad in kimonos, Iris set up a laptop in the living room while the children showed off their favorite gifts.

Miko's favorite was an art set that she wasn't so much showing off as playing quietly with. Bobby was fascinated with a model car assembly kit.

"Hey," Josh said, noticing the box. "Is that . . ."

"Kind of," Morgan said. "It was impossible to find a Pontiac 6000 with two doors, so I had to settle for four. And it's more black than gray, but that's as close to Zinger as I could get."

"What's a Zinger?" Bobby asked.

"It's a car that Morgan used to have," Josh said. "A mighty fine car at that."

"Dad's teaching me how to drive," Bobby told Morgan. "He lets me practice at the garage."

"He lets you drive a car?" Morgan turned to Josh as Bobby nodded. "What the . . . heck, Hampton? *You* are doing something illegal?"

"It's not illegal," Josh said. "It's on private property. No one's around when we do it and he barely moves the car."

Morgan shook her head and grinned. "So, has he taught you the most important thing about driving yet, Bobby?"

"He told me to always keep my eyes on the road," Bobby recited.

Morgan howled. "You *are* teaching him properly," she said to Josh.

"Why is that funny?" Bobby asked.

"It's a good lesson," Josh told him, "but it was also a thing Morgan and I used to say to each other when we were kids. It was our polite way of changing the topic of conversation."

"It was not," Morgan said. "It was a polite way of saying shut up."

"What?" Josh sputtered. "No it wasn't."

"It was when I said it."

"Kids," Trevor said, addressing Morgan and Josh as he and Iris rolled their eyes, "Iris has the video call ready."

Everyone gathered around the screen and moments later, Rab's face appeared.

"Merry Christmas," Rab said and adjusted the view on her end to include her husband David and their nine-year-old daughter Theresa.

Christmas greetings were exchanged all around, but soon the children became bored and returned to their presents.

"What's new in Bathurst?" Josh asked his sister.

"In Bathurst?" Rab gave a mock are-you-kidding-me look and laughed. "Well, I suppose you've heard about Shack and Mel."

"Shack and Mel? What happened to them?" Josh asked.

"I was just about to tell him," Morgan said, turning to Josh. "They got married yesterday."

"Seriously? Their kids are practically grown up," Josh said. "Why would they get married now?"

Rab laughed. "Because they're Shack and Mel. Anyway, I guess it goes to show they really do love each other. They didn't get married because they had to, that's for sure."

"I didn't even know they were dating," Josh said.

"They weren't, half the time," Morgan said. "But to each their own, right? They bought a house together over the summer and I guess the domestication thing just stuck."

"How old are their kids?" Josh asked. "It's been so long since I've seen them."

"Kayla's fifteen and Edward's thirteen. Kayla is as sweet as ever, but that Edward . . ." Rab lowered her voice and moved closer to the screen. "I think Shack Jr. would have been a more appropriate name."

"Yikes," Josh said.

"Yikes indeed. So what's new out your way?"

"Kittens," Josh said and called for the kids to wrangle the cats to show Rab.

After that was complete, the cats took off and talk turned to Morgan's art, Trevor's success at building his own law firm in Toronto, and the Mayans' prediction of the end of the world that had not come to fruition.

They signed off with e-hugs and e-kisses, which every adult in the room still found strange, and headed to the dining room.

Everyone helped bring the dishes of food from the kitchen. Wine and sparkling grape juice was poured, a blessing was said, and then they feasted.

After dinner, as was the Hampton/Shackleford tradition, Josh and Morgan settled in armchairs in the living room by the crackling fire and sipped on glasses of brandy while Trevor and Iris cleaned up.

"Why brandy?" Josh asked and made a face as he took a sip.

"You ask that every year. Because that's what they drink in the movies after Christmas dinner," Morgan said.

"But what movie did you get this from?"

"I don't know. All of them. Stop complaining. Our spouses are thoughtful enough to give us this time every year and we're not supposed to be bickering."

"Isn't that what we do best?" Josh asked.

"Well, it is one of my favorite things," Morgan said, "but let me break the mold for a second. Have I ever told you how lucky I feel to have you and Iris and your children as part of my life?"

"Are you drunk?" Josh kidded.

"Hardly. I'm serious, though."

"Yes, I know. And I feel the same way about you and Trevor."

"It's still kind of weird when I come back here to Silverdale. It's kind of like turning back time. I feel like a kid again. Oh, speaking of kids, did I tell you Damian is going to have one?"

"No," Josh said. "You told me he got married. When are they due?"

"Not until summer. I just found out. We're going to stop by and see them when we leave tomorrow."

"Are they still in Seattle then?"

"Yeah, they moved back to be closer to Lisa after Randy left her. She's not doing well, health-wise. That Randy . . ." Morgan shook her head. "But that's all in the past. And that's kind of what I was talking about. Every time I come back here, I relive our first trip. You know, the summer of '95."

"It was a life changing year," Josh agreed. "It was like the first link in a chain of events and decisions that brought us here today. Without the trip, we may still have found our respective spouses, but without our friendship."

"It would have been a lot easier if we had just been able to figure out who we were to each other to begin with, wouldn't it?"

Josh laughed. "I definitely could have done without all the drama."

"Yeah, well, you were the cause of more than half of it."

"Says you. But we can't deny the importance of the summer of '95. It was the beginning of all this."

Morgan and Josh toasted and sat back in their chairs.

Soon, Trevor and Iris appeared, followed by two sleepy children.

Morgan and Trevor moved to the loveseat and the Hamptons gathered round as Trevor read the Night Before Christmas. On any other day, the kids would claim they'd outgrown such a tradition. But Christmas was special.

As eyelids grew heavy inside, snow continued to fall outside. The town of Silverdale glistened and snowflakes sparkled with what could only be Christmas magic. Out of all the homes with cozy lamps burning in windows, and out of all the families gathered round fireplaces, one would be hard pressed to find a happier home than the one where these two families merged.

And yes, they all lived happily ever after.

The End

About the Authors

Canadian, multi-genre author Kerri Davidson currently lives in Elbow, Saskatchewan with her husband Travis. She has lived in numerous other locations throughout Saskatchewan and Manitoba. She used to list all the communities in her bio but has finally run out of room.

A reluctant vegetarian, she loves vodka, potato chips, all animals, and some humans.

Author website: KerriDavidsonBooks.com
Twitter: @bagoflettuce

Mark Gelinas was born in New England but didn't stay there long. As an Air Force dependent and while in the Navy, he lived throughout the United States and Canada. During his Navy career, he enjoyed three tours as an instructor. This prepared him for later work as a technical writer.

While enlisted, he wrote shorter pieces for various magazines. In 2005, NaNoWriMo showed him he could write longer pieces.

Mark now lives in Georgia with his wife, Kate, his youngest daughter, and cats. His writing career continues.

Twitter: @Elderac

Bee and Badger Books

CPSIA information can be obtained
at www.ICGtesting.com
Printed in the USA
BVHW050800050123
655294BV00001B/2